# DEAD DROP

# DEAD DROP

## ROSS McKENRICK

**Last Post Publishing**
**Pacific Grove, California**

Book and cover design by William H. Henderson

ISBN: 978-0-9793466-2-0
LCCN: 2008925072

Published by
Last Post Publishing
1120 Forest Avenue PMB 274
Pacific Grove, CA 93950
http://LastPostPublishing.com

Manufactured in the United States of America
Published May 2008

**IN MEMORY OF**

CW4 Ronald T. Suzuki
Major Maurice B. McBride

U.S. Army Counterintelligence Corps
(CIC)

# PROLOGUE

SUNDAY 6:00 P.M., 11 NOVEMBER 1990

He watched and waited from the darkness of his car. Across the street a red 1954 Porsche Speedster rolled out of a driveway and headed toward Monterey. His pulse quickened as he slid down in his seat and listened to the sound of the car's tires against the wet pavement. When the Porsche disappeared into the fog, he started his own car and pulled out after it. Within a minute he closed the distance and regained sight of its taillights.

The Porsche wove its way across town toward Cannery Row, then turned into a large parking lot. He slowed down at the entrance and let the car get out of sight before following it into the lot.

The parking space he chose along the south side of the lot gave him an unobstructed view of the three routes into the area. The air was dead calm. Only the faint intermittent wailing of a foghorn in the distance and the occasional closing of a car door interrupted the silence. A harsh orange light was cast over the area from three lampposts.

He slipped a magazine into the nine-millimeter Glock's black polymer frame. The gun sat well in his hand, though it just missed feeling comfortable because of the large grip. He threaded the suppressor onto the muzzle of the automatic, pulled back the slide, and let it slam forward chambering a round. Too bad he had to use the suppressor. Without it the pistol was evenly balanced, an instinctive pointer that could be brought on target quickly. He cradled the pistol in his lap and draped part of his gray plastic raincoat over it. He reached up and removed the bulb from the car's dome light.

Across the lot two white pillars supported a large sign painted with the words "American Tin Cannery." Just beyond that, a footbridge over a narrow street carried an occasional shopper to the parking lot from a tower above the upper level of a small indoor shopping mall. Ahead and to his left, half shrouded in fog, concrete steps led down to the street. Behind him, beads of water clung to the chilled metal strands of a chain link fence that capped a six-foot retaining wall. To his right, the only vehicle exit emptied onto Eardley Avenue. The Porsche was parked forty meters away near the center of the lot. It wasn't an ideal location, but it would do.

Again he watched and waited. The dampness made it feel colder than it really was. As time passed, shoppers entering and leaving the parking lot became fewer and the fog grew thicker.

It was seven-forty when Howard McGuire walked out of The Tavern and turned onto the main concourse of the small shopping mall near Cannery Row. He enjoyed seeing Stan and reminiscing with him, but more importantly he got what he came for.

Howard lingered in front of a large display window filled with shoes. His right hand adjusted his glasses and brushed a strand of gray hair back away from his weathered face. He studied the images of nearby people reflected in the window. He pulled a crush hat out of his coat pocket, set it squarely on his head, and walked to the escalator that led to the American Tin Cannery's upper parking lot.

The mall wasn't normally open this late on Sundays, but Monday was Veteran's Day and the shops were having sales with extended store hours. "Operation Desert Shield" was grabbing all the newspaper headlines and retailers were eager to capitalize on the patriotic mood of the country.

Howard McGuire was forty-eight and hadn't been in the Army for twenty years, but there was still a military cadence to his stride. He surveyed the area as the elevator took him up to the bridge tower. There was no sign of Indians. Only a few shoppers strolled near the storefronts as merchants prepared to close for the night. He loved the game; it didn't matter what he was playing for. The purpose and objective ceased to have meaning for him long ago. The process, the successful execution of the task, was its own reward.

As he came out of the tower, Howard turned up the collar of his Burberry trench coat and stepped out onto the footbridge to the parking lot. He stopped in the middle of the bridge to light a cigarette and glanced at the entrance to the mall. It was the same routine he'd used an hour and a half earlier.

His mind wandered for a moment. Had it been five years since he last spoke with Stan? He knew Stan had arrived at the Defense Language Institute in June. They had given him orders to avoid all contact with Stan, but what Howard had wanted—and had gotten—was more important than following the orders of some faceless men thousands of miles away. His last contact with Stan had been in Pusan, Korea, just after everything had come unstuck—just after his fatal mistake. Stan didn't blame him for it, but everyone else did. Shortly after that Howard began playing the game by his own rules.

Their meeting tonight at The Tavern reminded Howard of old times. To arrange the meeting, he had to come up with an appropriate pretext and devised a short cryptic phone message. Under the circumstances, he would have preferred to have someone watch his back for him, but there wasn't anyone suitable. Wedge would've done it, perhaps even without an explanation, but he had no right to expose Stan to Wedge. And he wasn't sure how far he could trust Wedge. And

. . . this was different. If Wedge became involved in this, even unwittingly, it could ruin Wedge's career.

He stood there on the bridge and finished his cigarette. No one had come near the mall entrance. Except for the foghorn in the distance, it was quiet. Satisfied, he discarded his cigarette and walked to the end of the bridge. On the other side of the parking lot a car door closed.

The leather heels of Howard's shoes clicked softly against the pavement as he headed across the lot toward his car. He jammed his hands deep into his coat pockets, tucked his chin into his chest, and walked slowly. The brim of his hat shielded his glasses from the mist.

Halfway to his car he stopped to light another cigarette and glanced around. The only person he could see was a man in a gray raincoat walking in his direction from the far side of the lot.

Howard maneuvered between two cars to get to his red Porsche just beyond them. The parking lot lights, filtered by the fog, reflected off the wet black asphalt. He reached his car and stopped to fish his keys out of his pocket. The man in the gray raincoat came around the back of his car. Howard looked up just as the man raised the pistol. Trapped between the parked cars, there was nothing he could do. He tried to mentally record as much as he could—six foot tall, medium build, dark hair—before two rapid muffled blasts jolted his chest and head. He fell back onto the pavement.

The gunman knelt over the body, noted the placement of the two bullets, and rifled his victim's clothing. The target's face was a disfigured mess. There was no telltale bubbling of blood near his mouth. Within seconds he found the wallet, stood up, and looked around in all directions. A silver Dodge pickup truck passed behind him and slowly came to a stop. Two men got out of the truck and appeared to look around for the source of the sounds. The truck cut off his route back to his own car.

The gunman crouched and wove his way between three parked cars, then stood and walked briskly toward the steps at the corner of the parking lot. He disappeared into the fog.

The steps took him down to the Sloat Street entrance to the mall. Inside was an unfinished blend of mauve metal trim, bare concrete, and safety glass. It was well lighted, even though all the stores and most of the other establishments were about to close. The doors to The Tavern were open and out of them drifted the indistinguishable babble of mingled conversations.

The gunman descended the stairs to the lower level of the mall and crossed the main concourse. Only a few people lingered in front of display windows. From there he went out the other side of the mall, headed east along Oceanview Avenue, and turned onto Cannery Row.

The street curved sharply near the entrance to the Monterey Bay Aquarium. The area nearby was deserted, but just ahead the sidewalks were crowded with tourists. The street passed under an enclosed skywalk connecting the second stories of the two Monterey Canning Company buildings.

On the eastside of the building he found a secluded spot where he took off the cheap gray plastic raincoat, wadded it up, and dropped it in a garbage barrel. Under the raincoat he was wearing a navy blue car coat.

He walked back to the Monterey Canning Company building, which housed a small shopping arcade and a restaurant. The area was brightly lit and bustling with people. He browsed along a row of shops until he reached a wooden walkway on the eastside of the restaurant. The restaurant and the walkway extended out over the water on large wood pilings. High tide covered most of the small sandy beach beneath it. The sky to the east was clear; he could see the dark expanse of the bay. The city lights appeared to rise out of the water and spread out toward the east and south. A few stars were visible in the eastern sky. The aroma of seafood escaping from the restaurant mixed pleasingly with the smell of the ocean and stimulated his appetite.

At the end of the walkway he leaned against the railing and glanced around before dropping the pistol into the dark water below. He pocketed fifty-eight dollars in cash from the wallet and dropped the wallet over the railing. Satisfied that no one had observed his furtive movements, he sauntered to the street and headed back to the American Tin Cannery.

Despite the silver pickup truck getting in his way, he was pleased with the way it went. It was foolish to return to the scene of the shooting. He told himself he wanted to do something about the car, but he knew it was unnecessary. What he really wanted was to see the faces of the policemen as they tried to discover what had happened. He wanted to stand near them knowing what they would never know.

It had been a slow night, but now it was approaching prime time. O'Donnell put away his paperwork and prepared to get out on the street for the remaining two and a half hours of his shift. He was what taxpayers pray for in a cop—not too tall, not too muscular, mature without looking old, competent, maybe even half-clever, but certainly not brilliant. At fifty Francis Xavier O'Donnell was the oldest sergeant on the Pacific Grove Police Department. No one dared to call him Francis. Some of the younger patrolmen hesitated to call him Frank.

O'Donnell heard Kenneth Graves, the swing shift desk clerk, coming down the hall. As O'Donnell got up from his desk, Graves entered his office and approached him. He straightened himself up to his full height, turned and looked down at Graves with a practiced glare. He strapped on his utility belt and said, "What is it?"

Graves quickly back pedaled two steps and braced himself in the doorway. "Ah, Ybarra called in. Says he's . . . ah . . . not feeling well. Wants to go home early," Graves said. Normally the department had three patrolmen on duty during the swing shift, one in each of the two beat areas plus a follow-up unit.

"Tell him he can go," said O'Donnell. "I'll take over as the follow-up unit from Mosley. Have Mosley cover beat two."

Graves nodded and scurried back to the front desk.

O'Donnell cruised the main business district in his patrol car and headed west down Oceanview Avenue toward the Point Pinos Lighthouse. O'Donnell was testing his spotlight when the call came over the radio.

"Five-eighty-two, Center."

"Five-eighty-two." Monk Mosley answered the call.

"Five-eighty-two, man down and bleeding, upper parking lot, American Tin Cannery, handle code three."

"Check."

O'Donnell glanced at his rear-view mirror. He switched on his emergency lights and siren and spun the steering wheel hard to the left as he jabbed at his brake pedal. The patrol car responded perfectly on the wet pavement and spun around a hundred and eighty degrees. O'Donnell smiled broadly and checked his rear-view mirror again as he slowly pressed the accelerator halfway to the floorboard. He grabbed his microphone just as Mosley's voice came over the radio.

"Center, five-eighty-two. I'm ten-ninety-seven, ATC." Mosley had arrived at the scene.

O'Donnell waited an extra second before keying his microphone. "Center, five-eighty. I'm in the area and responding."

As he passed the Hopkins Marine Station, O'Donnell's radio crackled with static. "Five-eighty, five-eighty-two. I've got a man down. He's bleeding bad from gunshot wounds."

"Five-eighty-two, ten-four. I'm two blocks away." O'Donnell's grip tightened on the steering wheel and his foot pressed down harder on the accelerator.

# CHAPTER ONE

SUNDAY 8:00 P.M., 11 NOVEMBER 1990

Keith McGuire had spent most of the day cleaning his apartment. It was something he forced himself to do every month or so. It was a small apartment that shouldn't have taken long to clean, but he'd spent two hours just dealing with the mildew on the walls of his bedroom closet. Hundred-foot-tall Monterey pines surrounded his and most of the other apartment buildings in the complex.    The rustic wooded setting attracted retired people, young singles, and fungus. Between the fog and the tall trees little direct sunlight ever penetrated into his apartment.

At five he had turned on the television and watched the Forty-Niners humiliate the Cowboys until halftime. By six-thirty he had finished eating what passed for dinner, added one more dirty dish to the stack in the sink, and placed the empty box of macaroni and cheese in the garbage. Dishes rarely found their way into a cabinet; they generally rotated between the sink and the dishwasher. At the moment there were still a few clean plates in the dishwasher.

McGuire slouched down in the sofa with a book cradled in his hands. No hint of his thoughts showed in his angular face. His deep-set mobile eyes darted across the page, then stopped abruptly. Damn these Russian names, he thought. There were way too many characters to keep track of, and they all had names that were impossible to pronounce and remember. He identified strongly with Colonel Vorotyntsev, whom he saw as a dashing figure, close to forty, medium height and build, and somewhat athletic with rugged good looks—much like himself.

McGuire pulled a business card from his shirt pocket, used it as a bookmark, and laid Aleksandr Solzhenitsyn's *August 1914* on the coffee table. He went into the kitchen for another beer. Now that he was well into the battle of Tannenburg, he felt vindicated for having had the patience to suffer through a hundred boring pages of prologue. He had found the book buried under a pile of neglected sports gear on the floor of his bedroom closet. It was a hardcover edition someone had given him. Judging from its musty smell, the book must have been sitting in the closet for some time. Earlier he had given some thought to going out for the evening and doing what single guys are supposed to do, but the book was interesting, the beer was cold, and the couch was comfortable.

The telephone rang as he opened the refrigerator and reached for another beer. It had to be the department. Alycia was up in Santa Cruz at some meeting trying to save the world from nuclear war, ozone depletion, de-forestation, Styrofoam, or disposable diapers. No one else ever called, even on a weekend night. He grabbed the wall phone by the breakfast bar before the second ring.

"Hello."

"Sergeant McGuire, this is Kenneth at the station. There's been a shooting at the American Tin Cannery. They need you down there, code two and a half."

"And?"

"And what?"

"Is there a suspect? A victim? Was anyone killed or wounded?" McGuire asked.

"I don't know. I'm pretty sure someone was shot. I wasn't listening to the radio very close."

"Have you contacted Upham yet?   He's the on-call detective this week."

"I paged him, but he hasn't called in yet. Sergeant O'Donnell told me to call both of you in."

"Okay, call O'Donnell and tell him I'm on my way.

Three patrol cars, a fire department medical van, and an ambulance were haphazardly parked with their red and blue emergency lights flashing in chaotic rhythm, creating a frenzied scene. A small area of the parking lot surrounding a red Porsche was cordoned off with yellow police tape. A few people gathered just beyond the tape. As Keith McGuire got out of his Chevy Blazer, he saw Frank O'Donnell walking across the wet pavement toward him. O'Donnell held up his hand, motioning to him to stop.

"Wait a minute, Keith." His breath was steaming and labored. Sweat covered his face and neck, and blood glistened on his hands.

"You okay, Frank?"

"Look, I'm not sure, but . . ." O'Donnell paused for breath. "I think the victim might be your brother."

McGuire's eyes shifted over to the ambulance, then back to O'Donnell. He stared at O'Donnell without responding.

O'Donnell hesitated, then continued, "He's been shot twice—once in the chest and once in the face. There's no wallet, no ID, but the keys in his hand fit the red Porsche and the car's registered to your brother."

McGuire started toward the ambulance. O'Donnell blocked his way. "Why don't we let the ambulance crew take him away before we go over there. We'd just be in the way."

"How bad is he?"

"We gave him CPR until the EMTs got here."

"And?" McGuire stared at O'Donnell's eyes, searching for an answer.

"I don't know. They're doing what they can. They won't know till they get him to the hospital."

"I want to know now whether or not it's my brother."

O'Donnell stepped aside to let him pass and fell into step behind him. McGuire covered the distance to the ambulance in a few swift strides and peered over the heads of the EMTs. Even with blood covering half his face, there was no doubt; it was Howard.

McGuire backed away from the EMTs until he bumped into the side of O'Donnell's patrol car. He leaned against the wet car and reached into the pocket of his leather flight jacket for a cigarette. All around him he could hear the squawking and garbled voices coming over police radios. He took a long deep drag from his cigarette before he turned to O'Donnell.

"Okay, Frank, so what happened?"

"The shooting occurred about fifteen minutes ago. Two soldiers driving out of the parking lot heard some sounds, stopped, and went over to check it out. They found the victim lying next to the Porsche. They also saw a man walk away from the scene." O'Donnell's breathing gradually became more controlled. "Mosley has them over by his unit. We still haven't heard from Upham. Why don't you go over to The Tavern and have a cup of coffee? I'll send a patrol unit over in a few minutes to take you to the hospital."

McGuire looked over and saw the gurney being hoisted into the ambulance. "No, Frank. I should question the witnesses and start processing the scene before it becomes a total loss. Who the hell knows when Upham will get here." McGuire reached into O'Donnell's patrol car and dropped what remained of his cigarette into the ashtray, then headed over to where Mosley was talking to the soldiers.

When McGuire walked up, Mosley took a step back, motioned his head toward McGuire, and said, "This is Detective McGuire. Keith, this is Specialist Vernon and Corporal Landrey. They're assigned to Fort Ord. They found the victim and called it in. Tell Detective McGuire about the sounds you heard."

McGuire quickly looked the two men over from top to bottom. Both wore blue jeans and cowboy boots. He settled his gaze on Landrey who spoke up first.

"Well, we were on our way out of the parking lot," he said. "Heard two sounds—one right after the other—loud enough to get our attention, but not like gunfire. Well, maybe like muffled twenty-two rounds. I stopped over there." He pointed to his truck several yards away. "If my window hadn't been down, probably wouldn't have heard it. Got out of the truck to see where the sounds came from and saw a man walking away in the other direction. I went to where I first saw the man and found the body lying nearby."

Landrey paused for a second, nodded his head toward Vernon. "Sent Vern, I mean Specialist Vernon here, back into the mall to call nine-one-one. Checked the man for a pulse; couldn't find one. Officer Mosley got here real quick, even before Specialist Vernon got back."

Landrey knew how to brief a situation. Direct and to the point, he'd make a good witness in court. McGuire guessed he was about twenty-six, perhaps five years older than Vernon. Corporal had become an uncommon rank in the Army—a rank usually reserved for those busted back from sergeant.

"Corporal Landrey, can you tell the difference between the sound of a twenty-two caliber and that of a larger weapon?" McGuire asked.

"Sure. Had a twenty-two when I was a kid; fired a lot of M-16 rounds, as well as forty-five caliber and nine-millimeter in the Army." Landrey zipped up the front of his gray canvas tanker's jacket and stuck his hands into his jacket pockets.

"You know, weapons sound different in town than they do on the range"

"In Panama City last December there was a lot of different kinds of gunfire; guess I can tell the difference."

"What about the man you saw walking away?" McGuire jotted down a few words in a small spiral notebook.

"Already out of sight by the time we found the body. Looked for him, but . . . think he might've gone down those stairs." Landrey pointed to the northwest corner of the parking lot.

McGuire glanced in the direction he was pointing. He returned his gaze to Landrey and continued his questions. "What did he look like?"

"Don't know. Only saw his back. Medium height."

"Did you notice anything else?"

"He was wearing a dark-colored raincoat."

McGuire turned his attention to the other man who had been fidgeting non-stop for the past few minutes. Vernon wore a gold and red "Forty-Niners" warm-up jacket. "Specialist Vernon, what were you and Corporal Landrey doing before you heard the sounds?" McGuire asked.

Vernon jammed his hands into his pants pockets, but his feet continued to shuffle about as he answered. "Ah, we were . . . ah, just on our way out of the parking lot."

"No. I mean before that."

"Oh, ah . . . we were shopping."

McGuire got their address and phone number and arranged to see them at the station Monday morning to get written statements. McGuire and Mosley thanked the two soldiers and walked over to the Porsche. McGuire crouched down next to Sergeant O'Donnell.

O'Donnell fixed the beam of his flashlight on an empty bullet casing and said, "It's a nine millimeter."

McGuire examined the markings on the base of the casing and confirmed O'Donnell's observation.

"Yeah, let's find the other one. Monk, did anyone else see or hear anything?" asked McGuire.

"I didn't have time to question anyone besides Landrey and Vernon. I'll go around and F.I. the rest of 'em now." Mosley lumbered off in the direction of the small crowd that had gathered behind the yellow police tape and continued with his field interrogations.

McGuire got an oversized gray plastic tackle box and a large black nylon camera bag from his car. He methodically went about taking the photographs he needed and was putting his camera back in its bag when Mosley interrupted him.

"Keith, there's a man over there, the dark-haired guy in the blue coat, says his name's Karasov. The blue sedan parked over here is his, and he wants to go home."

"So?" McGuire said without looking up.

"Your Blazer's got him blocked in."

"Oh, okay." McGuire zipped up the camera bag and looked up at Mosley. "Has he been F.I.'ed?"

"No. I didn't get that far."

"I'll take care of him." McGuire went over to the crowd of people that had gathered, spotted Karasov, and walked up to him. Karasov stood just over six feet tall and weighed about two hundred and ten pounds. He appeared to be in his mid-fifties, but there wasn't a hint of gray in his straight black hair.

"Mr. Karasov, I'm Sergeant McGuire." McGuire opened his jacket enough to expose the gold badge clipped to his belt. "Would you come over here with me?"

Karasov carefully stepped over the police tape and followed McGuire to the side of Karasov's car.

"Is this your car?" McGuire asked.

Karasov nodded a reply. Just under his chin he had a vicious looking two-inch scar that ran from one side of his jaw to the other.

"What's your full name?"

"Sergei Ivanovich Karasov."

"Where do you work?"

"I am teaching Russian at Defense Language Institute."

"Where do you live?"

"In Pacific Grove on Ransford Avenue, number twenty-four, fifteen, apartment four." Karasov spoke slowly with a heavy Slavic accent.

"Did you see what happened?"

"No."

"Do you know the man who was shot?"

"No. Who was he?"

"Do you know who was driving that red Porsche?" McGuire pointed to his brother's car. Karasov seemed to hesitate momentarily before answering each question, but maintained eye contact. Perhaps too much eye contact.

"No."

"When did you first see the red car?" McGuire watched Karasov more closely as he answered.

"Maybe ten minutes ago when I return here. It was not here when I park my car." Karasov moved a half step closer to McGuire as he answered.

McGuire instinctively took a small step back with his right foot and unlocked his knees. "Did you notice anything unusual when you parked here?" McGuire asked.

"No."

"What time did you park here?"

"Perhaps two hours ago."

McGuire reached into his shirt pocket and pulled out a business card. "Mr. Karasov, here's my card. If you remember something later that might help us, please call me. You can get in your car now. I'll move the car in front of yours; when I do, you can drive out."

McGuire moved his car, then went back to the Porsche and pulled a clipboard and tape measure out of the side pocket of his camera bag. He began making a rough sketch of the scene showing the different positions from which he had taken his photos and distances between objects.

McGuire saw Neal Upham's BMW negotiate its way slowly through the crowd toward him. He glanced at his watch. It was 8:55 P.M.

At thirty-one Upham was the department's youngest sergeant and at five-foot-eight he was the shortest officer. He got out of his car and closed the door. The woman in the passenger seat remained in the car. McGuire couldn't make out who she was. Upham was wearing an off-white linen suit and a black silk crewneck shirt. His nickel-plated Colt Python revolver bounced noticeably in its shoulder holster as he strutted across the parking lot.

"Good of you to join us, Neal," McGuire said.

"I was at the Whaling Station having dinner. I came as soon as I could."

"The Whaling Station's less than four blocks from here."

"The waiter just brought out our food when I got the page. If I'd known it was something serious, I'd have called in right away."

"Didn't you hear the sirens, Neal?"

"Well . . . Keith, I guess I'm just lucky you don't have a social life and could cover for me."

McGuire turned his back on Upham and continued diagramming the crime scene. This was no place for an argument.

Upham paraded around the area and spoke with O'Donnell and each of the patrol officers. Before he finished his tour, McGuire yelled over to him, "Upham! I'm going to the hospital now to check on the victim. Have the Porsche taken to the city yard. I'll see you back at the station."

"Wait a minute, Keith! I need to take Carmen home first." Upham walked over to McGuire.

"You mean the bimbo in your car? Just give her some cab money." McGuire packed away his equipment.

"That happens to be Carmen De La Silva from the Public Defender's Office," Upham said.

McGuire stood up with his camera bag in one hand and his tackle box in the other and turned toward his car. "Give her your keys," McGuire said over his shoulder. "She knows . . . ." He stopped abruptly when he saw the television news van pull into the parking lot.

Karl Waldrip hopped out and bounded across the pavement before Max, his cameraman and driver, brought the van to a full stop. "Hey, guys. *Que pasa?*" Waldrip walked right past them without waiting for a reply. "Ooooh! . . . this is good; we can do this with the emergency vehicles in the background and the police tape in the foreground. This is great. Max! Get your stuff over here."

"I can handle this, McGuire," Upham said. "Why don't you go up to the hospital and check on the victim."

"Kiss my ass," McGuire muttered under his breath as he walked over to his car.

# CHAPTER TWO

SUNDAY 9:30 P.M., 11 NOVEMBER 1990

At the crime scene Keith McGuire had concentrated on the task at hand and refused to think about his brother. Now he could think of nothing else as he negotiated the winding road to the hospital.

Since his brother returned to the area four years ago, Keith had only seen him a dozen times, mostly on business. They had dinner together twice in the past twelve months—once before and once after Keith's divorce. Both occasions had been awkward for Keith. His mind drifted back to earlier years and experiences he had shared with Howard as a child and a teenager.

They had been close when he was young, but just after Keith turned seven, Howard went away to college. Since then Howard had been more like a favorite uncle than a brother. He'd show up unexpectedly for a birthday or Christmas bringing presents from foreign countries. Keith was a sophomore in high school when he first fully understood the nature of Howard's work. That was the year Howard was at the Defense Language Institute studying Japanese. He was in Army Intelligence at the time. Later he joined the CIA and remained with them until early 1986. The following year he got a job with the Defense Investigative Service in Monterey conducting security clearance investigations for the Department of Defense.

McGuire's car glided quietly into the fog-shrouded parking lot of the hospital. He pulled into a space, killed the engine, and sat there looking at the large low-slung white building. He half-expected a flood of emotion and didn't want to leave his car until it had passed and was under control. He sat and waited, but nothing happened.

McGuire waited for the doctor. He sat sipping coffee at one of the dozen groupings of rattan furniture around the hospital's big indoor pond. A small island in the pond supported a twenty-foot tree and a few tropical ferns. Several potted ficus trees and bamboo plants were scattered around the dimly lighted area. An elaborate pattern of illuminated water in the pond gushed up three feet and danced in the air. A geodesic dome skylight forty feet across reflected back some of the light from the pond. Orange and white koi carp swam about aimlessly. The sound of the falling water drowned out all other noises, creating the feeling of being next to a waterfall in a tropical forest.

In the snack area a gray-haired Filipino man in a white uniform quietly stacked chairs as a prelude to mopping. Against the far wall near the unmanned information desk wheelchairs were clumped together like abandoned shopping carts. Occasionally an orderly or nurse would stroll by.

It was 11:43 P.M. when the doctor, dressed in a pale green scrub gown, came over to McGuire. The Main Operating Room was directly across from the pond. McGuire felt better when he saw the doctor was an older man, over fifty, perhaps a few years older than his brother.

"Detective McGuire?"

"Yes." McGuire rose to his feet.

"I'm Doctor Hernandez. They're taking the patient directly to ICU instead of the Recovery Room."

"How is he?"

"Not good. One bullet entered the right side of his chest, pierced his lung, and lodged at the rear of the thoracic cavity. The second bullet entered the left side of his face near his nose and exited behind the left jaw. A major blood vessel was severed and there was massive bleeding. His breathing's being supported by a respirator, but his heart is functioning on its own. His blood pressure is back up to ninety over sixty and his pulse is down to a hundred. It's hard to tell if there's any brain damage—"

"Brain damage?"

"We don't know how long his heart stopped before they started CPR. Under these circumstances there's always the possibility of brain damage." The doctor paused. "There's also the possibility of coma. Right now he's still under the effects of the anesthesia. We'll know more when it wears off in a couple hours."

"Where can I collect his clothing and the bullet you extracted?" McGuire asked.

"They're in the custody of the OR nurse. You can see the patient in ICU, but as I said he's still unconscious."

McGuire sealed the mushroomed bullet into a clear plastic zip-lock bag and examined it briefly before putting it in his jacket pocket. He turned his attention to the bag of clothing. At the bottom of the bag was a school ring. Stanford University, 1964. The inside of the ring bore the inscription "HCM." He could check out the remaining contents of the bag later.

McGuire pressed a buzzer by the door to the Intensive Care Unit. In a few seconds a young nurse came to let him in. There was a nurses' station situated in the center of the horseshoe-shaped main room. Surrounding the area on three sides were a number of small glass-walled rooms. The nurse led him to one of the fishbowl-like rooms, pulled a curtain halfway across the glass wall, and returned to the nurses' station.

With his hands in his trouser pockets and his shoulders slumped forward, he stood over the bed and stared down at his brother. Howard's face was heavily bandaged and a ventilator tube was taped to his mouth.

McGuire settled into an armchair next to the bed. He sat quietly, alternately looking at his brother, the bellows of the ventilator, and the monitoring equipment mounted on the wall. The room was in semi-darkness. The only light came from the nurses' station and the various displays and indicator lights of the monitoring equipment hooked up to Howard. Again he waited for an emotional response, but there was none. This wasn't really happening. It couldn't be his brother lying there. It came to him—the Solzhenitsyn book. Howard had given it to him for Christmas three years ago.

His eyes settled on the IV bag hanging a few feet above Howard's head. The clear liquid dripped from the bag into the tube leading to Howard's left arm in a slow mesmerizing tempo. Any minute now Howard would open his eyes and regain consciousness and everything would be fine. He kept waiting, but nothing happened.

A long time passed before he looked up and saw a nurse standing in the doorway speaking to him. He recognized her face and saw her lips moving, but no sound seemed to escape from her mouth. He felt confused for a moment, then began to hear sounds that slowly became words.

"Keith . . . Keith, are you all right?"

"Uh, I'm okay, just a little tired," McGuire said and rubbed his eyes.

"What are you doing here?"

He motioned with his head toward the bed and said, "My brother, Howard."

"I didn't know you had a brother. Keith, are you sure you're okay? Can I get you anything?"

"Thanks, Gayle, I'll be fine. I'd just like to sit here with him for awhile longer if it's all right."

Keith knew a few of the nurses at the hospital. During his years as a patrol officer, he had transported a lot of people to the hospital for treatment and had been treated there himself more times than he cared to remember. Many of the nurses had worked in the emergency room at one time or another. It's where he had met his second wife, Cristina.

He sat motionless in the chair for about an hour, looking at his watch and at Howard's eyelids. His mind wandered aimlessly, unable to focus and hold a thought. He felt helpless, unable to do anything for his brother. Gayle came every fifteen minutes to check on Howard. Each time she looked at her watch and shook her head, but said nothing.

There was something he could do. He could get the person who shot his brother. He made a silent promise to himself and to Howard, then got up and walked to the nurses' station. Gayle Fantes looked up from her charts. It was just past 3:00 A.M.

"It doesn't look good, does it?" McGuire asked.

"He can regain consciousness at any time."

"I'd appreciate it if someone would contact me through the department the minute he comes out of it." McGuire placed a couple of business cards on her desk.

"I'll call you. Hiroko's on the next shift. I'll ask her to do the same. I can have Dr. Hernandez call you later today. He usually makes his rounds about noon when he has patients here."

McGuire got to the station at 3:30 A.M. He spent the early hours of the morning putting the incident out on the teletype, preparing the bullet and the two empty nine millimeter casings for shipment to the state crime laboratory, and reviewing the news release Upham had written and left for him. He went home long enough to shower, shave, and find a photograph of Howard. After a quick breakfast, he made eight Polaroid copies of the photo, met briefly with Upham at the station, then went to the city yard to check out his brother's car.

Upham had agreed to stay at the station to give out the photographs and press release and answer questions. Maybe he'd get some more camera time. At least Upham was dressed more professionally this morning. Upham rarely wore a suit to work, but on this occasion he had on a dark blue suit with subtle gray chalk stripes, a white shirt, and a yellow tie. McGuire was glad Upham was so eager to handle the press. If he dealt with the press himself, it would only draw attention to his relationship to the victim, which was something he didn't want.

McGuire returned to the station at ten. His examination of the car failed to turn up anything of value. He and Upham reinterviewed Corporal Landrey and Specialist Vernon separately and got their statements in writing. After enduring lunch together, the two detectives went to the American Tin Cannery and spent the next few hours canvassing the stores and restaurants, talking to store clerks and waitresses, and showing them the photo of Howard. No one remembered seeing him. Before the light faded, they took daylight photos of the crime scene.

Upham was clever, perhaps even smart, and the Chief had selected him two months ago to temporarily fill a vacant position in the two-man Investigations Section. He would return to Patrol as soon as Toshiro Noguchi came back from the Middle East. When Upham first joined Investigations, McGuire tried to guide him along and consciously made every effort not to be patronizing. But Upham refused any assistance and chose to do things his own way.

McGuire was too used to partnering with Noguchi and had no desire to work with anyone who wouldn't meet him halfway. In the past eight years there had been five murders in Pacific Grove. McGuire and Noguchi had worked well together; there had been five arrests and five convictions. This case was classified as armed robbery and attempted murder, but that could change any day.

Noguchi was also a CID Agent in the US Army Reserves. Two months ago he was called to active duty for Operation Desert Shield and deployed to Saudi Arabia to join a few hundred thousand other American servicemen, leaving McGuire no choice but to work with Upham.

Back at the station McGuire settled in at his desk and reviewed the written statements of the two soldiers. Corporal Landrey impressed McGuire. He was very direct in his answers and sure of himself. Specialist Vernon equivocated a bit, but he'd probably be okay in court. McGuire looked up from the statements as Upham entered his office.

"I didn't get a chance to ask earlier, how did your meeting with the press go?" McGuire said.

Upham took off his coat, hung it on the coat rack, readjusted his shoulder holster, and settled into a chair before answering. "It went well enough. They'll run the photo with our phone number. Maybe we'll get lucky."

"Hey, the news will be on TV in a few minutes. We ought to check it out and see how you look." McGuire baited him, knowing Upham had probably set the timer on his VCR to record all the local news programs.

"I'll catch it on the late news tonight, if I can stay awake till then."

"So, what do you think of this case so far?" McGuire asked.

"Expensive car, nice overcoat, not to mention the Rolex Oyster. Made him a good target. Probably did something to spook the robber and got shot for it," Upham said. "There's been a few armed robberies and strong-arm robberies in that area. Should've taken the watch though . . . unless Landrey and Vernon scared him off before he could get it."

"I checked Howard's clothing for pocket litter last night. There wasn't anything that suggested any recent activity." As he spoke, McGuire played with a staple remover trying to occupy his hands and resist the urge to light up another cigarette.

"You know," Upham said, "Landrey's description of the two shots sounding like muffled twenty-two caliber rounds makes me think our robber might have used a silencer. Frankly, that plus the apparent speed and placement of the two rounds suggests a professional, not your average crook. Kind'a makes you wonder what your brother was up to."

McGuire kept his mouth shut and clinched his teeth.

Upham continued, "I'm curious to know how your brother could afford those expensive things."

"We don't have any evidence, except for one slug, two spent casings, and what two G.I.'s thought they heard, and you've got my brother being shot down by a professional hitman because of what . . . drug trafficking . . . Mafia involvement . . . what?"

Upham folded his arms on his chest. "I'm sorry it was your brother who was shot, but it's questionable whether you should even be on this case, and you sure the hell shouldn't be in charge of it, if you can't approach it objectively."

"Objectively? I'm not the one drawing conclusions from supposition; I usually try to gather some evidence first."

"Look," Upham said, "your brother works for the government at a pay grade of GS-11. That equates to about thirty-three thousand a year, gross. He probably barely clears enough to pay for food and housing around here. I make more than that and I sure the hell can't afford a Rolex or a Dunhill lighter or Burberry trench coat."

"Not good enough, Neal. Hey, I've got a novel idea." McGuire got up from his desk. "Why don't you collect some evidence, perhaps even investigate the matter?"

"That's exactly what I'm going to do."

McGuire left the office without replying.

In a larger police department McGuire wouldn't be allowed on the case because of his relationship to the victim, but the department only had two investigators and Upham had never handled a major felony investigation. McGuire knew Upham wanted to be in charge of an investigation like this, and he wouldn't hesitate to try to get McGuire taken off the case. If Upham could show McGuire's judgment was being influenced by personal considerations, the Chief would have to take him off. What really bothered McGuire was he had already considered the possibility of a professional gunman and couldn't rule it out. He would have to be careful around Upham and not give him any excuse to go to the Chief.

# CHAPTER THREE

McGuire pulled up near the front entrance of the police station. He was careful to avoid parking directly under the two fifty-foot palm trees. They attracted flocks of birds that perched there for hours and did indescribable things to objects under them.

The station had dark red roof tiles and wall panels framed by concrete columns and beams. The panels looked like paving tiles. Unlike the rest of the building, which was windowless, the entrance was surrounded with glass. Portraits of current and past Chiefs lined the walls of the lobby. At the far end was the front desk and to its immediate right was the door that separated the public area from the interior of the building.

Pinkney Grant was at the front desk when McGuire walked in. She was an attractive, long-legged woman with medium-length red hair and large green eyes. She seemed effortlessly pretty, but McGuire knew better. It took some work to look twenty-three when you're actually thirty-something. She hadn't allowed herself to put on any extra weight. The only bulges in her clothing were the ones that made men stare a little longer than was polite.

The Chief knew how to pick 'em—well, at least some of them. McGuire recalled the Chief had also made the decision to hire Kenneth Graves, the swing shift clerk. It was a lot easier to overlook Pinky's shortcomings, not that there were many. In fact it was pretty easy to lapse into all kinds of sexual fantasies whenever you saw her and forget she actually had a job to do.

"Good morning, Pink."

Pinkney looked up from her computer console. "Good morning, Keith. I'm so sorry about your brother. How is he?"

"Not too good, but he's a tough old bird. He may fool everyone and pull through okay." McGuire paused at the door next to the front desk and waited for Pinkney to let him in.

"Are you okay?" she asked. "Is there anything I can do?"

"I'm fine. Thanks for asking." He noticed she held eye contact just a little longer than normal before she glanced down and pressed a button causing the familiar buzz of the electric latch. He pushed open the door and decided he was confusing genuine concern with something else.

McGuire grabbed a cup of coffee in the break room, went straight into his office, and closed the door behind him. Pinkney's concern and expression of sympathy made him a little uncomfortable. There wasn't much he could say in response to people's offers of condolence. He had experienced the same thing when his parents died six years ago and again when Cristina divorced him ten months ago. He didn't like people feeling sorry for him.

McGuire rocked back in his chair and sipped his coffee. It was a medium-size windowless office with two desks separated by a seven-foot partition. Both sides of the partition were covered with police posters, calendars, newspaper clippings and photographs of crimes he and Noguchi had investigated. The calendars depicted seductive young female models wearing abbreviated police uniforms over captions that asked, "Do You Have Court Today?" The wall space that wasn't hidden behind filing cabinets was covered with framed commendations and school certificates.

McGuire drank half of his coffee before he gave in and lit his first cigarette of the day. He knew if he was ever going to quit smoking, he would have to give up coffee too, and alcohol, and probably sex. For a moment he saw himself lying in bed next to a beautiful young redheaded woman with large green eyes and thick sensuous lips, languishing in post-coital bliss, and reaching out with his hand toward the nightstand for a pack of . . . chewing gum. A shudder ran through him and the vision dissipated.

McGuire had worked until 8:00 P.M. last night drawing up a detailed diagram of the crime scene. Later he had gone up to Community Hospital to check on his brother's condition. Nothing had changed. He had returned home around 10:00 P.M. and crashed.

He started his morning with a review of his unfinished work from last week. There was a juvenile matter he could back out of and let Child Protective Services handle. He still had some follow-up work to do on a pair of residential burglaries. The problem with the library books he could put on permanent hold; it was one aspect of his job he really hated, but the Chief was big on community service.

Every few months McGuire had to go to the city library. The head librarian would give him a list of ten or twelve grossly overdue books and he had to go around reminding these library patrons of their errant behavior. Mostly they were little old ladies in their seventies or eighties who had so many books checked out they lost track of them. No matter how gentle McGuire was in his approach, once he identified himself as a police officer, they would go into a panic, fearing their delinquency might result in a criminal record. McGuire worried that sooner or later one of these geriatric misde-meanants might keel over with a heart attack when con-fronted about their overdue books. The newspaper headline would be ugly.

McGuire telephoned the Defense Investigative Service's Monterey Field Office and made an appointment to see

Howard's supervisor, Clayton Butler, the Special Agent-in-Charge at ten o'clock. In the meantime he could take care of some other matters.

McGuire consulted his business card file before dialing. A woman's voice answered the telephone. "Good morning, Holcomb, Tarantino, and Eisner."

"This is Keith McGuire. Is Mr. Tarantino in?"

"Mr. Tarantino is on another line. Would you like to hold?"

"Yes, if it won't be too long."

"May I tell him what this is in reference to?"

"I'm a former client of his. My brother was involved in a near fatal incident Sunday night, and I need some help in connection with his affairs."

"Please hold, Mr. McGuire. Mr. Tarantino shouldn't be long." The secretary's voice was replaced by unidentifiable background music.

McGuire's parents had died in a car accident in 1984 and Tarantino had handled the probate. His parents hadn't left much of an estate. His father had been crippled by a land mine at Omaha Beach during the Normandy Invasion. He had made a comfortable living as an accountant after the war, but never accumulated any wealth. When Keith's parents died, the only thing they had of real value was their home. At the time Vincent Tarantino had just quit the DA's office, joined a small private practice, and was eager for any work no matter how small. McGuire had worked closely with Tarantino on a number of criminal cases and trusted him.

"Keith, I'm sorry to hear about your brother. How is he?" Tarantino had a deep rich sincere voice that could enthrall a jury. He now did a lot of product liability cases and spent more time in court than most lawyers. That's where the money was; there sure wasn't any money in criminal defense.

"He's in a coma and, well, his condition's kind of iffy. The doctor doesn't give him much of a chance."

"How can I help?"

"I'll need to attend to my brother's personal affairs. If there's no change in his condition and he remains in a coma for awhile, I want to make sure his assets are protected and his bills are paid."

"As I recall you don't have any other siblings?"

"There was only Howard, and he never married."

"I'll need a letter from the attending physician indicating Howard is not physically able to manage his own affairs. I can have you appointed conservator. In the meantime you can do whatever is necessary and reasonable. I'm sorry about this, Keith. Is there's anything else I can do?"

"No, I don't think so."

"Well, if you need anything, please call me."

"Thanks, Vince." McGuire set the phone down. He knew Tarantino would handle the matter for him. From the very first case they had worked on together, they had treated each other as professional equals and had respected one another's abilities. That hadn't changed. But eight years ago Tarantino's salary as a relatively new Deputy District Attorney was just a little more than McGuire's pay as a brand new sergeant. Since then McGuire's income had increased about fifty percent, whereas Tarantino's had increased about three hundred and fifty percent. They lived in two different worlds now.

The Naval Postgraduate School occupied the grounds of what was formerly the Del Monte Hotel. It covered a quarter of a square mile within the City of Monterey, less than a mile east of the main business district. Herrmann Hall, the old hotel building, was a multi-winged five-story wood structure with white stucco walls and steep-pitched red tile roofs.

The fifth floor of Herrmann Hall was an unlikely place for the offices of a federal investigative agency. Never having been to the DIS office, McGuire began to wonder if he hadn't misunderstood the directions Clayton Butler had given him.

McGuire entered the building's east wing and found the elevator out of order. A wide, red-carpeted stairwell next to the elevator went up to the fourth floor. From there he ascended a narrow, uncarpeted set of steps to the fifth floor. About ten yards down a tall narrow bare corridor McGuire saw a blue, plastic sign indicating he had arrived at the right place.

He identified himself to the secretary who seemed vaguely familiar. She asked him to wait and announced his presence to Clayton Butler over the intercom. She was an attractive Japanese woman with long straight raven-black hair. Her age eluded him, but he placed it somewhere between thirty and forty. She returned to her typing without a second look at McGuire.

The ceiling in the secretary's office sloped down at strange angles towards the outer wall and jutted out into a dormer window. The bottom half of the walls were covered with wood grain contact paper that tried to pass as paneling, but was betrayed by bubbles of trapped air. Otherwise, it was a fairly typical old government office—institutional beige walls adorned with unframed travel posters, a mismatch of tan and gray metal office furniture, uncovered florescent light fixtures suspended from the ceiling, and surface mounted electrical conduit. Standing behind the secretary's desk were three heavy gray Mosler four-drawer safes with reversible magnetic "Open" and "Closed" signs stuck to the front of each control drawer.

Butler had a coffee mug in his right hand as he emerged from a narrow passageway that looked like it had once been a small closet. He was younger than McGuire had expected, perhaps thirty-five. He stood about five-foot-nine and was stocky with prematurely graying hair. The tan corduroy sports coat he wore should have been retired years ago.

"I'm Clayton Butler. I don't believe we've met."

"Never had occasion to come up here before."

Butler pointed his coffee cup at his secretary. "This is Michiko Thurgood, my secretary. Michiko, this is Howard's brother, Keith McGuire."

Michiko acknowledged McGuire's greeting, expressed sorrow for Howard's condition, then promptly turned away and returned to her typing. McGuire thought her eyes seemed a little moist.

"Would you care for some coffee?" Butler asked. Before McGuire could answer, Butler stepped out of the office, across the corridor, and into another room. McGuire followed him into a room that was a mirror image of the secretary's office.

"Yes, black please," McGuire answered and glanced around the room.

"This is our bullpen. It's where the agents come in to do their paperwork. These rooms were once maids' quarters back when the building was a hotel." Butler handed McGuire a mug of coffee. "We're tenants here; we rent this space from the Navy."

If office space was any indication of status, the Navy certainly didn't hold DIS in very high regard.

Butler leaned against a desk and motioned McGuire to a nearby chair. "I'm sorry about Howard. How's he doing?"

McGuire remained standing. "If he survives, there may be brain damage. If there isn't any brain damage, the doctor says it will take several months for him to fully recover. Under the circumstances I thought it'd be best to collect his personal items. There might be something among them that could assist our investigation, and I figured you'd be needing the space for his replacement."

"I don't expect a replacement for Howard." As he spoke Butler seemed to be inspecting the cracks in the angular ceiling. "There's a hiring freeze because of federal budget problems. Even with this Iraq problem I doubt our agency'll be hiring any new employees for some time." Butler stopped speaking for a few seconds while a large jet airliner passed over the top of the building with a deafening roar. Until the noise died down to a reasonable level, he intently studied the inside of his coffee mug as if some foreign object were floating around in it.

When the noise subsided, Butler continued, "Howard worked with Gordon Wedgwood at our office at the Defense Language Institute. I'll have Wedge meet you at DLI and help you with Howard's things. I've already instructed him to take over Howard's caseload. He's in the best position to help you sort through his things." Butler's voice had an irritatingly detached and disinterested tone.

McGuire took a sip of coffee and asked, "Who were my brother's closest associates?" It was good coffee, much better than they had at the station. He covertly inspected the inside of his own mug, but didn't see anything unusual.

"Howard wasn't really close to anyone here . . . well, except for Steve Wepsala. He's retired now. They knew each other from the Agency. Steve recommended him for this job. I don't know any of Howard's personal friends, other than Steve. Frankly, I don't think he had any. Your brother is a very private person, almost secretive in some respects."

McGuire stared at Butler and allowed an uncomfortable silence developed before breaking it. "What can you tell me about his recent activities?"

"Not much. His work was all fairly routine, except for an occasional hostage case at DLI."

"What's a hostage case?"

"That's a term we use for cases involving people who have relatives in communist-controlled countries . . . because of the possibility the relatives could be used as hostages to pressure a person into cooperating with hostile intelligence agencies. In fact, Wedge has been working a hostage case with Howard for the past few months. He'll be able to tell you more than I can. As for Howard's personal activities, I'm afraid I don't know anything about what he did after work hours."

McGuire grew bored watching Butler talk to his coffee mug about Howard's health insurance and other personnel matters. Butler promised to call the hospital and give them the necessary information from Howard's personnel file. McGuire agreed to return any DIS property at Howard's home, particularly his badge and credentials. Arrangements were made for McGuire to meet Wedgwood that afternoon.

# CHAPTER FOUR

TUESDAY 2:00 P.M., 13 NOVEMBER 1990

McGuire returned to the office and worked through lunch. He managed to successfully divest himself of the juvenile case and close out the two residential burglaries before heading over to Howard's office.

He drove onto the Presidio through the Taylor Street Gate and wove his way downhill. Classes had resumed about an hour ago and the streets were relatively empty. He turned his Ford Crown Victoria left into the parking lot in front of the Tin Barn. He was high on the hillside. McGuire admired the view of the wharf, the harbor, and the bay stretched out in front of him. The water was a bright teal blue. He could faintly hear the barking of sea lions coming from the Coast Guard pier. The morning fog had burned off and the sun warmed the air, raising the odor of damp fallen leaves. The sky was clear and offered a crisp view of the Gabilan Mountains to the east and Santa Cruz to the north. This had once been a perfect position for a battery of cannon to command the harbor and protect the Spanish port from Russians.

The DIS office at the Presidio was in the Tin Barn, a large tan building covered with corrugated metal. The main part of the structure was a theater used for graduation ceremonies, but along the north side were offices.

McGuire entered the side door at the front of the building. He looked down the long hallway and saw a cardboard sign with red stenciled letters "Defense Investigative Service" at the end of the hall. The door to Room 6 was open and a man with rolled-up shirtsleeves was sitting in front of a personal computer with his back to McGuire.

McGuire stood in the doorway and said, "Excuse me. Are you Gordon Wedgwood?"

Wedgwood jerked his head around toward McGuire and looked surprised. "Oh, hi . . . you must be Howard's brother. I didn't hear you come down the hall. Clayton Butler told me you'd be coming." As he got up his right knee smashed against the side of the computer stand causing the video monitor to shake violently. He grabbed his knee and fell back in his chair. Wedge pushed himself clear of the computer stand, then rose slowly to his feet. He grimaced, limped over to McGuire, and extended his right hand. "You can call me Wedge."

Wedge's hand was large, and his handshake firm. He was probably six-foot-two when he stood erect.

"I'm Keith, Keith McGuire. Is this Howard's office?"

"Yeah, I was like, just going through his computer files trying to sort things out. I'm really sorry about Howard. How is he?"

McGuire shook his head. "He hasn't regained consciousness yet."

Wedge looked at the floor for a second before raising his large boyish face with its limpid blue eyes. "Can he have visitors? I'd like to see him, and I'm sure Steve Wepsala would too—I'm sorry, you wanna sit down?" Wedge motioned toward a gray straight-back chair in front of the desk and remained standing as McGuire sat down.

Wedge was about twenty-five and looked as though he weighed two hundred and forty pounds. He had strong sloping shoulders, chunky arms, a massive chest, and a thick waist. His hair was short-cropped and relatively straight.

Dark brown cowlicks sprouted up at the back of his head. "How about some coffee or something?"

"No thanks," McGuire said and reached in his coat pocket for his cigarettes. "My brother's in the Intensive Care Unit at Community Hospital. They don't allow visitors in ICU, except for family members, but they may move him out of there in a few days. I'll let you know." He looked around for an ashtray. When he didn't see one, he put his cigarettes back in his pocket.

"If there's anything at all I can do to help," Wedge said.

McGuire fished around in his pockets until he found a pack of gum and offered a stick to Wedge.

"*Spaseeba*," Wedge said and accepted the gum.

McGuire looked at him quizzically.

"It means thank you in Russian. I'm trying to learn a few words in each of the languages they teach here."

McGuire nodded absently and asked, "How well do you know my brother?"

"I met Howard almost a year ago when I hired on with DIS. I saw him around office every day, but we really didn't talk much until Steve Wepsala retired in April. Since then I've worked with him every day." Wedge tested his knee before moving around the desk and carefully settling into the swivel chair next to the computer. As he did, his gut strained against his belt and rolled over his low-slung slacks just a little.

"Steve was my training officer," he continued, "so I didn't have much contact with Howard during my first four months. With Steve busy training me, Howard had to take care of some of Steve's caseload. I think Howard didn't want to interfere in my training. But once Steve retired, I started going to Howard for advice . . . but then, we all do."

"Can you tell me about the cases Howard was working on?"

"Most of his work was fairly routine stuff—security clearance investigations on the students here. We have our share of the usual drug, alcohol, and credit problems young people get into—"

"Any heavy-duty drug trafficking?"

"No. Nothing like that, mostly low-level recreational use."

"How about people involved in violent crimes?"

"He got a confession out of a rapist last month and there was a guy at D Company involved in a murder conspiracy. That one went to polygraph before he was able to get a confession."

"What happened to them?"

"Both were kicked out of the Army. There was nothing more they could really do to the rapist." Wedge loosened his tie and unbuttoned the collar of this shirt. "The statute of limitations had expired. The other guy was extradited to Virginia. I think he was convicted and sent to prison."

"Where's the rapist now?" McGuire began to feel too warm, so he took off his sports coat and draped it on the back of his chair. He noticed Wedge sneak a look at the Browning Hi-Power he wore in a brown leather pancake holster on his right hip.

"He's in some mental institution in Arizona. The guy like, flipped out after he left here. It was his sister he forcibly raped . . . at knife point." Wedge added, "This building doesn't have any insulation. When the sun's out, it gets a little warm in here."

McGuire nodded an acknowledgement and let his eyes wander over to two large oriental scrolls with Chinese writing on them decorating one wall. He had no idea what they said. He turned back to Wedge. "I always thought most of the young people here at DLI were former Boy Scouts."

"Most of them are. Only a few turn out to be real nasty cases." Wedge made small popping sounds with his gum. "A few thousand students come through here each year, but we only get involved with the ten percent that have had serious problems."

McGuire checked out a large map of the world held in place by thumbtacks on a framed corkboard just to the right of the Chinese scrolls. Dozens of red map tacks identified most of the major cities in Europe and the Pacific Rim. Places Howard's been, McGuire wondered. "Has my brother ever been physically threatened by anyone he's investigated?"

"Not since I've been here," Wedge said. "Well, he did receive a couple of hate letters, but he didn't take 'em seriously. Steve would know if there was anything serious like that in the past."

McGuire's brow furrowed. "Who were the letters from?"

"I think one was from a guy who got bounced out of here and wound up in Saudi Arabia as a 'grunt' in the 82nd Airborne Division."

"And the other?"

"He's still here, assigned to Company D. When his security clearance was denied, they yanked him out of class and placed him in a casual status. That's kind'a like the military equivalent of purgatory. They're processing him out of the Army for fraudulent enlistment."

"What was that case about?" McGuire asked.

"Well, they're discharging him because of undisclosed pre-service drug use, but the main issue was his involvement in satanic cult activity. It's not as bad as it sounds. He was into some really strange shit, but nothing criminal other than the drugs." Wedge got up and walked carefully around the small office, limping slightly.

"Can I get a copy of the threat letter from the second guy?"

Wedge stopped pacing and rested his hand on a document shredder sitting on a table near the door. "If the letter isn't here in Howard's files, he may have given it to Butler. I should be able to get a copy for you." He must have noticed McGuire staring at a sign taped to the document shredder, dedicating it to Fawn Hall. "I think this is Howard's idea of a joke," he said. "Steve thought it was funny. It has something to do with the Iran/Contra hearings."

A smile spread across McGuire's face. "Well, if you find a copy of the hate letter, just fax it to me at the station."

"I would, but we don't have a fax machine."

"Doesn't your agency have a lot of offices spread around the country?" McGuire asked.

"Yeah, about two hundred."

McGuire just shook his head. "We should get started sorting through Howard's stuff. I brought two cardboard boxes with me; they're out in my car. I'll be back in a minute."

When McGuire returned, Wedge had already emptied the desk drawers onto the desktop and was sorting through the items. McGuire went to the credenza. Lying flat in the bottom of the first drawer he opened was a framed photograph of himself when he was fifteen. He was wearing hip waders and standing in the middle of a mountain stream with a fly rod in one hand and a large cutthroat trout in the other.

He grasped the photograph and stared at it intently. As he wiped the dust off the cold smooth surface of the glass with his hand, he realized a lump had formed in his throat. Howard had taken the picture on their last fishing trip together, twenty-two years ago, just before Keith's interest in fishing was displaced by a preoccupation with cars and girls. He set the photograph aside so he could place it in the cardboard box last.

McGuire cleared his throat and said, "Clayton Butler mentioned a hostage case Howard was working on."

"He started a SOVBEAR case in August, actually two of them."

"SOVBEAR?"

"Oh, that's what Howard calls hostage cases involving Soviet Block Émigrés And Refugees. There's like, a few hundred instructors here at DLI from Warsaw Pact countries. They don't need security clearances as such, but because they have such close contact with students who are all going on to intelligence jobs, the instructors are investigated to determine their loyalty to the United States." Wedge placed a thick blue three-ring binder and a DIS telephone directory into the bottom desk drawer. "Butler had me work with Howard on the case. As I said, it's actually two cases, a husband and wife who work as instructors in one of the Russian Departments."

"What can you tell me about the cases?"

"Well, they're not classified . . . but there are some aspects of the case that are like, kind'a sensitive." Wedge stopped what he was doing and turned toward McGuire. "I'm not sure what I can tell you."

"Skip it for now. If we need to, we can deal with it later. Who were Howard's closest friends?"

"The only person I know is Steve Wepsala," Wedge said. "There really wasn't anyone else Howard was particularly close to."

"How did he spend his free time?" McGuire wondered how others would answer the same questions if they were asked about him—one intermittent girlfriend, one close work associate, one distant brother, no outside interests.

"He reads a lot. I don't think he had any other interests, except maybe fishing." Wedge paused and looked quizzically at McGuire. "Look, what is it you're not telling me?"

"What do you mean?"

"I thought Howard was shot and robbed outside the American Tin Cannery."

"Yeah . . . well, he was shot, and his wallet was taken. That doesn't necessarily make it a robbery." McGuire paused as the image of his brother lying in a hospital bed with his head bandaged and a hose taped to his mouth invaded his thoughts. "I think there might be something else involved. Perhaps it was only made to look like a robbery. I'm not sure of anything yet, and I don't have much to go on. Whoever shot my brother took his wallet, but didn't take his Rolex watch. Two witnesses are fairly certain the gunshots sounded muffled, indicating a silencer may have been used."

"What about Howard's years in the CIA? Maybe something from his past caught up with him," Wedge said and placed two thick volumes on interrogation techniques into a cardboard box.

"It won't do any good to speculate about that until I've looked into things that are closer to home. I could use your help. Howard and I haven't had much contact recently. I hardly saw him, even after he moved back here in eighty-six. I don't know who his friends are or anything about his recent activities. I didn't even know he could operate a computer."

"Is your department letting you investigate this case?" Wedge asked.

"For the moment anyway. There's only me and one other detective at the department."

"Look, what I told you about Howard's casework has to be off-the-record. If you need some of it for your report, we'll have to go through official channels. I'm sorry, but I can get into a lot of trouble for not following procedures." Wedge's face began to redden. "I'm still in my probationary year with DIS. What did Butler tell you when you talked to him?"

"Hardly anything at all. He said you knew more about Howard's work than he did, and I should ask you about it."

Wedge's mouth tightened. "He just didn't want to bend the rules himself."

"Rules or no rules, I'd still like your help." McGuire loosened his tie and rolled up his shirtsleeves.

"I'll help in any way I can, as long as you don't put any of this stuff in your reports."

As they talked they continued to rummage through Howard's belongings. It was amazing the things a person accumulated in a few years—coffee cups, plaques, radio, pictures, books—things that transformed a sterile office into a personal workspace. They were barely able to fit all of it into the two boxes.

McGuire learned Wedge was recently married. He graduated from San Jose State University in 1987, majoring in Administration of Justice. For two years he tried to get hired as a police officer, but he was never able to pass the physical agility test. In the meantime he tried selling cellular telephones to support himself, but being a salesman just didn't appeal to him. In fall of 1989 DIS needed additional personnel, and they had no physical agility test. Wedge applied and was hired in December.

They finished at a little after five. Howard's personal effects contained nothing that shed any light on his activities. As they loaded the boxes into the trunk of his Ford, McGuire's stomach growled noticeably. "I missed lunch today," he said. "Do you want to join me for dinner? There're still a few things I'd like to go over with you. That's if you don't have other plans."

"Dinner sounds great," Wedge said. "Tonight's a school night for my wife. Katherine's taking night classes to finish her degree in business. She won't get home till late. Where do you want to go?"

"It doesn't matter. I want to drop these boxes off at the station first. It won't take a minute. Why don't you leave your car here and ride over with me?"

Wedge glanced at McGuire's left hand and didn't see a ring, but decided to ask anyway. "What about your wife?"

"I'm not married . . . anymore."

# CHAPTER FIVE

TUESDAY 5:30 P.M., 13 NOVEMBER 1990

Wedge saw a battered green Toyota Corolla sitting in front of the police station. McGuire parked right behind it. In the lobby of the station, a man was standing at the front desk talking to the desk clerk. The clerk was shaking his head from side to side, then he saw McGuire and pointed to him.

The man turned around to face McGuire and Wedge. He was tall and lanky in his mid-forties. He extended his right hand toward McGuire. "Keith, I'm so sorry about Howard. I just can't believe it."

McGuire, balancing a cardboard box in his right arm, parried his outstretched hand by gesturing toward Wedge. "Eugene, this is Gordon Wedgwood. Wedge is a federal agent. Wedge, meet Eugene Leach."

Wedge shifted the box he was carrying to his left side and reached out with his right hand to shake Eugene's. He disengaged his hand quickly and shot McGuire a sideways glance.

McGuire introduced Wedge to the Kenneth Graves, the desk clerk, and Graves tripped the electric latch to the door to the interior of the station. Wedge got into step behind McGuire as he pushed his way through the door. He could feel Leach looking him over from head to toe.

Leach caught the door before it closed. "Wait a minute, Keith, I need to talk to you about Howard."

"Well, come on back to my office."

Wedge set his box down on the floor and found himself a chair near McGuire's desk. McGuire remained standing and appeared to be reviewing items in his "in" basket as Leach seated himself next to Noguchi's desk.

"I saw Howard Sunday night," Leach began.

McGuire turned and stared at Leach.

A half-smile appeared on Leach's face creating a smug look. "I've been trying to get hold of you since Monday morning, but every time I called, you were either out or in an interview."

Wedge noticed McGuire's face soften as he spoke. "Well, I'm here now. Tell me about it." Leach looked at Wedge, back at McGuire, and hesitated for a moment. "It's okay," McGuire said, "you can talk in front of Wedge. He's Howard's partner."

Wedge had never thought of himself as Howard's partner, but in a sense he was. They'd worked together on the two hostage cases. That was enough to establish a partnership. The idea appealed to him.

"Well, I'm at The Tavern Sunday night around seven," Eugene said. "I see Howard sitting at a corner table with another man. I've got some information for him, so I walk over toward his table. But . . . he sees me and he gives me one of those hard looks out of the corner of his eyes, like he doesn't want to be recognized. So, I just go back to my table, finish my drink, and leave."

"Who was he with?" McGuire asked.

"Don't know. Never saw him before." Eugene crossed his legs exposing part of a hairy calf above his gray and maroon argyle socks.

"What did he look like?"

"Early fifties, short black hair, dark leathery complexion with thick eyebrows, a big man, larger than Howard. He was wearing a green plaid shirt, buttoned at the collar but no tie, pleated tan corduroy slacks, and cordovan penny loafers."

"Anything else?"

"They were huddled together talking quietly. I couldn't make out what they were saying." Leach folded his arms across his chest and occasionally pulled at his chin with his right hand, displaying long slender fingers with a large signet ring on his little finger and a heavy gold bracelet on his wrist.

"How long did you stay there?" McGuire asked.

"About twenty minutes. They were still there when I left if that's what you mean."

Wedge noted Leach had a full head of wavy blonde hair that was just a little too blonde and a little too thick. His gray Harris tweed jacket was patched at the elbows and under it he wore a maroon turtleneck sweater. His navy wool slacks had a sharp crease and his black oxfords were highly polished.

"You had some information for Howard," McGuire said. "What was it?"

Eugene pulled out a notebook from the inside pocket of his sports coat and leafed through some pages. "Ran into Howard at The Gilded Cage last Thursday. It's about noon, and he's sitting at a table with Louie Joubert. When I come in, Howard gets up and asks me to step outside. He tells me he's interested in someone called Dale who's a client of Louie's. Howard says Louie won't tell him shit. Well, I don't know who Dale is, but Howard says it's important and involves national security, so I promise to find out for him. Frankly, I'm a little suspicious. I think Howard might be throwing up a smoke screen to cover his meeting with Louie. Anyway—"

"Why did you think that?" McGuire interrupted.

"Because I saw Howard hanging around Lovers' Point a couple of times last month, trying to look inconspicuous. That's where Louie meets most of his, ah . . . clients. I do some checking and find out that Dale's an officer in the Navy. I think he works at the Naval Postgraduate School. I don't know his full name yet, but he lives in an apartment on Sloat Avenue."

"Is there anything else?"

"No, but there is something you can do for me."

"What's that?" McGuire asked.

"It seems Bruce got himself into a minor jam at Lovers' Point. Maybe you could talk to the DA's office about it."

"Who was the arresting officer?"

"Sergeant O'Donnell."

McGuire grimaced. "That's going to be tough, but I'll see what I can do. Call me if you get anything more on Dale. Oh, and Eugene, let's keep this just between the three of us, okay." He walked Leach back out to the lobby, then returned to his office.

"Well, what do you think?" McGuire asked.

Wedge shook his head in disbelief. "Who in the hell was that?"

McGuire smiled and reached into his coat for his notebook. As he talked, he jotted down some notes. "Eugene's one of my snitches ... I mean, one of my confidential informants. I introduced him to Howard when he was working a case that led to a group of homosexual students at DLI."

"What's he do?"

"I think his parents left him some property. He doesn't have to work. I've helped him once or twice and he's given me some good information." McGuire pulled an ashtray out of a desk drawer and set it on his desk. He patted down his pockets until he located his cigarettes and a lighter. He lit up and inhaled deeply.

Wedge got up and moved to where Leach had been sitting, away from the cloud of gray smoke forming over McGuire's desk. "Like, who's Louie and Bruce and what's The Gilded Cage?" he asked.

"Bruce is Eugene's sometimes boyfriend. Probably got caught giving someone a blowjob at the public restroom at

Lovers' Point. Louie Joubert is a local dope dealer. He's been in and out of jail on a number of drug offenses. Mostly he sells cocaine and ecstasy to gays. Sometimes he trades it for sex . . . sometimes with kids." McGuire settled into his swivel chair and propped his feet up on his desk. "The Gilded Cage is one of our local gay bars. I'm surprised you haven't heard of it."

"Is Joubert gay too?" asked Wedge.

"I wouldn't label him as gay. He's either bisexual or just totally indiscriminate. Was my brother working any cases at the Naval Postgraduate School?"

"No. I'm sure he wasn't."

McGuire dusted a long ash off his cigarette into the ashtray. "How about Navy officers at the DLI?"

"What about 'em?"

"Well, did Howard have any cases on Navy officers at the DLI?"

"No. There weren't any among his cases," Wedge said.

"Any idea why he would be checking on Dale?"

"Well, Howard could have like, received information about Dale from a walk-in informant . . . but we're not allowed to do any investigative work in those situations." Wedge fell silent. He didn't like what he was thinking, and he sure the hell didn't want to raise any suspicions about Howard.

McGuire interrupted Wedge's thoughts. "I don't understand. What do you mean you can't investigate?"

"We can only report what we're told by an informant. If someone at a higher level decides to open a case on the matter, then it's sent back down to us for the appropriate investigative work."

"So, if you find out someone with a security clearance is, for example, doing drugs, you can't open an investigation on your own initiative?"

Wedge said, "Yeah, kind'a sucks doesn't it?"

McGuire shook his head. "Let's go eat. I'm getting a headache."

From their table at the Tinnery Restaurant Wedge could see the tall stately cypress trees and jagged rock formations of Lovers' Point Park across the street. Beyond it the shimmering reflection of the moon rising in the east made a wide silvery stripe across the bay. Only four other tables in the restaurant were occupied. There was a low murmur of conversations and the occasional clatter of silverware against china.

Over dinner they kicked around a few possible explanations for Howard's visit to The Gilded Cage, but wound up discarding all of them. After a prolonged silence, McGuire broached the topic Wedge had previously considered, but had chose not to bring up.

"Look, my brother's not gay, but I can't rule out the possibility that he might have been involved in something shady . . . maybe even something to do with drugs."

"I respect Howard a lot," Wedge said. "I can't believe he'd be into anything illegal." The thoughts that crept into his head bothered him, but he was having trouble saying them out loud. "Look, your brother, he—"

"What?"

"He . . . ah, had an appointment book. Have you gone through it yet?"

"What appointment book?"

"He kept a pocket calendar, the type you record your appointments on."

"It wasn't in his clothing."

"Maybe it's at his house."

"We ought to go over there and look around," said McGuire.

"I don't know. I don't have any authority to search his house."

"It's all right. I'm being appointed his conservator by the court. I'm supposed to go over there and handle his personal matters." McGuire pushed himself away from the table.

"Wait a minute," Wedge said. "That doesn't give me any authority to rummage through his house with you."

"Well, Butler asked me to return Howard's badge and credentials along with any other DIS property I find."

"So?"

"So," McGuire said, "we're going there to recover DIS property. And if we find any, you'll be there to take custody of it."

"Okay, but I need to call home and leave a message for Katherine, so she won't worry if she gets home before me." Wedge got up and handed McGuire a twenty-dollar bill. "Here, can you take care of the check while I make my phone call?"

# CHAPTER SIX

TUESDAY 7:45 P.M., 13 NOVEMBER 1990

A heavy cloud cover had moved in and obscured the moon. A street lamp cast a harsh light across the front of Howard's townhouse. Cream-colored duplex and fourplex units with dark brown roofs stood primly behind uniformly manicured lawns. The buildings were all the same yet different. One had aluminum siding, another was stucco, and yet another was board and batten.

Wedge got out of the car and cleared his throat. "Keith, you know, the thought occurred to me earlier that your brother was, ah . . . well, Howard was in a position to—"

McGuire stood on the concrete path to Howard's front door and signaled Wedge to stop. "Did you see that?" he whispered.

"See what?"

"Something in the window on the second floor."

Wedge looked up at the window, but saw nothing.

"Are you armed?" McGuire asked.

"No."

"Don't you guys carry guns?"

"Guns. We can't even carry Mace. I have to rely on my good looks and charm to get me out of a bind," Wedge whispered.

"It's a wonder you're still alive." McGuire bent over and pulled up his left trouser leg. From an ankle holster he slid out a stainless steel Walther PPKS. "Here take this. Flip the safety up. Leave the hammer down. There's a round in the chamber. It's double action."

Wedge hesitated before accepting the gun. "Do you think whoever's in there is armed?"

"Howard was shot forty-eight hours ago. Now someone's burgling his house in the middle of the night. Do you want to operate on the assumption he's not armed?" McGuire pulled a key ring out of his coat pocket and selected one of the keys. "Here, I think this is the key to the front door. Give me a couple minutes to get around back, then make a lot of noise opening the door, but don't go in until I call for you." McGuire slipped quietly through the gate at the side of the duplex and disappeared into the backyard.

Wedge stood in front of the building staring at the gun in his hand, wondering what he had gotten himself into. Wasn't this what he had always wanted; wasn't it what he had spent four years in college preparing himself for? He hefted the gun. The cold metal made an audible click when he flipped the safety off. Adrenaline pumped into his blood, and the muscles in the middle of his back began to tighten up as he made his way up to the front door. He had often day dreamed of situations like this, but somehow he never really imagined how it would feel.

As he reached the door, he heard something move inside. His body froze and tensed up. Make some noise, he thought.

He tried to insert the key into the lock, but his hand was trembling. Wedge steadied his hand against the doorframe and managed to force the key into the lock. He pushed and pulled the doorknob, then twisted it back and forth. He waited a few seconds before he turned the key and shoved the door. The door swung wide-open and slammed up against a wall.

When Wedge realized he was silhouetted in the doorway by the street light, he jumped to one side and pressed his back against the outside wall of the house. Both hands tightly gripped the gun. He felt sweat trickle down the side of his face.

McGuire crept around to the rear of the townhouse. He opened the screen door and found the door to the kitchen ajar. With his Browning drawn, he crouched down and slowly pushed the door open. It was dark inside the house. He listened intently before stepping into the kitchen. He strained to see into the dark corners of the room. There was a faint glow of light beyond a doorway straight ahead.

McGuire stepped cautiously across the vinyl floor, out of the kitchen, and into a carpeted hallway. The light was coming from a stairwell to his left. With his Browning held in both hands at chest level, he pressed his back against the wall and sidestepped until he reached the corner of the stairwell. He crouched down again before pivoting around the corner and looking up the stairs over the top of his pistol. The sudden loud rattling of the front door and the sound of the door slamming made him jump before he could remind himself it was only Wedge.

A dim glow coming from a skylight made it possible to barely see the carpeted treads of the stairs and the broad landing halfway up. Just as he got to the landing, he heard the latch of a door close. He stood motionless and strained to hear, but there was only silence. Let it be him; let it be the man who shot Howard, he thought.

His attention was focused on the top of the stairwell as he resumed his slow ascent. There was a hallway at the top. About twenty feet to his right at the end of the hall, he could see a thin ribbon of light escaping from under a door. His pulse quickened. He inhaled slowly, held his breath momentarily, then exhaled completely. Relax, be calm, be controlled, he told himself. With his gun in front of him, McGuire took one step toward the light when a closet door in the narrow hall swung open forcefully.

The door knocked the gun out of his hand and sent him sprawling to the floor and onto the stairs. As he struggled to get up, a knee smashed into his face. He grabbed desperately at the leg attached to it, wrapped his arms around an ankle, and yelled out for Wedge.

The person fell over on top of him, and they both rolled down the stairs to the landing. McGuire crawled up onto his knees, but the intruder wrestled him back down. He couldn't make out the person's face as they struggled in the darkness, but he was certain it was a man. Where was Wedge?

A bone-crushing blow from nowhere slammed against the side of his neck. He felt his body go limp just as he lost consciousness.

From outside the front door, Wedge heard a loud crash and the scuffling of feet. He heard his name being called, but he felt paralyzed, unable to move. More scuffling sounds came from inside the house, then another loud crash. He stood there motionless for what seemed like minutes and felt his heart pounding. He was suddenly cold and shivering.

When it was apparent no one was coming out his way, he took two deep breaths and forced himself to step over the threshold onto a tiled foyer. In the semi-darkness he could barely make out the shape and contents of the room in front of him.

Wedge clutched the Walther with both hands and stepped warily into the living room. All the curtains must have been closed. The only light came from the open door behind him. His right foot struck a stack of books lying in the middle of the floor and scattered them about. He dropped to his knees and strained his eyes for any movement in the room.

To his right was a hallway and just beyond that, a stairwell. As his eyes adjusted to the darkness, he saw more books lying about. The contents of a cabinet drawer had been emptied onto a coffee table. Sofa cushions were in a disheveled pile on the floor. Ahead and to his right, he could see the kitchen.

He traversed the living room as if he were in a minefield and made his way over to the kitchen. At the right rear corner of the kitchen a door leading to the backyard was open. Wedge stepped softly across the kitchen floor and peeked out the doorway. The upper hinge of the screen door was ripped out of the doorframe, and the screen was barely held in place by the twisted bottom hinge. The backyard appeared to be empty.

He walked through the hallway toward the stairwell. Just as he got to the foot of the stairs, he heard a moaning sound and stopped. Something moved on the landing above him. He shifted the pistol to his left hand and kept it pointed up toward the landing as he ran his right hand over the surface of the wall next to him. He found a light switch and flicked it up. The light was blinding as it reflected off the white walls and cream colored carpeting. A crumpled body lay on the landing.

"Is that you, Keith?" He heard another moan. He treaded up the steps one at a time, holding the pistol with both hands and keeping it pointed at the body. "Oh Christ, it is you. Keith, are you okay?" He knelt down and shook McGuire's shoulder.

McGuire rolled over and lay there for a moment, then reached up with his right hand. "Help me up will you," he groaned. Wedge pulled him to his feet.

"What happened?"

"I'm not sure." McGuire staggered into the kitchen, grabbed a dishtowel, and ran cold water over it in the sink. "Turn on some light."

The right side of McGuire's face was red and swollen. He stood over the sink and buried his face in the towel. "The back door was open. I came in and looked around. I just made it up to the top of the stairs and turned to the right when someone came busting out of the hall closet. The closet door hit me and knocked me for a loop. A knee caught me in the face. We both went ass over elbows down the stairs. Then it felt like he hit me on the side of the neck with a lead pipe."

"Who was it?" Wedge asked.

McGuire turned off the water, rung out the towel, and pressed it against the side of his face. "I don't know, but I think he stepped on my arm. It hurts like hell and so do my face and my neck. Did you see him?"

"No." Wedge avoided looking directly at McGuire.

McGuire looked over at the broken screen door. "I guess he must have gotten out of here pretty fast. Did you hear a car drive away?"

"No," Wedge said. Why didn't McGuire come right out and ask him where he had been while McGuire was getting his head stomped?

"Then he must have parked some distance away and walked over here." McGuire turned around and faced Wedge. "How bad do I look?"

"It may take a few days for the swelling to go down."

"I don't think he'll be coming back," McGuire said. "Let's take a look around."

The living room, kitchen, and laundry room had been thoroughly rifled.

"Whatever he was looking for, I don't think he found it down here," McGuire said. "Let's check out the rooms upstairs first."

The second floor, which included a bedroom, bathroom, and den, showed no signs of disturbance. The den contained a large bookcase, a four-drawer filing cabinet, a large old walnut desk with a wooden swivel chair, a separate typewriter stand with an Underwood Five manual typewriter, a dark brown leather sofa, and a television stand.

"We must have interrupted him before he got started up here," McGuire said.

Books were two deep on each shelf of the bookcase. Wedge perused the titles. They were mostly historical, political, and socioeconomic works on European and Asian countries. There were some classical books on warfare and intelligence along with some old novels by English, American, Russian, and Japanese authors. "He's got books here written in Japanese and Russian," Wedge observed out loud.

"Yeah," replied McGuire. "My brother attended DLI in the late sixties before he went to Japan. We had a great time together that year. He taught me how to drive."

"Did he study Russian too?"

"I don't know." McGuire paused and wrinkled his brow. "Out in the driveway you started to say something about Howard. What was it?"

"Well . . . at the restaurant you suggested Howard might've been involved in something illegal," Wedge said. "Of course I don't suspect Howard of anything, but I think you should know all DIS agents are like, in the perfect position to blackmail people."

"You think my brother was shot because he was blackmailing someone?"

"It's just something to think about. He digs up a lot of dirt on people; dirt some folks might pay serious money to keep out of their security file."

"Who for example?" McGuire opened the drawer of a filing cabinet and rummaged through the folders.

"What if he identified Dale before Leach did? If Dale's a Navy officer, and just about all Navy officers need a security clearance, he'd be a prime target for blackmail.

The walls of the den were lined with framed certificates and photographs bearing personal inscriptions. Wedge recognized a few of the names on the photos—a former Director of Central Intelligence, a famous Army Special Forces Colonel, and a retired three-star general. A shadow box contained a neatly arranged display of military medals—a Silver Star, Bronze Star, Purple Heart, Meritorious Service Medal, Army Commendation Medal, Vietnamese Cross of Gallantry, Vietnam Campaign Medal, and Vietnam Service

Medal. Wedge couldn't remember Howard mentioning any decorations he received in the Army.

McGuire finished searching the filing cabinet and moved over to the desk. On top of the desk was an envelope addressed to Keith. Inside was a birthday card with a drawing of a rainbow and a handwritten inscription: "Wishing you a rainbow on this and every birthday. As always, Howard." His birthday was still two weeks away. A surge of emotion rose from his chest to his throat and up to his eyes. He fought it off and regained his composure. He opened a desk drawer to put the card away.

In the drawer lay an eight-millimeter camcorder. McGuire picked it up, popped out a cassette, and read the label. He looked through the desk drawers for other cassettes, but found none. He slipped the cassette back into the camcorder. There was a patch cord already connected to the camera, so he plugged the free end of the cord into the back of the television and turned it on.

"What're you doing?" Wedge asked.

"What's it look like I'm doing?"

"Do we have time to watch videos?"

McGuire shrugged. "It's labeled 5 November 1990—kind of a strange way to label a video cassette, don't you think? Let's see what Howard video taped last Monday."

The picture was dark, but it was obviously a restroom viewed from an overhead position. In the center of the TV screen was an empty toilet stall.

"What the shit is this?"

"That's exactly what it is," McGuire said. "It's a shitter in a public restroom."

"Why in the world would he have something like—"

"Wait a minute. Look, someone's going into the stall."

"I don't want'a watch this." No sooner had Wedge spoken, then a second man entered the stall, closed the door, and dropped his trousers. The first man was seated on the toilet and the second man stood facing the first. "Oh, Jesus Christ . . . this is disgusting. Turn it off!"

"He's getting a mouthful, isn't he." McGuire let the video run for a few more seconds before switching it off. "Did you recognize either of those two?"

"Christ, all I could see was like, the top of their heads."

"Yeah, all three of them," McGuire quipped.

"I can't believe that belongs to Howard. Let's get this over with and get out of here."

McGuire placed the camcorder back in the desk drawer and led the way over to the bedroom. On top of a chest of drawers McGuire found what he was looking for. "Is this the pocket calendar you told me about?" McGuire held up a four-inch-by-seven-inch brown vinyl notebook.

"Yeah, that looks like it."

McGuire found Howard's badge and credentials on a nightstand. "Here, take this and turn it over to Butler in the morning," he said and handed the black leather case to Wedge. "Let's call it a night. We can go over the notebook tomorrow."

"What're you going to do about the guy that was in here?"

"I'm not sure yet. It doesn't look like he was after anything of value . . . well, at least not the usual things . . . unless it was drugs."

"Damn. Who do you think he was?" Wedge asked.

"At first I was hoping he was the man who shot Howard. Now I'd rather he was just a common household variety burglar, but there's not much chance of that. I've got no idea who he is or what he's after. If you've got any ideas, speak right up, don't be bashful."

Wedge just shook his head.

"Look, why don't you go out to the car and wait for me," McGuire said as he headed down the stairs. "I'll lock the place up. No sense leaving anymore fingerprints than we already have. I'll come back in the morning, give the place a thorough going over, and collect whatever latents might have been left.

Maybe we can meet for lunch and try to make sense out of some of this."

After dropping off Wedge at the Presidio, McGuire drove home. What information would he share with Upham? Much of it put Howard in a bad light and would only fuel Upham's suspicion that Howard was into something illegal. Upham wouldn't hesitate to use it to get McGuire taken off the case. Even McGuire couldn't help speculate about his brother's activities. It was okay for him to speculate, because he would try to disprove any wrongdoing. Upham, on the other hand, would make it the primary focus of the investigation. Perhaps he could just avoid discussing the case with Upham for a while.

At home in his apartment Keith McGuire had trouble sleeping. The pain in his left forearm, his neck, and his face caused him to toss and turn, trying to find a comfortable position. The events of the day kept crashing in on his brain. Soon his thoughts were replaced by memories from his adolescence—scenes of Howard teaching him how to drive the family station wagon, Howard showing him how to fly fish, Howard taking him out to the pistol range—as he fell into a fitful sleep.

# CHAPTER SEVEN

McGuire was on his way out of the station when heard Upham. "Hey, McGuire! Wait a minute. I need to talk to ya."

"Is it important or can it wait till later?" McGuire yelled back.

"I think you ought to look at this. It'll only take a minute."

McGuire followed Upham into his office where he had some papers spread out on his desk.

"What'd you do to your face?" Upham asked.

"I had a fight with my girlfriend."

"Oh." He hesitated for a moment, then pointed at a credit report. "According to this, your brother has a $105,000 loan with Security Pacific Bank, his mortgage. He also has VISA, Diners Club, and American Express credit card accounts."

"Good. Make me a copy of that. I'll need it to report his cards were stolen."

"No, you won't. I've recovered his wallet along with all his credit cards."

"Where?" McGuire couldn't keep the surprise out of his voice.

"A young kid was playing under the Outrigger Restaurant on Cannery Row at low tide yesterday afternoon around four. He found it wedged between some rocks and turned it over to a meter maid who was working the area." Upham had a smug look on his face as he pulled a clear plastic evidence bag containing a brown wallet out of the bottom drawer of his desk and dropped it on top of the credit report.

"That should be secured in the evidence room, not left lying around in your desk."

Upham ignored his comment. "While you were out screwing off yesterday evening, Monterey PD phoned us, and I went over to pick it up. The meter maid turned it in to the Admin Sergeant at Monterey. He recognized the name and called us. The only obvious thing missing from the wallet is cash. The fact his credit cards weren't taken supports my theory that your brother wasn't simply the victim of an armed robbery."

McGuire glanced at the papers on Upham's desk. "And it appears you've decided to pursue the investigation based on that premise."

"That's right, I have. Someone needs to take charge of this case and get it going in the right direction. I checked county real estate records." Upham stood erect with his chest puffed out and both hands on his hips. "It seems your brother paid $195,000 for his town house last March. With a mortgage of $105,000, that means he made a down payment of $90,000. Any idea where he might get that kind of money?"

"No, none at all."

"Well, what have you turned up?"

McGuire hesitated, then lied, "Nothing yet."

"Who was the federal agent you were with last night?"

"My, my, you have been busy."

"Graves told me you and a federal agent met with Leach yesterday evening while I was over at Monterey PD."

McGuire asked, "Is Graves one of your snitches now?"

"If I find out you're hiding anything from me on this case, Captain Headley's going to hear about it, and you may wind up back on patrol working the grave shift."

"You seem to know everything. What could I possibly hide from you?  I'd really like to stay and shoot the shit with you, but I've got work to do. There are two boxes of Howard's stuff from his office sitting on the floor next to my desk. You're welcome to search through them. If you haven't already thought of it, you might want to search under the Outrigger to see if anything else was dropped there and question some of the merchants." McGuire turned and walked out of the office.

Well, now he had done it. He had intentionally withheld information about a crime from another detective. But if he shared the information with Upham, he had no doubt Upham would use it to have him taken off the case. If Upham investigated this case by himself, he might never find out who shot Howard and why.

McGuire drove to his brother's town house and spent the morning conducting a latent investigation. The intruder had left a pair of channel-lock pliers and a pry bar hidden under a bush near the back door. Neither had fingerprints on them. In some soft dirt next to the bush, he found a shoe print and made a plaster cast. There was no doubt the marks on the door and doorknob were made by the tools he found, but he photographed everything anyway, including the fingerprints on the door, doorknob, and door frame. He spent time in the living room and kitchen trying unsuccessfully to determine what the intruder was looking for by the way the search was conducted.

When he was through at Howard's place, he went to Community Hospital and obtained some elimination prints from his brother. He returned to his office and completed his report as he normally would, but filed it in his desk drawer. He tagged and secured the tools in the evidence room at the station.

The videocassette at Howard's place bothered McGuire more than he let on. What kind of shit was Howard involved in? He was starting to wonder if he had misjudged his brother all these years. He thumbed through Howard's pocket calendar. It was an ordinary appointment calendar with a separate section for addresses. Turning to Sunday, 11

November, he found a single notation: "18:30 meet Zagorsky
@ Tavern." He looked back through the week and found each
day had only a few phrases inscribed, except for Saturday,
which was blank.

> *FRI, 9 Nov: DLI Day, case review w/Wedge.*
> *THU, 8 Nov: 08:00-12:00 Poly Willis*
> > *12:30 Gilded Cage*
> *WED, 7 Nov: 07:30 SI Ashton 2hrs*
> > *17:30 L.Pt. "S"*
> *TUE, 6 Nov: 07:30 SI Harris 1hr*
> > *09:00 SI Coggins 3hrs*
> > *13:00 SI Glazeman 2hrs*
> > *17:00 Election*
> > *20:00 Dinner w/Wepsala @ Fandango*
> *MON, 5 Nov: 09:00 SI Sowdon 3hrs*
> > *17:00 L.Pt. "S"*

The entries prior to Monday, 5 November, looked like
more of the same, except each Monday and Wednesday
evening in October had a location near the shoreline listed,
followed by an "S."

In the address section of the notebook were entries for
Wedgwood and Wepsala, but nothing for Zagorsky. In the
back of the address section was a page for recording important dates. Keith's name was written at the very top:

> *Keith Elliot McGuire*
> *Born:  30 Nov 52*
> *Married:  ~~15 Jun 72~~    5 Sep 82*

Just below that were his parents' names, their birthdays,
their wedding anniversary, and their date of death. He had
also listed the names of Keith's former wives and their
birthdays.

Howard had always remembered the special dates with
cards, flowers, gifts, even when he was far away. Keith had
grown accustomed to finding a fresh bouquet of flowers at his
parents' gravesite when he would go there on the anniversary
of their death.

It was one-fifteen and Fisherman's Wharf was busy, but Dominico's Restaurant was almost empty. Dominico's was a large, clean, airy place, rather nicely decorated. There was a long window along one side of the restaurant from which you could see a boat dock next door and beyond that, the yacht harbor. McGuire selected a table next to the window and seated himself, so he would have a good view of the main entrance and the entire room. Wedge took the seat across from him.

Through the window McGuire watched a fishing boat pull in, and a few minutes later a fisherman appeared next to a large metal basin at the edge of the dock ten feet above the water. As he began cleaning fish, an assortment of sea lions, sea otters, pelicans, and sea gulls gathered around. The applause of tourists mixed with the barking and cawing, as the sea lions and gulls showed off their ability to catch scraps of fish thrown into the air. The pelicans and otters ate only when scraps were thrown directly to them and not intercepted by a gull.

McGuire finished his meal, he reached for a cigarette, and motioned to the waiter for more coffee. Wedge pushed his plate aside and examined the pocket calendar more closely. "I can go back to the office and check, but I'm fairly certain the entries like 'SI Glazeman 2hrs' indicate Howard conducted a two-hour Subject Interview of someone named Glazeman. I remember the Willis case. Howard had him—" Wedge stopped in mid-sentence when the waiter arrived and refilled their coffee cups. As soon as the waiter left he continued. "Howard had Willis polygraphed on the eighth. The ninth was like, DLI Organization Day. The school was closed for a day of special events and sports competition. We spent the day reviewing the Pavlenko case. Pavlenko's the SOVBEAR case I told you about. The only Wepsala I know is Stephen Wepsala. I have no idea who Zagorsky is, and I don't know what L.Pt.'S' might mean."

"At least we know Zagorsky has dark hair and is a relatively large man, and he met Howard at the Tavern On The Bay at the American Tin Cannery Mall. L.Pt. must be Lovers' Point," McGuire said. "That video cassette at Howard's place, what was the date on it?"

"Five November. That matches one of the dates in here," Wedge said and handed the appointment book back to McGuire.

"Surveillance . . . Howard was doing a surveillance at Lovers' Point. The video was made at the public restroom at Lovers' Point Park." McGuire took another sip of coffee. "We better find out who Dale is. He might be one of the two men in the video tape."

"DIS agents aren't authorized to do surveillances under any circumstances. Howard could get fired for something like that." Wedge shook his head. "He wouldn't risk his job by doing an unauthorized surveillance just to make a case on a homosexual. Besides, I double-checked and he hasn't had any cases involving Navy officers for over three months."

"This may not have anything to do with his job. He may have simply decided to go into business for himself." McGuire flipped through a few pages of Howard's appointment book and held it out for Wedge to see. "Look at all the Mondays and Wednesdays in October. See the S's? Those are all locations along the Recreational Trail. Lovers' Point is at the end of the Rec Trail."

"So what are you saying? Howard spent two nights a week trolling for queers along the Rec Trail, so he could make 'X' rated home videos?"

"I don't know, but I think it has something to do with Dale. Can you check over at the Naval Postgraduate School and . . . shit, I just remembered."

"Remembered what?" asked Wedge.

"I F.I.'ed a Russian guy at the crime scene. He was about six-foot-one, 220 pounds with short dark hair and thick eyebrows." McGuire pulled out his notebook and flipped through its pages. "Here it is—Sergei Karasov. He's a Russian instructor at DLI. But he claimed he didn't know anything."

"What's F.I.'ed?" Wedge asked.

"It's when you stop and question someone—Field Interrogation."

"Oh yeah, right. I knew that," Wedge said. "But the name in appointment book is Zagorsky."

"I'm going to pay a visit to Karasov, then talk to Steve Wepsala," McGuire said. "Could you try to identify Dale? Oh, and see what you can find out about Karasov through DLI records."

"Look, I don't know. Our agency keeps us on a pretty short leash. I don't have the latitude to like, investigate matters outside—"

"You're an investigator aren't you? Your partner's been shot for Christ sake," McGuire said.

"I don't need to be reminded of that."

"You're in a position to get it quickly and discreetly. I'm not." McGuire took one last angry drag on his cigarette and crushed it out in the ashtray.

"I'll do what I can, but remember, nothing I get for you can be used in court or attributed to me." Wedge shifted in his chair.

"Speaking of which, were you able to get me a copy of the hate letter that soldier sent my brother?"

"I couldn't find it at Howard's office, so I asked Butler. He said he would look for it, but I wouldn't count on him finding it. Anything more than 90 days old has to be destroyed. If he kept a bootleg copy of the letter, he won't admit it."

"Okay, let's plan on meeting at Howard's place tomorrow. I want to look around there a little more, and it'll give us a chance to go over whatever we're able to find out between now and then." McGuire swallowed the last sip of coffee in his cup and stood up.

"How about after work, say about six. It could take me the rest of today and most of tomorrow to come up with anything on Dale and Karasov." Wedge got up and dropped his napkin onto his plate.

"Fine," McGuire replied, "I'll meet you there at six. I'll bring some Chinese food."

# CHAPTER EIGHT

WEDNESDAY 2:30 P.M., 14 NOVEMBER 1990

Wedge wanted to be involved in this investigation with McGuire, but he knew he had to be extremely careful and hide his activities from others in DIS. During his training at the Basic Agent Course in Virginia, they had repeatedly cautioned the trainees not to play cops and robbers. They were background investigators and nothing more. They were not allowed to conduct investigations without proper authorization. As a probationary agent he could be fired for any infraction. He knew it would be useless to discuss the matter with Butler. Butler did everything by the book and always made sure his ass was covered. Still, McGuire's comment about being Howard's partner had an effect on Wedge. DIS Agents almost always worked alone, but Wedge had worked together with Howard on the Pavlenko case and they had fallen into a mentor/protege relationship.

He was ashamed of how he had been paralyzed by fear last night and how his inaction had contributed to McGuire's injury and the burglar getting away. Sure, he had been scared before, but never like that. He had thought about it on the way home Tuesday night, reliving each second of it. He kept thinking of how it might have turned out if he hadn't frozen. He desperately wanted another chance to prove to himself that he wasn't a coward.

It was a good thing Katherine had been asleep when he got home; otherwise, he probably would have told her all about it, except for the part about being afraid. This morning he had been in a more rational state of mind and knew she would become upset if he told her he had been involved in anything that had to do with guns. She wanted him to pursue a career with a real future, but she didn't object to him working at DIS, because there was no danger involved. Well, what he was about to do, he would have to hide from both his boss and his wife.

He was lucky his caseload wasn't too heavy. The crisis in the Middle East had resulted in the deployment of a few hundred thousand G.I.'s to the Persian Gulf. And more were being sent there every day. Consequently thousands of security clearance investigations had been put on hold and the number of new requests had declined significantly. Even counting the twenty cases he had taken over from Howard, Wedge only had thirty-eight pending cases. Of course two of them were hostage cases—the Pavlenkos—which took considerably more time than a regular case. But the casework on the Pavlenkos had nearly been completed. Still, if he were going to help McGuire, he would have to find some way of accounting for his time.

DIS was extremely numbers oriented. Each agent had to account for his work day in five-minute increments and accomplish at least seven interviews or record checks a day. At times the pressure to complete a high number of leads and case closings had a negative impact on the quality of the investigations.

Wepsala had repeatedly told him not to worry about lead count and case closings. "Just do the best you can, put in an honest day's work, and the numbers will be there for you at the end of the month." It was easy for him to say. He was an experienced efficient investigator whose monthly stats weren't scrutinized like that of a probationary agent.

At the DIS Field Office Wedge wandered into the agents' bullpen. It was late afternoon and the room was empty. He listened for foot steps in the hallway. He grabbed a binder containing a computer printout of all Navy personnel stationed in the Monterey area and sat down at a desk in the corner of the room, out of view of the secretary across the hall. There were over three thousand names listed alphabetical.

There was an easier way to do this, but he knew asking for a computerized search by first names would invite questions from the people at the Navy Personnel Support Detachment, particularly because he wasn't one of the agents who worked cases at the Naval Postgraduate School. Any request of that type would be unusual enough for someone to mention it to one of the agents who normally worked here, and they would in turn want to know what Wedge was doing on their turf.

He had gotten to "Byrne" when he heard someone approaching. He quickly closed the binder and turned around. Butler and Miles Quinlan walked into the bullpen. Butler had his coffee mug in his right hand. The two men stopped talking when they saw Wedge. "Miles, you've met Wedgwood before, haven't you?" Butler asked.

"Sure, I know Wedge." Quinlan walked up to Wedge with his ready smile and his outstretched hand. "How've you been?"

"Just fine, sir. And you?" Wedge replied. Quinlan was the Director of Investigations of the Northwestern Region. Wedge had met him once before when he came down to Monterey from San Francisco to attend one of their office meetings. Had he really remembered Wedge, or had Butler and Quinlan just gotten through talking about him? The region covered more than seven states and had about two hundred investigators assigned.

Butler interrupted, "Miles, do you take cream or sugar?"

"Black," he said without turning away from Wedge. "Terrible thing about Howard. I came down today to look in on him at the hospital and check with the chief of police in Pacific Grove."

"Did you meet Howard's brother there?" Wedge asked.

"No, he was out of the office. Had a nice chat with the chief though. He briefed me on the status of the case."

"Mr. Wedgwood, what brings you to the office?" Butler asked as he handed Quinlan a mug of coffee.

"Oh, nothing. Just trying to track down a possible reference here at the school," Wedge said.

"Do you need any help?" Butler said.

"No. I found what I was looking for."

"I meant, do you need any help with your caseload at DLI?"

"Uh, no. I can handle it."

"Well, I don't like leaving you up there by yourself. I want Martha Pembroke to work with you part-time until I figure out how I want to reshuffle our resources." Butler glanced over at Quinlan, as if expecting a nod of approval. Instead, Quinlan grimaced and headed across the hall to Mrs. Thurgood's office.

"Really, everything's fine. If I need any advice, I can like, phone you or one of the more experienced agents." Wedge grabbed a file folder out of his briefcase, walked over to the duplicating machine, and turned it on. It made a terrible screeching sound as it warmed itself up.

"How many cases are you carrying now?" Butler asked.

"A little under forty, but I've got it under control."

"Nevertheless, I've decided to send Martha over to work with you starting on Monday." Butler watched Wedge intently as he spoke. "Things have slowed down a little here at the School and at Fort Ord. Bob can manage without her for a while."

"If you think it's necessary, couldn't you send Bob?" Wedge started feeding pages of a sworn statement into the copier.

"Do you have a problem with Martha?" Butler raised his voice slightly.

Wedge turned around to face Butler. "No, now that you've put it in that tone of voice, I guess I don't."

"Martha's an experienced investigator, and she's been with this organization a lot longer than you have," Butler said.

It was pointless to push the issue. Butler never changed his mind after he announced a decision. The trouble was he never consulted anyone before making his decisions. Sure, Pembroke had been with DIS for a long time—as a secretary. She had completed college by attending night school and gotten her degree in music. Her investigative experience consisted of three years of conducting police records checks and one year of handling totally clean cases on junior officers at the Naval Postgraduate School.

"Institutional nepotism at its worst" was how Wepsala had once referred to Pembroke's appointment as a special agent. She was forty years old, grossly overweight, and had the charm of a rutting elephant seal. What bothered Wedge more than her appearance was her demeanor. She was too officious and always referred to herself as Special Agent Pembroke.

"Well, I've gotta run. See you later." Wedge gathered up the copies he made and returned the file folder to his briefcase.

"I want you to cut out fifteen of your cases and give them to Pembroke by the end of the week," Butler said as Wedge walked out of the room and headed toward the stairs.

"Yessir," Wedge called back and continued down the hall. He could finish going through the personnel roster later. Right now his time would be better spent at the DLI Security Office checking out Karasov.

Wedge tried to act nonchalant as he accepted Sergei Karasov's DLI Security file from Betty Lou Thompson, the file clerk.

"Mr. Karasov's security investigation was just completed in September. Why do you need his file now?" Betty asked. She was a spindly older woman, perhaps fifty-eight, with pinched features and wire-rimmed glasses that she wore low on her nose.

"I'm like, one of the mushrooms, Betty. No one bothers to tell me why they want anything done."

In the back of the Security Office Wedge spread out Karasov's file on the duplicating machine and leafed through it wondering who had conducted the background investigation. He was fairly certain no one in the Monterey DIS office had worked on the case. The file indicated "Hostage BI completed favorably by DIS 26 Sep 90. Loyalty determination only—No clearance granted." The file also included a copy of Karasov's federal employment application, Personnel Security Questionnaire, National Agency Check Request, an ID photograph, and a fingerprint card. He made duplicate copies of the documents and slipped them into his briefcase along with the original ID photo and fingerprint card. He refastened the papers back into the file folder, walked over to Betty's office, and handed her the folder. "Betty, this file doesn't have any investigative reports in it."

"That's because I file the investigative reports separately. If you need them, I'll have to open the safe," she responded in a slightly irritated tone.

"If you don't mind, I'd like to see them."

Betty looked even more irritated as she fought with the combination lock on her security container. "You'll have to excuse me for a minute, I need to go to the ladies' room." Betty went to her desk and removed a handbag from its large bottom drawer. She left the office quickly without looking back.

She was only gone two or three minutes. Just long enough to check the safe combination, which she probably had written down on a slip of paper inside her purse, Wedge thought.

When Betty came back into the office, she placed her handbag on top of the safe and began rotating the lock dial without saying a word. She opened the safe on her first try, fished out a thin file marked "For Official Use Only" and handed it to Wedge. She stood in front of him waiting for him to return it to her, so she could lock up the safe. "Will this take long? I don't like to leave the safe open."

"A couple of minutes. I just need to verify a couple of things." Wedge found a report with the DIS Monterey Field Office code. The investigating agent's name on the report took him by surprise—S/A H.C. McGuire. Wedge glanced down to the bottom margin of the report where the initials of the investigator, the typist, and reviewing official were typed. Howard's initials appeared in the block for the investigator and the one for the typist. Butler's initials were typed in the reviewing official's block, but he hadn't penned his initials above his typewritten initials as he normally would, if he had reviewed the report. Wedge realized he had a shocked expression on his face, so he composed himself before slowly closing the folder and lifting his head. "I need to make a copy of two reports in here. I'll be back in a minute." After he returned from the back of the room, he handed the file to Betty, thanked her, and quickly left.

Wedge sat in his '85 Plymouth Reliant and stared out the front windshield without looking at anything in particular. In his hands was the copy of the report written by Howard. Attached to the two-page report was a twelve-page typewritten statement signed by Karasov. He also had a copy of a report from the Chicago Field Office. The typeface on Howard's report and the written statement were the same. Wedge recognized it as having been made on Howard's office computer printer. The typeface on the Chicago report was different. It looked as though it had been typed on an old manual typewriter. There had only been two field reports in the file. The rest of the reports were merely the results of name traces at various government agencies, all of which were favorable.

It was strange that Howard had never mentioned the Karasov case. When Howard briefed him on the Pavlenko case in early September, he had given Wedge bootleg copies of a few of his most recent hostage cases to review. Karasov's case was not one of them, yet Howard's report on Karasov was dated 3 September 1990.

Wedge went back to his office at the Tin Barn and tried to catch up on his report writing. When he finished his second report, he glanced at his watch. It was four o'clock. If he hurried, he could get to Herrmann Hall by four-fifteen. The DIS office would be completely empty by then. Everyone who worked there, especially Butler, went home promptly at four. He could search for Dale in the Navy personnel roster in the bullpen without being disturbed and try to get home in time to help Katherine prepare dinner.

By six he had gone through the entire roster. It wasn't glamorous investigative work, but it produced results. There were only three sailors in the Monterey area with the first name of Dale: Petty Officer Third Class Dale Zackary Maitland at DLI, Lieutenant Dale Margaret Treherne at NPS, and Lieutenant Commander Dale Carston Ellis at Fleet Numerical Oceanography Center. In the morning he'd sneak a peek at the office case files and see if there was a closed case on Ellis.

On the telephone Karasov didn't sound eager to cooperate, but he agreed to meet McGuire at his apartment at four-thirty. Karasov's second-story apartment was on the fringe of Pacific Grove's low-rent apartment area, if you could call $650 a month for a cramped, one-bedroom unit low-rent. The apartment looked out onto Ransford Avenue and was accessible from an outside stairway and landing. McGuire drove up in his unmarked Ford. He could see a man watching him from behind the heavy drapes of Karasov's apartment window.

"Mr. Karasov, Sergeant McGuire, we spoke on the telephone earlier. May I come in?"

Standing in the doorway in broad daylight, Karasov looked older than he had on Sunday night. He nodded and stepped back from the door. McGuire entered the apartment and noticed a large silver samovar in the middle of a table in the small dining area to his right. It was next to an even smaller kitchen.

Karasov guided him into a dark crowded living room furnished with an eclectic mix of chairs and tables that looked as though they might have been purchased at garage sales. The room had a musty odor.

"You are exactly on time. I appreciate punctuality," Karasov said. "You have more questions for me, Sergeant McGuire?"

"Yes, a few. I won't take much of your time." McGuire sensed a bit of arrogance in his voice and manner, but at the same time he seemed somewhat guarded. Karasov motioned him to a gray leather tub chair near the window through which Karasov had watched his arrival. He seated himself in a brown corduroy wingback chair opposite McGuire.

Karasov had wide square shoulders and a trim waist. Thick thighs bulged against his slacks and his small feet contrasted sharply with the rest of his body. He had a small tight mouth and an aggressive Roman nose. The scar under his square chin was just as nasty looking as McGuire remembered it. Deep lines creased his broad face. It was a face you took seriously, one that probably didn't tolerate much frivolity in others.

"I read in newspaper, the man who was shot is also named McGuire," Karasov said. "May I ask, is he a relative?"

"My brother."

"Then, you and your family have my sympathy. There was no picture in newspaper. He is younger than you?"

"No. He was older by ten years. What was your reason for being at the American Tin Cannery on Sunday evening?" asked McGuire.

"I am suspect?"

"We have no suspects yet. It's necessary to question everyone who was there that night." McGuire pulled out a small notebook and pen. "Perhaps you saw or heard something that might be of value to us."

"Of course. I am willing to help. I went to mall to do shopping." Karasov drummed the fingers of his right hand against the arm of his chair as he spoke. "By chance, I meet old friend of mine, Charles Howell. We have drink together at Tavern and talk about old times."

"Where does he live?" McGuire wrote down the name and waited for an address. He noticed a momentary change in Karasov's facial expression and a slight hesitation in his response. Karasov's fingers stopped drumming against his chair.

"He is moving to new house in San Francisco, 5210 Pacheco Street."

"What's his phone number?"

"No telephone yet. He will give it to me later."

"Well, where does he work then?"

Karasov shifted in his chair. "He starts new job in January. Transamerica Corporation."

"Oh?" McGuire sat mute and watch Karasov intently. He waited for Karasov to fill the void with an explanation. After a full fifteen seconds of silence, McGuire gave in. "Mr. Karasov, do you know Howard McGuire?"

"No."

"How long have you been in the Monterey area?"

"Almost five months already."

"Where did you live before?"

"Illinois. I move here in June, this year, for job at Defense Language Institute."

"You said, you went to the mall to shop. I didn't notice you carrying anything when I spoke to you Sunday night. Did you make any purchases?"

Again Karasov hesitated before answering. "As I said before, I meet Charles Howell by chance. I plan to buy clothes, but we talk, we drink, then it is too late to do shopping."

"Thank you." McGuire got up and began moving toward the door. "Mr. Karasov, how long have you been in the United States?"

"Five years." Karasov opened the door for McGuire.

"Your English is very good. Thank you again." They shook hands and McGuire started down the stairs to the driveway.

# CHAPTER NINE

THURSDAY 10:00 A.M., 15 NOVEMBER 1990

Wedge had lost track of time preparing a report, and now he had to rush to get to the office before Michiko Thurgood took out the mail. He was in luck; the elevator was working. He rode it up to the fourth floor, praying it would make it without a problem. The elevator was old, unreliable, and chronically in need of repair. Last month it had taken a woman hostage and held her for two hours before repairmen were able to free her. Wedge bounded up the small stairs from the fourth to the fifth floor and made it to Mrs. Thurgood's office just as she was sealing her last envelope.

"Michiko, how's it going?"

"It is going just fine, Mr. Wedgwood. And how are you today?"

"Please, Michiko, you promised to call me Wedge."

"I'm sorry Wedge-san, I keep forgetting." Michiko gathered up a stack of large envelopes.

Wedge motioned his head toward Butler's office and whispered, "Is he in a good mood this morning?"

She shook her head. "He left a little after nine for a doctor's appointment." Michiko started out the door with the envelopes. She came back and laid the envelopes down on her desk. "I almost forgot to lock up." She walked over to the three heavy gray metal Mosler safes behind her desk.

"Hey, don't worry about them. I'll watch the phones and stand guard while you make the mail run," Wedge said.

"Oh, thank you, Wedge-san. You know how fussy Mr. Butler is about the files. I will only be a few minutes." Michiko gathered up her envelopes again.

It was the first time he had heard her say anything even mildly critical of Butler. As she made her way down the hall toward the small stairwell at the end of the wing, Wedge checked his watch and called after her, "No need to rush, take your time."

Butler was more than just fussy about the case files. Agents weren't allowed in the file drawers. If an agent needed a file on a closed case, Michiko would get it for them and have them sign a "charge-out" card for the file.

The "case control ticket" boxes were even more inviolable. The boxes contained card-size pieces of paper on which were recorded data needed to track each case from opening to closing and to determine how much and what type of investigative work was completed and by whom. Butler spent hours each day counting, analyzing, and recording information on the tickets. During the first week of each month, he used this information to produce the most impressive statistical reports in the region.

Wedge looked up and down the hall to see if anyone was nearby. He carefully closed the door with just enough force, so it sounded like a door being intentionally closed. The hallway floor was old brittle linoleum. He'd have no trouble hearing anyone approach.

He stood in front of the safes. His eyes darted from one safe drawer to the next until he found one labeled "September G to L." He pulled the drawer open and searched till he found Kaminske . . . Kane . . . Kaplan . . . Kato. He started again from the beginning and searched through all of the files that started with "K." He checked the cases closed in October and the ones closed in November. No Karasov. Precious minutes were passing. His anxiety made him move faster. He went through the same routine looking for a file on Ellis. No Ellis. Maybe Ellis was an open case assigned to another agent and Howard was only helping on the case.

Wedge tiptoed through the closet-like passageway from the secretary's office into Butler's private sanctum. The air was warm and stale, heated by the morning sun that flooded in through his dormer window. The three wooden ticket boxes were sitting in the middle of Butler's desk. Just as he lifted the lid to the box marked "Open—Blue," the telephone on Butler's desk rang. Startled, Wedge's whole body jerked violently.

Instinctively he reached for the telephone, but stopped himself before he lifted the receiver. The phone continued to ring, as he stood tensed, leaning over the desk with his hand resting on the receiver.

He heard footsteps running down the hall. A key unlocked the door to the secretary's office. Someone snatched the secretary's phone from its cradle, silencing it before the sixth ring. Wedge let go of the telephone receiver and crept to the corner of the room. He pressed his back against the wall and stood motionless, sweating.

"Defense Investigative Service, Special Agent Pembroke. . . . No, she's away from her desk. . . . I don't know, maybe in the restroom. . . . Why don't you try back in 10 minutes. . . . Right, goodbye."

Wedge heard the receiver being replaced in its cradle, the door slam, Pembroke mumbling to herself, and footsteps trailing off down the hall.

His heart was pounding. He looked at his watch. Ten-fifteen. What if Butler returned early? How would he explain his presence in his office? Don't think about Butler. Concentrate on what you're doing. He wiped his sweaty palms on the sides of his trousers and went back to the box marked "Open—Blue." It had blue tickets filed alphabetically by investigator. He checked each set of tickets, except those behind his own name. No Ellis.

He grabbed the box marked "Closed." Its blue tickets were grouped alphabetically by month. There was no ticket for Karasov or Ellis. He froze at the sound of footsteps. They came down the hall from the direction of the main staircase in the center of the wing. He gently closed the lid of the wooden box. As the footsteps neared Butler's office, he edged into the passageway and waited. The footsteps stopped. A key turned the lock on Butler's hallway door.

McGuire stood viewing the immaculate landscaping of the front yard as he waited on the porch for someone to answer the door. The house sat on the ocean side of Scenic Road just south of the Carmel city limits in an area known as Carmel Point. Very expensive. He was about to push the doorbell for the third time, when he decided to go around to the side of the house. It was late morning. There was a Toyota pickup in the driveway. As he walked past it, he placed his hand on the hood of the pickup truck and felt a little heat rising from the engine compartment.

In the far end of the side yard, he saw a man wearing khaki work pants and a plaid flannel shirt under a gray sweatshirt, kneeling on the ground, spreading mulch around the base of some rose bushes. As he approached the man, he called out, "Pardon me. Are you Mr. Wepsala?"

The man rose and turned slowly. "I'm Stephen Wepsala. And who might you be?"

McGuire detected a faint, unidentifiable accent. "Keith McGuire, Howard's brother."

Wepsala's eyes smiled. "Please excuse my appearance. As you can see Mother Nature requires considerable help." He removed his work gloves before extending his right hand. "I'm pleased to meet you, Keith. I have some coffee brewing. Will you have some with me on the back deck?" Wepsala stood five foot eight and weighed about a hundred and fifty pounds. His handshake was firm and sincere.

He spoke in a low deep voice characteristic of someone with considerable experience commanding others. McGuire followed him into the house. In the kitchen Wepsala poured coffee from the pot into a carafe and found two thick cream-colored ceramic mugs. "I'm glad you came by. I've wanted to meet you for a long time. Howard has spoken of you often and fondly. I read about what happened to him. I tried to see him at the hospital, but without success. How is he?"

"Not well. He's in a coma."

"I am sorry to hear that. Your brother and I go back a long way. I have known him for over twenty years." He loaded everything onto a tray. "He is one of the few I regard as a friend, a good friend. Is there something I can do?"

"Howard's probably told you I'm a detective with Pacific Grove P.D. There are a number of unusual facts related to the shooting. Can I speak with you in confidence?"

"To the extent that I am able, yes." Wepsala picked up the tray from the smooth granite counter top and motioned with his head toward a sliding glass door at the far end of the living room. "The deck is out there."

McGuire went ahead of him and slid the door open. He followed Wepsala out onto a large redwood deck built in the shape of a ship's prow. The deck was built over an outcropping of rock that rose about sixty feet above the waterline. A small winter storm was brewing out at sea. The wind was light, but gusty. Not far away, white surf pounded against the rocky coastline. It was a million-dollar view, perhaps closer to two million.

"You probably know a lot more about Howard than I do," McGuire said. "Because of our lack of contact over the years, I don't know much about his activities. I guess we haven't been very close lately."

"You mean before he moved back to the peninsula?"

"Even after he came back."

Wepsala set the tray down on a round glass patio table. "I never measure relationships by the frequency of contact.

During the first fifteen years we knew each other, I doubt Howard and I saw each other more than thirty times. Based on the things Howard said about you, I had the impression he felt very close to you. After your parents died, you were the only relative he ever spoke of."

Wepsala's thick gray hair had recently been trimmed and barely touched his large ears. He looked as though he was in his early sixties and extremely fit for his age. Sad brown eyes, tired mouth, slightly hooked nose, and short gray beard combined themselves into a martyr's face—a face you immediately trusted.

McGuire had never considered his relationship to his brother from Howard's perspective. "I suspect that whoever shot Howard, planned and executed the shooting to make it look like a robbery. Is there anyone who might have a reason to want Howard killed?"

"A few, but none who would actually try it themselves or even have someone else do it for them." Wepsala poured coffee into the mugs.

"Why did my brother leave the CIA?" McGuire had to speak up a little to be heard. Sitting on the deck was like being near an airport. The heavy surf made the ocean sound like jet engines off in the distance, idling before takeoff.

"I heard from former associates that he was fired in early '86 as the scapegoat for a failed operation that ended in someone accidentally getting killed."

Wepsala paused and seemed to mentally compose what he would say next. "Howard never spoke specifically about the operation, but I had the impression he was the case officer for a Soviet agent. Somehow the operation was blown, but Howard was able to get his man out, one step ahead of the KGB. I heard that a number of CIA Soviet-East European Division human assets were lost about that time. Some of the old-timers in the agency suspected a mole. Others wanted to blame it all on Edward Lee Howard, the CIA employee who defected to Moscow in late 1985." He reached under his sweatshirt, pulled a pack of cigarettes out of his shirt pocket, and offered McGuire one.

"Is it possible the KGB might seek revenge against my brother for something he did during his intelligence career?" McGuire accepted the cigarette. He had resisted the urge to light up one of his own. There was an attractive piece of raku pottery on the table, but he couldn't tell if it was an ashtray or an empty flower vase.

"No. They don't operate like that." Wepsala screwed a short plastic holder onto the end of his cigarette before lighting it and pulled the raku bowl closer to them. "They pride themselves on their ability to track down and punish defectors, especially former KGB agents, but there is an unwritten rule against killing your opponent's intelligence officers."

"Have there ever been any exceptions to that rule?"

"Not exactly." Wepsala pulled thoughtfully at his beard and gazed off toward the south where Point Lobos jutted out into the ocean. "A few years back, there was an Army Warrant Officer by the name of Siegler who died under questionable circumstances. He was involved in a joint FBI-Army Intelligence operation that went bad. They used Siegler as a double agent against the KGB. He was found dead in a hotel room. They officially tried to call it a suicide, but the evidence indicated otherwise." Wepsala paused and turned back to McGuire. "The only other exception is reprisal for killing one of their agents, a kind of *quid pro quo*. But that hasn't happened in decades."

McGuire leaned back in his chair and warmed both hands on the mug. He sat quietly for a few moments before he asked, "What was Howard's attitude like after he was fired?"

"Frankly, he was bitter and disaffected toward the Agency and the government in general, but surely he told you himself," Wepsala said.

"We never discussed it."

"But at the time he must have come to you for moral support, as well as assistance of a more practical nature." Wepsala seemed to look at McGuire in a questioning, almost accusatory manner.

McGuire's face flushed. "Well, he came to visit me of course . . . but he didn't talk about his work . . . only that he was glad to be through with it and able to settle down. He didn't ask for any help. He seemed to be fine."

"Would you expect your brother to ask for help?"

McGuire felt an icy tightness in his chest. He recalled Howard's visit and their conversation clearly now. He remembered how he had told Howard about his own problems. The entire evening had been spent talking about Keith's life. Howard must have sensed his preoccupation and withheld any information about his own problems.

"Of course, you're right. I should've offered my help." McGuire turned his face away from Wepsala and looked out at the ocean. "Would you tell me what you know about his termination from the agency?"

"He rightfully felt he had been betrayed. After all, between the Army and the Agency he had put in close to twenty years of service, allowed himself to be bounced around from one country to another, and denied himself some of the most important personal aspects of life—like a wife and children." Wepsala brought the steaming mug of coffee to his lips and sipped slowly.

"Why didn't he marry?" McGuire asked.

"The Agency frowned on its personnel marrying foreigners—it probably still does. If you spend your entire career outside the U.S., there are few opportunities to . . . well, there just are not that many unattached American women running around Asia. Even if there were, a case officer can't give his work the time it demands and have anything resembling a normal family life. Howard gave the Agency one hundred percent, literally. It was his home and his surrogate family." Wepsala stared off in the distance again and fell silent.

"Selling your soul is easy when you are young," he resumed. "Changing your mind later is much harder. Howard never complained when he was passed over for promotion. He always told me he preferred to work as a field operative and a promotion would force him to take a desk job. But when they terminated him, it totally broke his spirit."

The sun slowly disappeared into an overcast sky and the air became noticeably cooler. McGuire shivered and reached for his coffee mug.

"Would you prefer to move inside?"

"No, I'm comfortable. I enjoy being outside." McGuire motioned toward the rock outcropping flanked by two gnarled cypress trees. "And the view here is awesome."

Wepsala picked up the carafe and poured more coffee into their mugs. "This will help keep you warm."

"If Howard felt so bitter toward the government, what made him decide to work for DIS?" McGuire asked.

"He came to see me in October '86 shortly after he returned to Monterey, and I suggested he apply for a position with DIS. He dismissed the idea without even really considering it. He said he did not want anything to do with the government. Naturally I was surprised when he came to the office three months later for an interview with Henry Schwartz." Wepsala tapped a long ash from his cigarette into the raku bowl.

"Henry Schwartz?"

"Henry was in charge of the office back then. I guess during those three months Howard pulled himself out of it, set aside his resentment, and realized he had to play the cards he was dealt."

"What made him change his mind?"

"Retirement. Civil Service retirement benefits are not as good as most people think, but they beat the hell out of no retirement at all. At the time he was forty-four years old and had over twenty years invested. He needed ten more years of federal service to retire comfortably. You think twice about changing horses at that stage of the race."

McGuire nodded his agreement and asked, "Howard's calendar shows he had a dinner appointment with you last Tuesday, the fifth. Did you see him?"

"We met at the Fandango Restaurant in Pacific Grove. Since my retirement last April, Howard and I have gotten together about once a month for dinner. I think it was his way of getting me out of the house, so I would not become a recluse."

"What did you talk about?"

"Oh, we made some plans for a fishing trip in the spring, talked about my garden, and discussed how Gordon Wedgwood was coming along. Do you know Wedge?"

"We've met." The wind shifted and a light gust brought with it the faint sour smell of rotting seaweed. McGuire looked to see where the odor came from.

Wepsala turned his nose up and sniffed the air. "We get that smell once in a while. Seaweed washes up on shore and gets trapped between the rocks. After a week or two in the sun, it gets pretty ripe." He pulled the cigarette butt out of its holder and dropped it into the ashtray. "Wedge is a sharp young man. In a few years he'll make a fine investigator."

"Did Howard talk about his work?"

"He groused about his boss, Clayton Butler, and about Miles Quinlan, the Regional Director of Investigations. He voiced the usual complaints about their emphasis on quantity instead of quality. Quinlan is a better man than Howard gives him credit for, but like many managers, he has lost touch with how things really are out in the field."

"Did he mention any specific cases?"

Wepsala seemed to ponder the question for a moment as he reloaded his cigarette holder. "He was angry about Butler's attitude toward hostage cases. Quinlan had chewed out Butler because of the large number of overdue cases the Monterey office had during the summer months. Butler took it out on

Howard and criticized him for spending too much time on hostage cases."

"I understand Wedge was working with my brother on his latest hostage case," McGuire said. "Did he talk about that?"

"Only in generalities. He seemed pleased with the way Wedge was handling himself on the case. Wedge deserves a lot of credit." A smile spread across Wepsala's face. "He digested a large amount of information on hostile intelligence methods of operation during the short time I had to train him."

"Did Howard talk about anything else?" McGuire asked.

"He asked me about my experiences with CDs."

McGuire raised his eyebrows. "He asked you about compact discs?"

Wepsala chuckled. "No, concealment devices. They sell simple ones now at retail stores. No doubt you have seen the hollowed out books and the empty beer cans that unscrew at the top. Howard asked if I had ever run across the use of a toilet paper roller as a CD. He also asked if I had ever known the Soviets to use flower arrangements as a method of agent communication. Neither was familiar to me."

"Did he tell you why he asked those questions?"

"No and I didn't ask."

"Was my brother ever the target of any reprisals or threats, because of his work with DIS?"

"Never anything really serious, just the occasional hate letter from people who were denied a security clearance or who had their security clearance revoked."

"Do you know a Sergei Karasov?"

"No."

"Did Howard ever mention his name?"

"Not that I recall. Who is he?"

"A Russian instructor at the DLI," said McGuire.

"He must be fairly new there. I knew the names of almost all the Russian instructors."

"How about a Zagorsky?"

"That name sounds familiar." Wepsala stroked his beard. "Zagorsky . . . there was a Zagorsky at the Soviet Embassy in Tokyo back in the late sixties. Stanislav Zagorsky. We suspected he was either GRU or KGB, but we never found out for sure. If he was one of them, he was very clever."

"Thanks, you've been very helpful."

"When will Howard be allowed visitors at the hospital?"

"Not until he's out of the ICU." McGuire took a last swallow of cold coffee and got up to leave. "The doctor expects they'll be able to move him to Garden North, the medical-surgical area, on Friday or Saturday. You should be able to see him just about any time of the day once they move him."

Wepsala rose to his feet and walked with him around the side of the house to the driveway where his car was parked. "If there is anything I can do, please let me know." He stood in the driveway and waved goodbye as McGuire drove off.

# CHAPTER TEN

Wedge waited in the closet-like passageway between Butler's office and the secretary's office. As soon as he heard Butler unlocking his office door, he quietly slipped through the passageway into the secretary's office. Quickly he opened her hall door, sat down behind her desk, and called out, "Is that you, boss?" Wedge pretended to review notes from one of his case files as Butler came through the passageway.

"Where's Michiko?"

"She went down to the post office. She should be back in a few minutes."

"What're you doing hanging around here?"

"I told Michiko I'd like, watch the phones for her while she went for the mail."

"Well, I'm here now. You can go back to work."

Wedge put his case file away and headed toward the door with his briefcase.

"By the way," Butler said, "I phoned you three times yesterday afternoon and you didn't answer. Where were you?"

"I must've been out running leads," Wedge replied with only a hint of sarcasm in his voice. Sometimes not having pagers or cellular phones had its benefits. "What did you want?"

"I want a copy of everyone's 'Work Time Report' for my mid-month review."

"I already made a copy and put it in your box." Wedge started to leave.

"Mr. Wedgwood."

"Huh." Wedge stopped and look back at Butler.

"Watch your step."

"Ah . . . right . . . sure. I'll be careful." Wedge strode off down the hall. He was more interested in getting out of there than he was in trying to fathom what Butler was saying or why.

Since there was no information on Ellis in the office case files, Wedge decided to risk a visit to the Navy Personnel Support Detachment on the first floor. On his way down in the elevator he puzzled over Butler's words. Was Butler just angry, because he wasn't respectful enough, or did Butler know what he was up to?

When Wedge arrived at the customer service counter, a young woman in a dark blue uniform was bent over near a bookcase, rearranging three-ring binders on a lower shelf.

He stood at the counter and called over to her, "Excuse me." She glanced over her shoulder at him and quickly straightened up. She looked barely nineteen and a just little on the plump side. The patch on her sleeve was that of a seaman apprentice. She ran her hands down her sides and smoothed out the wrinkles in her skirt.

"Yessir, can I help you?" She smiled.

Wedge still hadn't gotten used to having young women refer to him as sir. "Ah . . . yes . . . well, I'm Gordon Wedgwood with the Defense Investigative Service." He fumbled momentarily as he pulled out his credential case. He gave her a glimpse of the badge mounted on the outside of the leather case before letting the case fall open to display his credentials.

Her smile disappeared and was replaced with a blank expression. The only sound that escaped from her lips was "Uh-huh." She wasn't going to be any help.

"I need some assistance on an official investigative matter. Is your supervisor available?" Wedge asked.

"Yessir," she replied, "I'll get the Senior Chief." She disappeared into an office. Minutes later a man wearing a khaki uniform emerged from the office. He was in his early forties, of average height and build, with an air of authority. "VICKERS" was engraved on the black plastic nametag on his chest.

"You with NIS?" he asked before Wedge could introduce himself.

"No, Defense Investigative Service."

"You have some identification?"

"Sure." Wedge pulled out his credential case again and held it open on top of the counter. The Senior Chief Petty Officer grabbed the edge of the credential case to take a closer look, but Wedge held on firmly to the case. He eyeballed the credentials closely before releasing his grip and looking up at Wedge.

"I've never seen you before. You new?"

"Yeah, I've only been with DIS for a few months."

"I'm used to dealing with Martha and Bob." The Chief grabbed the telephone and tapped in a phone number from memory. "This is Senior Chief Vickers at PSD. Is Bob Stoddard there?"

Oh Christ, Wedge thought, he's calling the Field Office. The muscles in his back tensed up. He had no legitimate reason for being here. If Butler found out, he'd want an explanation.

"How about Martha Pembroke?" Vickers waited for a reply. "Who am I speaking to?"

Moisture popped out on Wedge's forehead and his stomach knotted up.

"Mrs. Thurgood, do you have an investigator by the name of Gordon Wedgwood assigned to your office?" Another pause. "No, that's all I needed. Thank you."

As soon as he heard Mrs. Thurgood's name mentioned, he felt his body relax. Thank God, Butler didn't answer the phone.

"When someone new turns up, I like to check 'em out myself the first time they come in. You gonna be working here at the school permanently?"

"No. I cover DLI, but once in a while I get a case that brings me over here."

"What'd ya need?"

"Well, I'd like to review the personnel file of Lieutenant Commander Dale C. Ellis. He's assigned to Fleet Numerical."

Vickers wrote on a slip of paper and called over his shoulder to the young seaman apprentice. "Dinwitty, come here for a minute." He handed her the slip of paper. "Get this officer's file for me."

Dinwitty headed out smartly across the hall to the file room. She returned in less than a minute with a worn, inch-thick file folder and handed to Vickers. He opened the file and perused it for a moment before turning it around, so Wedge could read the papers it contained. Wedge pulled a pad of lined paper out of his briefcase and made notes as he flipped through the file. Wedge could feel Vickers watching him intently and trying to decipher his scrawled notes upside down.

Ellis lived at 1045 Sloat Avenue, Apartment 6, Monterey. He had a Masters Degree in mathematics from MIT. His last assignment was at the Naval Tactical Interoperability Support Activity in San Diego. He transferred to Fleet Numerical Oceanographic Center last June. There was an ID photo taped to a page, but he kept going through the file till he reached the end.

Ellis had a Top Secret clearance with some special access authorizations. Any involvement with a drug dealer would certainly be of interest to Navy security officials, but without a plausible reason for knowing anything about Ellis, Wedge had no way to report Ellis's activities. He could figure that out later. At least for now he could show McGuire he had produced some results from his investigative work. He flipped back to the ID photograph and studied it carefully before closing the folder and putting his pad of paper away.

Vickers tapped his black government-issue ballpoint pen against the counter. Wedge handed the file to Vickers. "Thanks for your help, Chief."

Vickers merely nodded and walked away, dropping the file on Dinwitty's desk on his way back to his own office.

# CHAPTER ELEVEN

THURSDAY 6:10 P.M., 15 NOVEMBER 1990

They sat at Howard's kitchen table. The smell of Chinese food escaping from the open containers awakened Wedge's appetite. Wedge pulled a file folder from his briefcase and laid it out in the center of the table between the containers of cashew chicken and pork chow mein.

McGuire started skimming through the documents as he shoveled fried rice into his mouth with chopsticks. He stopped when he got to the photo of Karasov. "Can I borrow this photo for awhile? I want to see if Leach can identify him as the man he saw with Howard on Sunday night."

"Sure. What did Karasov say?" Wedge piled chow mein onto his plate.

"He said he was at the Tavern On The Bay, but that he was there with someone else. It might be a language or a cultural thing, but I sensed he was holding back something." McGuire gestured at the other documents in the file. "Is there anything important in this stuff?"

"The forms indicate Karasov's security investigation was completed by DIS in late September." Wedge leafed though the papers until he found Howard's Report of Investigation and handed it to McGuire. "You can see that according to Howard's report, he spent six hours interviewing Karasov on the twenty-seventh and twenty-eighth of August. Did Karasov say whether he ever met Howard?"

"He denied any knowledge of him."

Wedge shifted his attention back to the food. Between bites he said, "There's more, and I don't like any of it."

"What?"

"I went through our office files, and I couldn't find any record of Karasov's investigation. There should have been like, a closed case file and a separate case control form. I couldn't find either." Wedge started in on the cashew chicken. After he dropped a few slippery pieces onto his lap, he abandoned the chopsticks and switched to a fork. He looked around the table and over at the kitchen counter. "D'you bring anything to drink?"

"I knew I was forgetting something. Why don't you check out the refrigerator?"

"There's a couple of Beck's in here. D'you want one?"

"Yeah. You've got copies of the security forms requesting the investigation in here . . . and a DIS report from another office. DIS must have conducted an investigation."

"The request for investigation is fine, but the report from the Chicago Field Office doesn't look right." Wedge emerged from the refrigerator with two bottles of beer in his hand.

"What do you mean?"

Wedge set the beers on the table and pointed to the report from Chicago. "Well, look at it. It was typed on an old manual typewriter. Look at the bottom of the report. See the three sets of initials? The first initials belong to the typist, the second belong to the investigator, and the third identify the supervisor that reviewed the report. All the initials are different."

"So what?"

Wedge went back around to his side of the table and sat down. "If the first two sets of initials were the same, I'd have no problem with the report. There's probably a few older agents in DIS who type their own reports on manual typewriters, but there aren't any secretaries or typists who would use one today."

"If you think someone faked the report, let's call Chicago and ask them about it."

"I don't want to do that unless I like, absolutely have to. It'll raise too many questions." Wedge grabbed his beer and gave the bottle cap a sharp twist. "Ahhhh, shit!" He shook his right hand as he got up, went over to the counter, and started going through drawers until he found a bottle opener.

"Okay, we can let it go for now. Look, can I hold on to this file for a while? I need some time to digest all of this, and I may want to run some checks on Karasov."

"Go ahead and take it. Take it all. I'd feel better having you deal with it." Wedge passed the bottle opener over to McGuire.

"I almost forgot," McGuire said. "Wepsala didn't know anything about Karasov, but he remembered a Zagorsky assigned to the Soviet Embassy in Tokyo in the late sixties who might have been KGB or GRU." McGuire took a few more bites of chow mein and washed it down with a swig of beer.

"Jesus, you don't think that—"

"No, I don't think so. By the way, how can Wepsala afford that house of his out at Carmel Point?"

"It's something isn't it? With that view I can't even guess at what it would sell for. His wife inherited it. Her parents had money."

"What about Dale?"

"Oh, yeah. I'm pretty sure he's Dale Carston Ellis, a lieutenant commander assigned to Fleet NOC."

"Fleet knock?"

"Yeah, Fleet Numerical Oceanographic Center."

"Oh."

"Well, anyway, in the file folder with Karasov's stuff is a page of notes I took while I was reviewing Ellis's personnel file. I couldn't get a photograph, but I saw one."

"Good, let's go upstairs and take another look at that video tape," McGuire said and winked at Wedge.

"Don't do that. It's disgusting enough as it is."

"What's the matter?" McGuire smiled. "Hasn't anyone ever done that for you?"

"Well yeah, but that's different," Wedge insisted.

"Other than the person's sex, what was different about it?"

"For one thing it wasn't in a public restroom."

"Are you telling me, if a gorgeous babe offered to give you a facial in a public restroom, you'd turn her down?" McGuire said.

"Well . . . maybe not if the stall had a door I could close."

"So basically you're telling me it all comes down to preference?"

"Can we talk about something else while I finish eating?" Wedge resumed his assault on the cashew chicken with vigor. After a minute of silence, Wedge changed the subject himself. "By the way, do you have Howard's appointment calendar on you?"

"Yeah, why?" McGuire pushed his plate aside and lit up a cigarette.

"Is there like, a notation in it concerning his interview with Karasov on the twenty-seventh and twenty-eighth of August?"

McGuire pulled it out of his coat pocket and thumbed through its pages. "It looks like he didn't do much on those two days. There's no reference to Karasov for that entire week."

Cigarette smoke wafted across the table into Wedge's face. Wedge shook his head. "Today's the 'Great American Smokeout,' isn't it?" he asked.

"You know, I think it is." McGuire rocked back in his chair, sipped his beer, and took another long drag from his cigarette.

Upstairs in the study Wedge connected the eight-millimeter camcorder to the television and turned them on. They watched closely as the figures entered the restroom stall.

"Wait a minute," Wedge said. "I want to back it up to the point where the one guy looks up." Wedge played with the camcorder controls until he was able to pause it on the proper frame. "No. He's not Ellis," Wedge said.

"What about the other guy? The one that's sitting down?" McGuire asked.

"I can't tell?"

"Maybe there'll be a better angle of him when they finish."

Wedge was getting impatient. "Jesus. Like, how often does this kind'a thing go on at Lovers' Point?"

"Not much anymore. It looks like they're done. What do you think?"

Wedge laid the camcorder on top of the television, but allowed the cassette to continue to run. "From the little I could see, I'd say the guy's hair was too long, unless he was wearing a wig. I don't think it was him."

McGuire began rummaging through Howard's desk. Wedge stood in front of the television and looked absently around the room. Some movement on the TV screen caught his eye, and he focused his attention on a man walking into the restroom stall. The man was dressed in a blue warm-up suit and wore tennis shoes. His hair was light colored and military length. This could be the guy, Wedge thought. He watched the man intently, but he was in and out of the stall before Wedge could be certain.

Wedge stood in front of the TV, trying to get a clear image of Dale Ellis's photo in his mind. The figure of a young boy quickly passed across the edge of the TV screen. In a minute he passed across the screen again in the opposite direction. The thought of young boys using the restroom and accidentally seeing what he had just seen disturbed him. He turned his attention back to the TV screen as another man entered the stall. Wedge got a clear view of his face as he took off his bicycling helmet. He recognized the man, but couldn't immediately place his face. "That's Aleks Pavlenko," he muttered. "Hey, Keith. This guy on the tube looks like Pavlenko."

"The guy you're doing the hostage case on?" McGuire turned and watched as the man in the stall fumbled with the toilet paper dispenser. "What's he doing?"

"I'm not sure," Wedge said. "I thought I saw him take something out of his pocket. Look, I think he just put some toilet paper in his pocket." Pavlenko was only in the stall for a minute before disappearing off the screen.

"Maybe he's got a cold and needed something to blow his nose with," McGuire said. "You think Howard set up the camera to record Pavlenko or was it just a coincidence?"

"Let's see if he comes back." Wedge pulled a chair over from the desk and positioned it in front of the television. "A couple of minutes ago, I saw someone who might have been Ellis."

"Do you want to rewind the cassette, so you can look at it again?" McGuire asked.

"No. Let's let it run for awhile."

Time passed slowly. Wedge was about to reach for the camcorder when the man in the warm-up suit reappeared on the screen. "That's the guy I saw earlier. Look, he's messing around with the toilet paper too."

The man was bent over with his back to the camera, blocking their view of the toilet paper dispenser. He put something into his pocket, opened the stall door, and left. Wedge grabbed the camcorder, backed up the tape, and paused the frame. "I can't be sure, but he might be Ellis." They ran the tape to the end, but neither of them appeared on the screen again, so they rewound it and played it again.

"Do you know what a concealment device is?" McGuire asked.

"Yeah."

"Howard asked Wepsala, if he had ever heard of anyone using a toilet paper holder as a concealment device."

"Do you think they're using the restroom as a dead drop?"

"Tell me about Pavlenko while we make a thorough search of this room," McGuire said. "You take the filing cabinet; I'll do the closet and the desk."

For the next half-hour as they looked for anything related to Howard's activities, Wedge summarized what he knew of the Pavlenko case.

Aleks Pavlenko had been born in Kiev in 1960 of a Jewish mother and a Ukrainian father. He had graduated from the Maurice Thorez Pedagogical Institute in Moscow with a degree in English in 1982. At Thorez he had met and married Zhanna Ilyanova, a fellow student. During their summers at Thorez, they worked as tour guides for Intourist, the state tourist agency. After graduation, they were hired as instructors at Thorez and taught Russian to foreign students.

In 1984 they applied for exit visas under the Jewish émigré program. Both were immediately fired from their jobs, but were able to support themselves by tutoring private students in English. About a year later their exit visas were granted and they flew to Vienna. In Vienna they had to choose between emigrating to the United States or to Israel. Since they chose the United States, they remained in Vienna for six weeks, then traveled by train to Rome. They found a pensione in Rome. With the financial help of HIAS, the Hebrew Immigrant Aid Society, they were able to get by for the four months it took the U.S. Government to grant them immigrant alien status.

In June 1985 they flew from Rome to New York to San Antonio. They held menial jobs in San Antonio until December 1985, when they obtained employment at the Lackland Air Force Base branch of the Defense Language Institute. By mistake, the Pavlenkos and many other Russian language instructors hired at Lackland were only subject to minimal security checks.

In August 1986 the Lackland branch of DLI closed and many of the instructors including the Pavlenkos transferred to Monterey. Shortly after their arrival in Monterey, they had a baby and bought a $180,000 home with a $150,000 mortgage. All went well until Zhanna was laid off from her job in October 1988. She was unable to get any outside work, so she became a full-time homemaker.

In July 1990 she was rehired by DLI. During her inprocessing at the Security Office, they discovered she hadn't received the right security investigation at Lackland. They also determined Aleks needed a complete background investigation.

Howard was assigned both cases in early August. He conducted local record checks, then waited for the results of the National Agency Check. The NAC was completed at the beginning of September and nothing of significance turned up. At that point Howard brought Wedge into the investigation. Together they interviewed the Pavlenkos' supervisors, work associates, friends, and neighbors. None of them were able to shed any light on the Pavlenkos' life in the Soviet Union.

A few people provided some information that caught Howard's attention. Aleks had reportedly taken up bicycling in July. One neighbor, an elderly man who suffered from insomnia, had noticed a light in the Pavlenkos' home would go on every other night at exactly 1:00 A.M. and would go off at 2:00 A.M. as if the light were controlled by a timing device. Somehow the Pavlenkos had been able to make their mortgage payments while Zhanna was laid off from her job at DLI. Both Aleks and Zhanna were GS-9's and each earned about $27,000 a year. During her twenty-one month lay-off from DLI, Zhanna only received a total of $5,000 in unemployment benefits. Their combined incomes were not nearly enough to cover their mortgage payments and other basic living expenses.

Howard interviewed Zhanna, and Wedge interviewed Aleks separately, but at the same time. The interviews took place on four consecutive mornings in late September. Howard had prepared two lists of nearly identical questions.

On the first day both Aleks and Zhanna were composed and confident. Their answers to the early questions were so similar there was no doubt the answers were rehearsed. Both claimed they were able to subsist during Zhanna's lay-off through frugal living, money from their savings, and unemployment benefits. They had not sought outside financial help. They had not returned to the Soviet Union for any reason. His only foreign travel since arriving in the United States had been four summer vacations to Mexico beginning in 1987. Zhanna and the baby had accompanied him on the first two vacations, but were unable to go on the last two.

On the seemingly unimportant questions that came later, their answers differed notably. Zhanna said they spent a week at a Black Sea resort near Odessa right after their marriage. Aleks stated they couldn't afford a honeymoon. They gave different answers for the location of their wedding reception, as well as different circumstances for their first meeting.

By the fourth day of the interrogations, Aleks seemed shaken and feigned embarrassment while correcting some of his responses from the previous day. Zhanna managed to maintain a relaxed demeanor and conversational tone. Howard and Wedge conducted the interviews in a friendly, empathetic manner. They accepted the Pavlenkos' explanations for mistakes without cross-examination. It was all reduced to separate written statements for Aleks's and Zhanna's signatures. They were also asked to sign releases that permitted DIS to review their bank records. The releases made an obvious impact. Even Zhanna became nervous and was unable to prevent her voice from cracking.

Their bank records showed only $2,000 in savings in October 1988. But in April and in November 1989 there were deposits of $10,000 each. Further digging produced a wire transfer slip for the second deposit. It was a stroke of luck, because wire transfer slips were normally discarded within six months. The slip showed only that the money was transferred from Suisse Credit Zurich as a family transaction. There was no record of where the April deposit came from, nor was there any record of the $30,000 Pavlenko used as a down payment for their house.

Howard finalized the investigative reports and had Wedge take a copy to the FBI. Howard didn't want to take the case there himself. The last time he had gone there, he had exchanged heated words with Walter Dombrowski, the Foreign Counterintelligence Specialist. Relations between the two were at a low point, so Howard had sent Wedge to see Dombrowski.

The FBI office was in a small nondescript office building near *El Estero* close to the Naval Postgraduate School. No signs indicating its presence were visible from the street or parking lot. Even the antenna on the roof appeared innocuous.

Dombrowski had sat at his desk, looking more like a gangster than an FBI agent. His tie had been at half-mast, his suspenders hung limp against his white shirt, and his sleeves were rolled up exposing his thick hairy forearms. He was smaller than Wedge, but his slightly crooked nose, deep set eyes, and square jaw made him look formidable. "So, what you're saying is you won't accept the case," Wedge had said.

"There just isn't enough to initiate an investigation." Dombrowski twirled a pencil around the fingers of his right hand.

"What else do you need?"

"Some evidence the Pavlenkos have passed information to the Soviets. I don't have the time to work a case based solely on the type of discrepancies you've got in your report." Dombrowski began lightly drumming the eraser end of his pencil on his desk. "I've got my hands full tying up loose ends on the Conrad case and working a couple of cases I have some solid leads on."

"We can't get that kind'a information through reference interviews and records checks." Wedge leaned forward on the edge of his chair. "You know we can't go any further than we already have. Besides, if we had the evidence you want to justify opening a case, what would we need you for?"

"Now, you listen to me, pal." Dombrowski slammed the pencil down. "I've been in this business for fifteen years. I don't appreciate you or anyone else coming in here and telling me how to do my job. I—"

Wedge threw up his hands and cut in. "Hey, I'm sorry; this case is important to me. I don't want to see it go unresolved."

Dombrowski rocked back in his chair. Frustration seemed to replaced the anger in his voice. "I'm not saying your case doesn't have merit, but I'm only one man, and I can only do so much. I have to be selective about what I spend my time on. Your office, particularly Steve and Howard, has turned over a lot of good stuff in the past, enough to keep two or three FCI specialist busy. But there aren't two or three of us here. There's only me. The other agents in the office don't work FCI cases. I can take the case, but I can't promise you I'll do anything with it."

When he had returned to the DLI, Wedge had given Howard a rundown on his meeting with Dombrowski. Howard had seemed neither surprised nor upset. He had decided to request a copy of the State Department records on Pavlenko. It would be a waste of time, but he did it because it would let him keep the case open a while longer.

# CHAPTER TWELVE

THURSDAY 8:00 P.M., 15 NOVEMBER 1990

McGuire closed the closet door and looked over at Wedge as Wedge wound up his account of his meeting with Dombrowski.

"Do you know Dombrowski?" Wedge asked.

"Well enough. He's okay. We worked a bank robbery together once. He normally doesn't get involved in that sort of thing, but they were shorthanded at the time. I've had more contact with the other guys in the Monterey Office."

Wedge picked up a photo album from the bookcase and began leafing through the pages. "Hey, there's a lot of pictures of Howard in here when he was really young." Wedge handed McGuire the album.

"Do you recognize the young boy he's playing catch with?" McGuire asked.

"Is that you? You must be seven years old in this picture."

McGuire recognized the pictures, but not the fine leather album cover. When their parents had died, Howard had asked if he wanted any of the old beat-up photo albums. He had no interest in them, so Howard had gathered them up in his arms like treasure. That was all Howard had wanted. He had left the rest of the personal property for Keith.

McGuire looked over at the bookcase. There were three more matching photo albums. Howard must have removed the pictures from the old albums and remounted them. Many of the pictures in the album showed Howard engaged in different activities with Keith.

He went to replace the album next to the others in the bookcase and noticed a small, black loose-leaf notebook jammed up against the back of the bookcase, partially hidden behind the photo albums. McGuire reached between the photo albums and pulled out the notebook. He flipped through its pages and came upon some photographs. "Yes!"

"You find something, Keith?" Wedge turned to see what he had found. McGuire was engrossed in the notebook. Each of the grainy black and white photos had been hand cropped with scissors and taped to a separate page of the notebook. There were photos, showing men going in or out of a small building.

"That's the restroom at Lovers' Point," McGuire said as he flipped through the pages. "Look, here's the guy in the bicycling outfit and here's another picture of him. Here's one of the guy in the warm-up suit."

Wedge jabbed his index finger at the man in the photo. "That's Ellis. I'm sure of it. And the other one's Pavlenko."

"Here's a picture of Joubert and Ellis," McGuire said. He flipped back to the front of the notebook and went through it page by page. "He must have spent a month on surveillance before he took these pictures. It looks like he set up a stationary surveillance at different points along the Recreational Trail between the Naval Postgraduate School and Lovers' Point. Where do the Pavlenkos live?"

"East of the school, near Laguna Grande," Wedge said.

"Sloat Avenue borders the west side of the school, so he could have been watching either Pavlenko or Ellis, and one led him to the other."

"My money's on Pavlenko," Wedge said.

"Okay, so we've got a suspicious Russian émigré possibly in contact with a Navy officer who has a security clearance, and the Navy officer is in contact with a drug dealer. One of them could have detected Howard's surveillance and tried to kill him." McGuire furrowed his brow and tapped the notebook against the palm of his hand. "But why? And how do we account for Howard's financial situation, and did he have some other reason for contacting Louie Joubert?"

"You want to focus on your brother instead of the others?"

"We can only work with what we've got. We need to figure out the motive for the shooting." He stuffed the notebook into his hip pocket, knelt in front of the desk, and opened the bottom desk drawer.

"Okay, what if Howard really went off the deep end? If he's been blackmailing people he's learned of through his job with DIS and either Pavlenko or Ellis was his latest victim, that could explain the money. Pavlenko or Ellis could've like, broken in here to search for things like the photos and the video tape." Wedge glanced around the room and walked over to the typing stand. "Or, if Pavlenko's a spy and he reported Howard's blackmail attempt to his boss, they could've sent someone to kill him."

"I don't think so, Wedge. When I spoke to Wepsala, I asked him if there was any possibility Howard might have been targeted by the KGB. He more or less ruled it out."

"There's also the possibility Howard began working for the KGB, then tried to quit after he found out about Pavlenko and Ellis. I hate to say it, Keith, but it works. Howard's known to the KGB, he gets fired from the CIA, becomes bitter . . . ."

"Wepsala said, when he first suggested to my brother that he apply for a job with DIS, he totally rejected the idea, but three months later he changed his mind."

"Suppose they approached him and offered to supplement his income, if he'd take the DIS job and fix a few investigations of Russian instructors at DLI like Karasov."

"Then why would he turn on them?" McGuire asked.

"Desert Shield," Wedge said. "There're U.S. soldiers at risk. With me working on the Pavlenko case with him, he would've had to go through the motions on the investigation.

He could've changed his mind near the end. What with the build-up of U.S. forces in the Persian Gulf, he could've decided to find out what Pavlenko was up to. That would've led him to Ellis. Ellis could be in a position to provide information that could endanger American lives." Wedge picked up a small manila envelope that was sitting in plain view, propped up against a typewriter.

McGuire asked, "What have the Russians got to do with the Persian Gulf?"

"Well, according to Howard, they have an interest in seeing Iraq succeed. They've been supplying Iraq with equipment and advisors. They're probably supplying them with intelligence too." Wedge opened the flap of the envelope and three Polaroid photographs dropped into his hand.

"Damn it. This is all speculation," McGuire said. "We don't have one piece of direct evidence—nothing I can use to get a search warrant for Pavlenko's or Ellis's residence. And the only thing I have that might identify the person who broke into Howard's place is a shoe print, and it may not even belong to him."

Both men lapsed into silence. McGuire became engrossed in a bundle of his brother's bank statements. He couldn't believe what he saw. His brother was a financially prudent man. He wouldn't leave large amounts of money sitting in a checking account. There had to be something wrong.

"Christ!" McGuire said, "he's got $32,000 in his checking account."

"Keith. You'd better look at this." Wedge spread the three photos out on the desk.

McGuire placed the bank statements back in the file and stood up. When he saw the pictures, he rocked back on his heels. "Whoa! She's a looker. Who the hell is she?"

"That's Mrs. Pavlenko."

"What? You're kidding. She could make it as a model. Looks like Howard was involved in a little hanky and/or panky."

"Are these considered boudoir photos?"

"That'd be stretching it. In boudoir photos they usually have at least some article of clothing draped over them, even if it doesn't cover much." McGuire leaned over the desk and took a closer look. Only Mrs. Pavlenko appeared in the photos. You never knew what a person was really like until you rummaged through their personal stuff. He grabbed up the photos and headed out of the den and down the hall. Wedge followed him into Howard's bedroom.

He held the photos in front of him and compared Howard's bed to the one in the photo. "I can't tell. The bedspreads don't match, but that doesn't mean anything. Where'd you find these?"

Wedge led the way back to the den. He picked up the manila envelope and leaned it up against the right side of the typewriter. "It was sitting just like that."

McGuire snatched the cover off the old Underwood Five typewriter and grabbed a sheet of paper from the desk. "Get me that DIS report from the Chicago Field Office."

When Wedge came back with the report, McGuire was already pounding out a few sentences. With the report lying on the stand next to the typewriter, he began typing the same words that appeared in the first paragraph of the report.

McGuire held up the two sheets of paper next to each other. "Shit, I'm no expert at this, but it sure the hell looks like the Chicago report was typed on this machine. It doesn't look good, does it? Thirty-two thousand dollars in his checking account, compromising photographs of a married woman, faked security reports."

McGuire drove behind the police station and parked his car. Rather than going back into his office, he radioed the desk clerk. There were no messages for him, so he told the clerk he was going off duty and walked across the street to his own car. Returning home at 9:00 P.M. was normal for him. Perhaps home wasn't the right word. His apartment was where he slept, showered, changed clothes and occasionally ate. It was a second-story unit in a relatively new apartment complex near Asilomar Conference Center in Pacific Grove. Many of his neighbors were young professionals, including a number of military officers attending the Naval Postgraduate School, who would only be there for a year or so. Perhaps because he knew they were temporary, he never made any effort to get to know them.

He flipped on the living room light switch with his elbow, walked over to the kitchen and deposited his briefcase and the mail on a small clear space on the kitchen counter. Dishes were piled high in the sink.

He debated with himself whether to relax with a beer or clean things up. He looked in the dishwasher for a clean glass, but the dishwasher was empty. The phone rang as he took his first swallow from the bottle of beer. Please, don't let it be the department.

"Hello."

"Hi, Keith. It's Alycia. Do you have plans for tomorrow night?"

"Well, ah. . . ."

"There's that new Japanese restaurant on 17th Street, Takara. I've been dying to go there. I heard they have excellent sushi." She was always enthusiastic about food, even when it was only raw fish.

"I'm sorry, Alycia. I just got home. Things are really hectic right now, and I don't know what I'll be doing tomorrow. Besides I wouldn't be good company."

"Why? What's wrong?"

"Oh. You haven't heard."

"Heard what?"

"My brother was seriously wounded last Sunday."

"Oh no, Keith, what happened?"

"He was shot and robbed at the American Tin Cannery."

"How is he?"

"He's in pretty serious condition." McGuire was getting tired of repeating himself.

"Oh, Keith, I'm so sorry. You must feel terrible."

"It hasn't been easy. I am a little tired."

"Don't do a thing. Just relax. I'll be right over."

They had met six months ago when he was helping erect a crime prevention booth for the "Good Old Days" festival. She was working on the "Friends of the Monarch" butterfly booth right next to him. Their relationship was developing slowly and had not yet taken any particular shape. So far there were no demands, no expectations, or so he thought.

Alycia was an anachronism. At twenty-eight she was too young to have experienced the 1960's, but she had the values and appearance of one who had lived in a commune in Big Sur without the drugs or the contempt for authority. Attending college in Santa Cruz was probably responsible for many of her attitudes. Having a wealthy mother and a modest inheritance of her own made it easy for her to pursue her interests. When she was not attending classes in yoga, Tai Chi, or Zen meditation, she volunteered her time to a number of charitable organizations. Leading the current list of good works was raising money for the monarch butterfly habitat.

She was an earth person, a nurturer with an exaggerated concern for humanity. McGuire prepared himself to be embosomed and coddled.

# CHAPTER THIRTEEN

FRIDAY 8:45 A.M., 16 NOVEMBER 1990

Captain Hosea Headley looked up from his desk as McGuire passed by his office. "Well! Good afternoon, Sergeant McGuire."

It wasn't a particularly subtle greeting, but then Captain Headley wasn't a particularly subtle person.

McGuire looked at his watch. "Morning, boss," he replied. He was just arriving for work. He normally didn't eat breakfast, but this morning Alycia had gotten up before him and made some awful fruit concoction with non-fat yogurt he felt obligated to eat.

She had used the word "relationship" at least twice over breakfast. McGuire had sat there mute not knowing how to respond and worrying his silence might be misunderstood. He needn't have worried. Each time she kept right on talking, carrying both sides of the conversation, seemingly unconcerned with his impassiveness. Somewhere in the conversation she hinted at the possibility of her moving in with him. He pretended not to pick up on it. She was cleaning up in the kitchen when he left.

McGuire poured himself coffee in the break room and settled in behind his desk when Headley came in. "I need another man to work security at the high school football game tonight." Headley was fifty-three, tall, and slender with narrow suspicious eyes. A bushy moustache partly streaked with gray hid his small mouth.

McGuire only put on a uniform about twice a year when helping out during the Feast of the Lanterns or the Butterfly Day Parade. He disliked getting into uniform because they all fit a bit tight. He kept promising himself he would lose a few pounds, so the uniforms wouldn't have to be taken to a seamstress to be let out.

"Sorry, boss, but I've been so busy during the days, the only chance I get to see my brother in the hospital is in the evening," he lied. He planned to sneak over to the hospital later around noon. "Upham said he wanted some overtime. You might check with him." Headley muttered to himself and shuffled out of the room. That'll be "Hosehead's" major project for the day, probably his only project for the day, McGuire thought.

He began sifting through papers that had been indiscriminately heaped into the tray on his desk. There were FBI Wanted Bulletins, copies of daily logs and case reports, departmental memos, police association newsletters, and an announcement for a training class. The last item seemed interesting—a three-day class in December in Palm Springs on the investigation of autoerotic death. McGuire smiled at the thought, death while having sex with a car. Upham stepped into his office and interrupted his musing.

"Why'd you tell Headley I wanted to work the football game?"

The smile returned to McGuire's face. "You've been complaining about all the over-time you've missed out on since you left patrol."

"That's different. Now I've gotta go out and baby-sit a bunch of high school kids on a Friday night." Upham shrugged his left shoulder as he tugged at his holster's shoulder strap to get it to ride a little higher.

"I thought you enjoyed high school football games. Didn't you go to last week's game between Pacific Grove and Carmel?"

"The only reason I went was because the Chief's nephew's a starting linebacker on the Breakers varsity team and the Chief had a couple of extra tickets he wanted to get rid of."

"You could've told Headley you were busy," McGuire said.

"Right. With a promotion board coming up in January, I'm going to tell the future chief of police I'm too busy to support the department. How'd you get out of working the football game?"

"When he asked me, he only needed one more man. I told him how keen you were on getting out into the community and working with teenagers, and you welcomed the over-time."

"You're a real pal."

"My pleasure." McGuire smiled broadly. "Did you search the area under the Outrigger?"

"I went there yesterday at noon, but the water was too high. Low tide wasn't until four-thirty, so I went back at four, but I ran out of light too soon. Low tide this morning was at three-thirty. I got Headley's okay to go out there this after-noon with three patrolmen and some flood lamps."

"Have we gotten anything back on the bullet and casings?" McGuire asked.

"Yeah. The lab faxed a preliminary report. The casings are Federal nine-millimeter. The bullet was also nine millimeter, six lands and grooves, right-hand twist, jacketed hollow point with a center post, 147 grains." Upham seemed to wait for a reaction, but when McGuire didn't respond, he continued, "Whoever shot him knew something about bullets."

Upham was right. It was heavier than normal for a nine-millimeter. Heavier bullets had slower muzzle velocities. A 147-grain bullet in a nine-millimeter pistol would travel under 1100 feet per second, the speed of sound. For a silencer to be effective it had to use a sub-sonic round. The heavier bullet coupled with a center post also had better stopping power. Most crooks wouldn't take the time to find a store that had them or pay the higher price for them.

"And what have you accomplished?" Upham said.

"I interviewed Howard's boss, a co-worker, and an old friend. I also re-interviewed the Russian guy I F.I.'ed at the scene. None of them provided anything useful. I'm going out now to talk to Howard's neighbors," he lied. "I'd better run or I'll be late." He felt bad withholding information from Upham. He had never before intentionally lied to another detective concerning a case they were working on.

"Before you go, tell me what you were doing at your brother's house yesterday." Upham leaned up against a filing cabinet and crossed his arms in front of him.

"I've been appointed Howard's conservator by the court." McGuire began straightening out his desk and putting things away. "I went there to check his mail and pay some of his bills."

"For more than three hours?"

"There was a lot of mail."

"Who was there with you?"

McGuire stopped what he was doing and looked up. "What makes you think anyone was there with me?"

"There was a white '85 Plymouth Reliant parked next to your car. It had cold plates."

McGuire kept his anger in check. "What were you doing, Upham, following me around?"

"Answer the question, McGuire."

McGuire rose to his feet. "If you want to solve this case and make your badge real shiny in time for the promotion board, get out on the street and do some investigating." McGuire grabbed his briefcase and headed for the door. "Don't waste your time following me and worrying about what I'm doing. If I find out you're running any more vehicle registration checks on my friends, you're the one who's going to have some questions to answer, in front of the chief." He walked out of his office and left the station as fast as he could to avoid anymore questions from Upham.

"Sorry I'm late, Wedge," McGuire said and pulled out a chair. "I had an appointment to see Dr. Hernandez at the hospital. I hadn't spoken to him since Wednesday, and we had a lot to discuss."

Kiewel's was half-empty. They sat at a corner table on the wooden deck next to one of the large white planters that defined the outer edge of the outdoor seating area. It was one-thirty, and the bright sun cast long shadows over the deck. Twenty feet beyond the planters was the Recreational Trail. The warm day brought out walkers, joggers, bicyclists, and rollerbladers in large numbers.

"How's Howard doing?"

"Better. His condition's stabilized. After Hernandez left, I went to check on Howard, but they had already moved him out of ICU over to Garden North. I'll have to go back tonight."

It was an unseasonable seventy-two degrees, and the shallow teal blue water in front of them between the Coast Guard pier and Fisherman's Wharf glistened in the sun. The sky was clear, except for some thin low clouds off to the north near Santa Cruz, and the air was still. They sat silently watching the steady stream of traffic along the Recreational Trail until the waitress disturbed their reverie.

After she took their orders and disappeared, a man and a woman two tables over got up and left. Within seconds five seagulls swooped down on the table, landed on top of the plates, and scattered the silverware onto the deck. Three of the gulls attacked the bread basket, squawking at each other as they fought over a quarter loaf of French bread. Wings flapped aggressively, beaks hammered at one another, and water glasses tumbled over. A busboy came running from the kitchen and routed the seagulls with a dishtowel. He gathered the debris from the deck and placed it on the table, then expertly grabbed the four corners of the tablecloth and carried everything away in one bundle. One seagull returned and stood watch from the edge of a nearby planter. Wedge and McGuire sat at their table momentarily dumbfounded by the aggressiveness of the birds.

McGuire collected his thoughts and got down to business. "It seems Howard made a $90,000 down payment on his town house last March, and according to his bank statements, his checking account has a balance of $32,000. Do you have any idea where he might have gotten that kind of money?"

"No. Did you ask Wepsala?  They occasionally talked about finances and investments."

"I'll have to call him later. About those photos at my brother's place, did you notice anything going on between him and Mrs. Pavlenko?"

"Are you kidding?  Nothing against Howard, but he's like, twenty years older than Zhanna. You saw how she looks. Every young stud in the School of Russian Language is strutting around trying to get her attention." Wedge's eyes kept wandering over to the Recreational Trail. "That's why Howard interviewed her and I interviewed her husband. He thought my hormones would stage a coup d'etat over my brain, if I was left alone with her in a small room."

"Did she ever come back to Howard's office after the last day of the interview?"

"No. I haven't seen her since then."

"Was my brother seeing anyone?"

"You mean like, dating?"

"Yeah, I guess that's what I mean."

"I don't know. He never said anything, and I never asked. It's not something we'd have talked about. In fact, we never really talked. I'd ask questions and he'd answer them. Sometimes he'd give me instructions." Wedge stopped talking while their waitress served their food. Once she left, Wedge started again, "I don't recall anyone, just bullshitting with him, except Steve. I don't think any of us ever had the nerve to ask him a personal question." The seagull perched on the planter was eyeing Wedge with great interest as he picked at his French fries. "What's our next step?" he asked.

"Dale Carston Ellis," McGuire said. "It shouldn't be too hard to get something on him and drag him in for questioning."

"How?"

"That's what we need to cook up. We know Ellis is connected with Louie Joubert and Louie is probably selling him drugs. We might be able to get to Ellis through Louie."

"Maybe we should think about this over the weekend and get back together on Monday," Wedge said.

"No, we have to do it this weekend." McGuire raised his voice slightly. He didn't want to tell Wedge about his problems with Upham. It was only a matter of time before Upham had enough information to get him taken off the case. "We need to do it either tonight or tomorrow night."

"Okay, I guess we could get someone to go to the Gilded Cage, pretend they want to buy some drugs, and see if they can contact Joubert. If they can get him to sell them some cocaine, you could arrest him."

"Wrong." McGuire's eyes narrowed and his lips were drawn into a thin line.

"What's wrong with it?" Wedge looked offended.

"Entrapment—that's what's wrong with it." McGuire was beginning to lose his patience. He had to remind himself that despite Wedge's training, he wasn't a cop. "If we initiate the contact and ask to buy drugs, it'd be a bad arrest, and it wouldn't get us anywhere. Louie's smart. He probably knows the law better than some cops. If we send someone in there, it'd have to be someone who's trained and can think on their feet."

"Okay, okay, what about this: I could go to the Gilded Cage and like, pretend to look for Ellis. I could play it by ear and see what I can find out. If Joubert offers to sell me some, I'll figure something out, so you can make a good bust."

"We'll have to wire you. It could be a little risky. Louie's a tough character."

"When?"

"Tomorrow's Saturday. I'd say seven o'clock tomorrow is our best chance. I've got a Fargo unit we can use to wire you."

"Seven o'clock's good. We could meet at Howard's place and go from there," Wedge said.

McGuire remained seated and lighted a cigarette. "I'm going to have some coffee."

Wedge pulled out his wallet. "God, it's way too gorgeous today. I'd really like to hang out here longer, but I've got to get back to work." He put some money on the table and weighted it down with the salt shaker.

"Don't work too hard," McGuire said and leaned back in his chair. "I'll see you tomorrow at seven."

"*Da sveedahnya.*" Wedge smiled and offered a mock salute before heading back to his car.

As McGuire walked by her office door, Lois, the Chief's secretary, leaned over her desk and called out to him. "Keith, the Chief and Captain Headley would like to see you."

McGuire stopped. "When?"

"They're both in his office now. Let me check." Lois picked up her phone and announced McGuire's presence. She looked up at McGuire and smiled. "You can go right in."

Unlike the rest of the station, the Chief's office was thickly carpeted and equipped with heavy dark wood furniture. Positioned in front of the Chief's oversized desk were two straight-backed leather-cushioned armchairs of highly polished mahogany. They were often referred to as the "uneasy chairs." Captain Headley sat in one of them and motioned McGuire toward the other one.

"Keith," the Chief started out solemnly, "I wanted to talk to you earlier this week about your brother, but some problems came up at city hall that demanded my attention. I'm truly sorry about what happened to him."

"Thank you, Chief. I appreciate your concern."

"Do you need some time off?" the Chief asked. He was just over sixty, but probably in better shape than half the officers in the department. His wavy bone-white hair could have given him a distinguished look, if it weren't for his bulbous red nose and the spider webs of busted capillaries near the surface of his cheeks.

"No. He's in a coma, and there really isn't anything I can do for him, except catch the person who shot him."

Headley spoke up, "That's something we need to talk about, Keith."

"What's there to talk about?" McGuire turned his attention to Headley.

The Chief cleared his throat and answered, "Captain Headley has ah, . . . some concerns about you being in charge of the investigation."

McGuire turned his head back toward the Chief. "Is there a complaint about the way I've been handling it?"

"Well," Headley responded, "Sergeant Upham feels you're not keeping him informed on all aspects of this case. He told me the evidence suggests your brother wasn't the victim of an armed robbery, and his shooting was only made to look like a robbery. He suspects there's another motive, one that would explain your brother's—"

The Chief cleared his throat again and cut him off. "Captain Headley is advising me to take you off the case. He feels your relationship to the victim could affect your judgment."

"Chief, this case is important to me," McGuire said. "I want the person who shot my brother arrested and punished. Neal's never investigated a major felony. He doesn't have the experience to do it right, nor does anyone else on the department. Don't make me sit on the sidelines and watch him screw it up."

The Chief listened thoughtfully and pondered the matter in silence. He looked at Headley first, then directed himself to

McGuire when he spoke. "Keith, I'm going to let you stay on the case, but I'm putting Sergeant Upham in charge. You'll keep him informed of every move you make, every scrap of information you develop, and you'll follow his instructions."

"I can live with that." McGuire looked over at Headley and saw a scowl on his face.

"If there's any improper conduct on your part," the Chief said. "I'll take you off the case and have Captain Headley personally take charge of it. He's had enough experience to handle it adequately—more than adequately."

Until this moment McGuire hadn't realized how important it had become for him to personally catch the gunman. He owed a lot to his brother, and he had treated him poorly since his return to Pacific Grove. McGuire needed to do something to make up for it, and catching criminals was what he did best. Whoever was responsible for what happened to Howard was going to pay the price, no matter how far McGuire had to step out of line to get him.

By getting the Chief to allow him to stay on the case, McGuire had bought himself some time, but not much. There was no way he could tell Upham about Joubert or Ellis without admitting he had withheld information from him. If he and Wedge were successful this weekend, it would only be a matter of a day or two before Upham would find out and complain to Headley. Hopefully it would be enough time. He could deal with the consequences later.

# CHAPTER FOURTEEN

FRIDAY 7:00 P.M., 16 NOVEMBER 1990

Wedge finished clearing off the table and carried the silverware and glasses into the kitchen.

"You know, Gordon, we haven't had much conversation all week. Anything new happening at your office?" Katherine asked. She opened the dishwasher and began arranging the dirty plates on the lower rack.

"No. It's the same old stuff," Wedge said. "Just more of it since Howard's been gone. Oh yeah, my boss sent Pembroke over from the Naval Postgraduate School to work with me at DLI. I hope it's just temporary until Howard recovers."

Katherine returned the salt and pepper shakers to the corner of the kitchen counter and asked, "Who's Pembroke?"

"You've met her, haven't you?"

"Her?" Katherine's left eyebrow arched momentarily.

"No, I guess not," Wedge said. "She wasn't at the office picnic last summer."

"I don't recall you ever mentioning her name before," she said in a disinterested tone.

"I haven't had much contact with her, but with George and Howard gone, I'm glad someone else'll be up there to help with the work." He hesitated, then said, "I think you'll like her, actually. Martha and I should work well together." He waited for a response, but she still didn't rise to the bait. He went on, "Yeah, we really need two people at DLI. Some of the cases get a little complicated and require two agents to work closely together."

"Is she married?"

He listened carefully to her voice, but it still had the same conversational tone. Maybe I can draw her out, he thought. "No," he said, "and it's really surprising because she's rather attractive . . ." Wedge glanced over at her. She was at the sink with her back to him. If she was interested, she was hiding it well. I'd better quit before I dig too deep a grave, he thought. "That is for a short, fat, forty-eight-year-old spinster."

"That's a terrible thing to say. I'm sure she's a very nice person." She turned toward him with a self-satisfied smile on her face. "How's Howard doing, poor man. Have you visited him in the hospital?" Katherine finished loading the dish-washer and closed its door.

"I thought I told you; I'm going there in a few minutes. You don't mind, do you? It seems kind of useless since he's in a coma, but I want to go see him anyway. Howard's brother's been keeping me posted on his condition."

"You didn't tell me Howard had a brother."

"Oh, didn't I? He's a cop in Pacific Grove." Wedge rolled up his sleeves and began scrubbing out a large pot in the sink. "Well, actually he's a detective sergeant. He seems very competent. I like him."

"How old is he?" She looked up from the bowl she was covering with plastic wrap.

"Keith? I'm not sure, probably in his late thirties."

"Is he married?"

"Divorced."

"What's he look like?"

Wedge stood over the sink with soapsuds up to his wrists. "Wait a minute. I know where this is leading and the answer is no. Besides, he already has a girlfriend."

"What do you have against Sally?" Katherine said. She had a hurt expression on her face.

"I don't have anything against your sister. I like Sally. She's got a great sense of humor. I just prefer not to get involved again in any of your matchmaking efforts."

Sally was a very touchy subject between them. At twenty-five Katherine was the youngest of four sisters, and at thirty-three Sally was the eldest and still unmarried. Katherine worried more about Sally's marital status than Sally did.

"I'm sorry, hon. Look, Keith's not her type. If I like, tried to fix her up with Keith, it'd be a disaster. What about Clayton Butler? He's a bachelor, and he's closer to her age."

"You mean your boss?"

"Yeah. You remember him from the office picnic, don't you—kind of stocky, brownish-gray hair?"

"He wasn't bad looking, but he seemed a little short and awkward. Why hasn't he gotten married?"

Probably because he doesn't have any social graces, he thought. "I don't know. Maybe he's moved around too much."

"How much does he make?"

Wedge guessed he was at least a GS-13, step 3. That put him at about $48,000 a year. Katherine began to show a little more interest, and the whole idea began to appeal to him. Maybe all Butler needed was to get laid to loosen him up a bit—a little attitude adjustment as Howard used to say. If Sally had half the sexual appetite of Katherine, it would certainly improve Butler's disposition. Having him date his sister-in-law could have its advantages, but the thought of him as a relative was still a bit repulsive.

It was Keith McGuire's fifth visit to the hospital during the past week in addition to the numerous telephone conversations with the two specialists and the attending physician. Each doctor had given him a slightly different prognosis.

The woman sitting next to Howard's bed had her head bowed as she dabbed her eyes with a facial tissue. Her straight raven-black hair flowed over her shoulders. Keith stood in the door and cleared his throat. Michiko Thurgood stood up slowly with her eyes cast down and glided across the room. She paused next to Keith. Without looking at him she whispered, "Pardon me for intruding."

"Please wait. You don't need to leave because of me."

"I have been here long enough, and you will want to be alone with your brother."

"I'd like to speak with you for just a minute."

"Words can change nothing." She stepped through the doorway and continued on her way. Keith watched her ascend the stairs and disappear in the direction of the lobby.

He sat down in a chair across from Howard's bed, and a nurse came in to change an IV bag. "Hello," he said.

"Hi, I'm Mona Damrash."

"I'm Keith McGuire."

"You're the patient's brother. Gayle Fantes in ICU told me about you. He's doing much better, you know." The nurse spoke as she finished making a few notes on her clipboard. "I'll be back in a while to bathe him."

"Excuse me, Mona, but the Japanese woman who was in here earlier, when did she arrive?"

Damrash glanced at her watch. "About four-thirty this afternoon, I think," she said and slipped out of the room.

Keith looked at his own watch. It was just after seven. There was a newspaper lying on the table next to Howard's bed. The headlines were about Iraq and deployment of U.S. troops to the Persian Gulf as they had been every day that week. Keith turned his attention back to his brother's motionless body. He felt the same sense of helplessness he did when his parents died. He sat there torturing his lower lip, thinking about all the things he had recently learned about Howard and how he wanted to know so much more. He could hear the sound of carts rolling down the hall and the occasional page for a doctor over the PA system.

On each of his visits to the hospital, memories of Howard, unrecalled for so long, had crept into his thoughts. During

Howard's first year back in Monterey, he had invited Keith on a few fishing trips. At the time Keith had been too immersed in his work to find time for him. Or for Cristina. Eventually Howard stopped asking, and Cristina simply gave up. It wasn't until Cristina moved out that he realized how he had allowed his work to consume more and more of his life until there wasn't enough left to support any personal relationships. But instead of trying to change, he took refuge in his work.

Just after his separation from Cristina and again after the divorce, Howard took him out to dinner and offered words of solace, but Keith's pride wouldn't let him accept Howard's support. After that, Howard had kept to himself and rarely intruded into Keith's life.

Now Howard was in a hospital. He deserved better than Keith had given him. Who had taught Keith how to throw a football, ride a bicycle? Who had repeatedly spent his precious time at home on leave taking him fishing and showing him how to shoot a pistol? Who had always remembered him on birthdays, Christmases, graduations? Who had flown half way around the world to be at his side at the weddings and the funeral? He owed his brother a great deal.

"Well, I thought I might find you here." Stephen Wepsala stood in the doorway, clutching a large vase brimming with flowers. He set the vase down on a shelf under the wall-mounted television set. "Very nice, a private room with his own bathroom. Is that a little patio out there?" Wepsala walked across the small room and peeked out the siding glass door.

"It's good of you to come."

"How is he doing?"

"Well enough, considering."

"And you? How are you doing?" Wepsala seated himself in the cushioned rattan armchair next to Howard's bed.

"It occurred to me a few minutes ago—I've spent more time with him this past week than I have in the past year."

"You always appreciate things more when you come close to losing—sorry, pardon the platitude."

Before Keith could reply, the nurse returned. "It's time for the patient's bath. There's a snack bar upstairs. I'll only be about twenty minutes. You're welcome to come back when I'm through." Her matronly smile made it clear they were being ordered to leave.

They got themselves some coffee, found a comfortable spot near the pond, and watched the koi carp slowly swimming around. "I'm glad to have this chance to talk with you again," McGuire said. The sound of splashing water masked all the noises around them. "I want to know more about my brother."

"There's a lot to tell. Where shall I start?" Wepsala asked.

McGuire sat forward in his chair and said, "Tell me about Michiko Thurgood."

Wepsala furrowed his brow. "How did you know?"

"She was here for two and half hours. She left a little while ago. When I was introduced to her on Tuesday, I knew I had seen her somewhere before. When I saw her here today, it jogged my memory. She was in the waiting area near ICU when I came here Monday night. Lord knows how long she sat there, unable to go into ICU to see him, and probably too timid to ask anyone how he was."

Wepsala had a pained expression on his face. "They have been, shall we say, keeping company for a couple of years now. No one at the office knows. I was unaware until after I retired. Even then he swore me to secrecy. Something must have happened in September because at our last two monthly dinners I asked about her twice and he sidestepped the question both times."

"Isn't she married?  I recall Butler introducing her as Mrs. Thurgood."

"I'm not sure what her marital status is. I know she was married to a Navy officer who was shot down over North Vietnam near the end of the war and listed as Missing In Action. That was over seventeen years ago. I think she still receives some compensation from the government."

"Was there anyone else?"

"No one I know of. Then, of course, if he hadn't told me about Michiko, I wouldn't have even known about her."

McGuire kept silent for a minute, but when Wepsala didn't volunteer anything more, he asked, "You said my brother may have been made a scapegoat by the CIA. Why?"

"The reasons go back a long way and involve internal agency politics. I don't think it will provide you any motives for Howard being shot."

"I'd just like to know more about my brother."

"All right, I guess you're entitled to a short professional history of Howard McGuire." Wepsala stroked his beard and pondered for a moment as he sipped his coffee. He seemed to reach some sort of decision, then began. "I first learned of Howard when we were both working in Vietnam in the mid-1960's. He was a fairly young Army Counterintelligence Agent based in Can Tho and working the entire Mekong Delta area. I was in Saigon at the Embassy. He did some pretty heroic things while he was there. Most of it had to do with 'Bright Light' reports and operations against COSVN—"

"Bright light, cosvin, what's that?" McGuire interrupted.

"Bright Light was the code word we used for matters pertaining to U.S. POWs and our efforts to locate and rescue them. COSVN was an acronym for Central Office South Vietnam, the Vietcong intelligence organization. I read a number of Howard's reports in Vietnam, but I didn't meet him until 1969 in Japan. He had just completed an undercover assignment and been promoted to Warrant Officer."

"You mean Howard was originally an enlisted man in the Army?"

"You sound surprised. Most of the Army's best agents started out in the enlisted ranks."

"But he was a Stanford graduate."

"In those days if you wanted experience in counterintelligence in the Army, it was not advisable to seek a commission. The Army was desperately in need of infantry officers at the time. If by chance you did get into intelligence after commissioning, there was little or no chance of working in the field. Young lieutenants were put in charge of the motor pool, the personnel section, the budget and fiscal office, the supply room. Most of the operational positions were filled by enlisted men and warrant officers."

"What was Howard doing in Japan?"

"He was assigned to the Special Operations Team of the 704th Military Intelligence Detachment at Camp Zama when I first met him. Over a dozen U.S. servicemen had deserted and eventually defected to the Soviet Union through Japan. Howard and his boss Chief Warrant Officer R.T. Tanaka led the Army effort to neutralize *Beheiren*."

"Beheiren?"

"The Japan Peace for Vietnam Committee. Under the guidance of the KGB, it assisted the defectors and helped set up the exfiltration route used to get them to the Soviet Union. By early 1971 R.T. and Howard were able to totally stop the flow of defectors."

McGuire looked up and saw Wedge lumbering toward them from the direction of Garden North. Wepsala looked in Wedge's direction and smiled broadly. Both men stood up as Wedge approached them. They shook hands and exchanged greetings before sitting down.

"The nurse said I'd find you up here," Wedge said.

"Steve was just telling me about Howard's professional history. It would be good for you to hear the rest of it."

The three men settled back into their seats and Wepsala continued. "In about 1968 a major problem began developing for Army Intelligence back in the States. By 1970 it became widely known the Army was investigating civilian anti-war activities. There was a tremendous negative reaction."

"I remember that," McGuire said. "I was in college at the time."

"Well, the Army found itself in an embarrassing position and grossly overreacted to the situation. In June 1971 the Army issued a directive to cease all investigations of American civilians. It did not matter that some of the American civilians, mostly students, were being used as unwitting pawns by the Soviets. The directive seriously crippled Army Counterintelligence. Its hierarchy became paralyzed by indecision, and for a long time it chose to do nothing rather than risk criticism and law suits."

"Howard told me it's even worse now," Wedge interjected.

"Unfortunately Howard is right. These days Army Counterintelligence devotes most of its time and energy reorganizing itself. Anyway, back in the summer of 1971 we heard rumblings about stripping the Army, Navy and Air Force counterintelligence agencies of their mission to conduct security clearance investigations in the US. On the face of it, it was a good idea to eliminate duplication of effort and reduce the cost of doing the investigations. That was how DIS came into being in 1972. The secondary effect was to reduce the strength of the military counterintelligence agencies in the US. It also eliminated the most valuable training ground for new agents, as well as a natural cover activity for covert counterespionage investigations."

"It must have been a fiasco trying to curtail the activities of three agencies and start up a new one the size of DIS from scratch," McGuire commented.

"Well actually, Keith, it wasn't that bad. Each of the three services transferred personnel and equipment to DIS when it started up. DIS used military personnel for several years before they were able to gradually civilianize all of the positions.

"We—that is the CIA—picked up a number of good case officers from the Army in the early seventies. Howard decided to apply to the CIA. He was in a strong bargaining position because of his experience, education, and language ability. While some others accepted work as contract employees, Howard held out for an appointment as a regular officer and got it in early 1972.

"Shortly after your brother was hired, he was handpicked to join the staff of the Counterintelligence Division headed by James Angleton. By 1973 Howard was one of Angleton's rising young stars. That same year James Schlesinger, the Director of Central Intelligence, the DCI, fired about seven percent of the personnel in the Clandestine Service. Then in late 1974 the new DCI, William Colby, forced Angleton to retire and three of Angleton's top officers resigned in protest. Colby broke up the Counterintelligence Division and reassigned its personnel throughout the Agency. Many of the Agency's most experienced counterintelligence officers chose to retire or resign. Howard was still a dedicated junior officer, and he adapted to the changes and distanced himself from the political infighting."

"Why did Colby get rid of the Counterintelligence Division?" McGuire asked.

"Probably because of 'Operation Honetol,' Angleton's witch hunt for a mole in the Agency. The operation ruined the careers of a number of good men. Some thought Angleton had become obsessed by his mole hunt and was destroying the agency. Others felt it was Colby who betrayed the agency and started it on its downward spiral.

"In 1976 a Senate Committee headed by Frank Church investigated the CIA and issued a very critical report. Things further degenerated after that. By 1977 I was down on the Farm—at the CIA training center at Camp Perry—teaching, Howard was in Asia, and Stansfield Turner was the DCI. Then came the Halloween Massacre. In late October 1977 over eight hundred officers were fired. Myself and over six hundred others resigned in protest the following year. Needless to say, there was a great deal of disarray. Howard was among those who managed to hold things together until the Reagan Administration took over and Bill Casey, the new DCI, began rebuilding the Agency. Howard and I kept in contact over the years, even after I resigned from the agency.

"Your brother was a successful field man until 1985, but he was repeatedly passed over for promotion. He was one of the few really experienced CI case officers assigned to the Soviet Counterintelligence Branch of the Soviet-East European Division."

"Why was he passed over for promotion?" McGuire asked.

"Howard was hired at the journeyman level. He did not have to work his way up the pay scale like his peers, and he was tainted by his limited involvement in Operation Honetol. These things combined to gain Howard the animus of others—others who were promoted over him during the Turner regime. I suspect one of them was waiting for an opportunity to discredit him. When Howard's operation was compromised in late 1985, his boss, Rick Ames, had left the branch to attend language training in preparation for his transfer to Rome. With Ames gone Howard was left holding the bag. It was easier to blame the compromise on Howard than to look into the possibility of some other cause."

"Why did DIS hire him, if he had been fired from the CIA?" McGuire asked.

"The CIA does not release any information concerning its former employees, even to DIS. DIS was only able to verify his dates of employment."

McGuire took a sip from his paper coffee cup. It had gone cold. "I didn't know any of that."

"How is your investigation coming along?" Wepsala changed the subject.

"Not very well." McGuire stared off at the water in the pond spouting into the air and fall back onto itself. "I'm having a lot of trouble trying to nail down a motive for the shooting. The hostage investigation Howard and Wedge have been working on might be tied into it. You could help clear up a few things for me, if you don't mind."

"About what?"

"Well, Howard had some strong suspicions about this hostage case he was working on with Wedge, but he wasn't able to put together enough evidence to get the FBI to accept and pursue the matter. But what could a pair of DLI instructors be spying on?"

Wepsala glanced around in all directions, leaned forward, and lowered his voice. "Not all spies steal secrets. There are primary agents, support agents, penetration agents, observation agents. Some are agents of influence. Others are sleepers—agents who remain dormant for years, assimilating themselves into the local society and developing their legends, before they are tasked to perform an espionage or sabotage mission. I always thought DLI presented an excellent opportunity for hostile intelligence."

"I still don't understand what the attraction is at DLI."

"A few hundred instructors at DLI were born in communist-controlled countries. Howard and I are convinced that many of them were propositioned by the intelligence services of their native countries before they were allowed to emigrate. It would not take much to make them agree to anything when they are in the final stages of getting permission to leave a country like Russia. Most would be willing to agree to cooperate with the KGB, if they thought it would make the difference between getting or not getting their exit visas. They probably figured once they were out of Russia, they could thumb their noses at the KGB."

"How much influence can the KGB exert on Russian émigrés because of some coerced agreement?" McGuire asked.

"Most of the émigrés are probably never contacted again by the KGB, but I am certain the KGB tracks as many of them as they can. When one of them lands in a position that might be useful, the KGB reminds them of their agreement. Usually that would not be enough to induce them to help the KGB. But if they have relatives or other loved ones still in the Soviet Union, the KGB can threaten the well being of their relatives."

"I see," McGuire said.

"Actually, most are probably able to stand up to the pressure and call their bluff, but a few are induced to do simple tasks," Wepsala said. "Perhaps they are only asked to report on the movements of other Russian émigrés."

"But once they start cooperating," Wedge added, "the hook is set deeper."

"Unfortunately, Wedge is right," Wepsala said. "On top of the original threat against their relatives, the KGB can then also threaten to expose their activities to the FBI. You can see the implications at DLI. Not only would the émigrés be asked to report on their fellow instructors, but they could also be tasked to report on the students. They could act as spotters and assessors to identify students who because of drugs, finances, or character flaws might be induced to spy against the United States. Each year a few thousand young military servicemen pass through DLI. They eventually have access to some of the military's most highly classified secrets." Wepsala paused. "I hope I am not sounding too didactic."

McGuire sat forward in his chair. "No, not at all. Please go on."

"We refer to émigrés who get trapped into that type of situation as low-level 'recruited' agents."

"I'm sorry, but could you explain that a little more?" McGuire said.

"It is not important, just terminology. The important distinction is they receive little or no training after they are recruited. If they do receive any training, they get it when they return to the Soviet Union on vacation."

"Wait a minute," McGuire said. "Are you telling me Russian instructors at DLI return to the Soviet Union on vacation? I thought they were mostly Jews who had been discriminated against and had to wait years to get permission to leave."

Wepsala nodded as he answered, "I know it is hard to believe, but many of them travel there on vacation. DLI encourages it by giving them extra time off from work, if they bring back things that can be used in the classroom. It's a perfect opportunity for the KGB to debrief and train the ones who have been recruited. In Moscow they have complete control of everything. Of course their training is nothing compared to what a KGB officer receives."

"How does the work of a KGB officer differ from that of a recruited agent?"

"It depends on whether they are dispatched as 'legals' or 'illegals.' Do you know the difference?"

"No."

"Those dispatched as legals are generally assigned to embassies and consulates and have diplomatic cover. They work primarily as case officers—agent handlers. Those dispatched as illegals enter the country illegally and use false identities. They can do the same work as legals, but they can also do much more. For one thing, they are not limited to cities where the Soviets have diplomatic offices. Illegals sent to DLI could be used as support agents to service a number of recruited agents. They could even be used to support an American who has already been recruited by the Soviets. DLI is also a good place for a sleeper. They could spend several years developing their cover as a trusted U.S. Government employee before applying for employment as a linguist at NSA, CIA, FBI, or State Department."

Wedge said, "Howard suspected the Pavlenkos might be trained intelligence officers, illegals, working as support agents. Howard told me that it's almost impossible to uncover a low-level recruited agent at DLI."

"Why is that?" McGuire asked.

Wedge seemed to ponder the question for a moment and looked over at Wepsala for help. Wepsala looked back at him and smiled, but said nothing.

"Well, they don't do anything unlawful, and they don't have to lie about their background." Wedge shifted around in his chair. "A professional intelligence officer has to have a legend, a cover story, about his life in the Soviet Union—education, employment, family history. He has to account for a couple of years he spent in training with the KGB. Most Soviet émigrés are Jews and Jews are almost never accepted into the KGB. They're not considered politically reliable."

"But you said the Pavlenkos were Jews," McGuire said.

"No. I only told you what they claimed to be."

Wepsala rose to his feet. "I think we can probably go downstairs now and check in on Howard."

# CHAPTER FIFTEEN

SATURDAY 7:30 P.M., 17 NOVEMBER 1995

As soon as Wedge got out of McGuire's unmarked car on Lighthouse Avenue, McGuire drove away. Wedge was four blocks from the Gilded Cage. There was no one within fifty yards of him and the darkness helped to cover his approach, but he still worried that someone he knew might see him. He walked a few feet past the entrance, turned around abruptly, and darted into the building.

The Gilded Cage was dimly lit, and it took a few seconds for Wedge's eyes to adjust. Two men sat at the bar. A mixed group of four people were at a corner table. Two women on a large dance floor clung to each other and moved slowly to music from a jukebox. Next to the jukebox was an elevated platform with some sound equipment, chairs, and musical instruments scattered about. It was a roomy establishment. Even the seven-foot gold birdcage on a raised pedestal fit comfortably in the far corner; though, it looked as if no one had danced in it for years.

Wedge sauntered over to the bar and felt everyone's eyes following him. If you're going to pull this off, you'd better loosen up, he thought. He selected a barstool near the middle of the bar and surveyed the room casually without looking directly at anyone. The bartender, a slender man of about thirty-five with a thick black moustache, came over. Wedge ordered a Tom Collins.

This wasn't what he had expected. Two of the male customers were wearing tight blue jeans and silky shirts, but no one sported any leatherwear with metal studs, except the bartender. Wedge had worried his clothing might be noticeably different. There was a gay rights poster behind the bar, but no one in the room looked particularly militant.

"That'll be four dollars. Can I get you anything else?" the bartender asked.

"No, thanks." Wedge put four dollars on the bar and stuffed a dollar bill into a glass that held two quarters and a dime. "My name's Wedge. What's yours?"

"You can call me Mack," the bartender said and raked in the four dollars.

"I was supposed to like, meet a friend here twenty minutes ago. I hope I didn't miss him." Wedge took a small sip of his Tom Collins.

"No one's left here in the past half hour. What's his name?"

"Dale. Maybe he was here earlier."

Mack scratched the scalp behind his right ear. "There's a Navy guy called Dale comes in here sometimes. I haven't seen him tonight. Ask Louie when he gets here. Louie knows him pretty good."

"Thanks." Wedge took another look around the room. "What time do you think he'll be here?"

"He usually comes in about this time every evening. I'll call him over when he gets here." Mack walked down to the end of the bar.

Once Wedge had started talking to the bartender, the other customers resumed their conversations and only seemed to eye him intermittently as he sipped his drink.

Mack stopped talking to the two men seated at the end of the bar and walked over toward the front door. A slender man in his early thirty's with an acne-scarred face had just come in. Mack whispered something to the man, then both of them approached Wedge. Joubert and Mack sat down on either side of Wedge. Wedge shifted slightly on his barstool.

"I am Louie Joubert," the newcomer said. He spoke with a French accent.

Wedge turned toward Joubert and rested his left arm on the padded bar. "I'm Marion Wedgeport. I'm looking for a guy named Dale. Mack suggested I ask you. You see, Dale's a friend of mine, and I was supposed to meet him here a little while ago and—"

"You, are a friend of Dale's?" Joubert said as he stared at Wedge's left hand.

Wedge stole a glance at his own hand and saw his wedding ring.

"How do you know Dale?"

"Ah . . . we met at Lovers' Point a few weeks ago. I know he . . . ah, lives on Sloat Avenue in Monterey, but I lost his address and phone number." Wedge quickly looked around the room. No one had moved. He looked back at Joubert. "Okay, he really wasn't expecting me to meet him here. He told me he came here a lot, so I like, took a chance and came here hoping to see him again." Wedge lowered his voice to a whisper. "Being married and all, I'm really kind of nervous about this. It's all new to me." He felt moisture beading up on his forehead. He lowered his head and covered his face with one hand. "I shouldn't have come here. It was a dumb thing to do. I've got a wife and a child," he mumbled.

"Hey, take it easy. Maybe I can help you," Joubert said. "Let us step into the office in the back where we can talk in private."

As Joubert climbed off his stool, Wedge saw the butt of a pistol peek out from his open jacket. Fear gripped him in the small of the back. It never occurred to him Joubert might be armed. Wedge desperately looked for a way out of the situation. Joubert had grabbed his left arm and was guiding him past the jukebox toward a room in the back. Seeing a sign for restrooms, he made his move. "Here, would you hold my drink while I go to the bathroom?" Wedge said. He shoved his glass into Joubert's hand and lunged for the restroom door.

He went into the first stall, locked the door, and stood there for a minute, expecting Joubert to follow him. No one came in. He opened the stall door slowly. The smell of disinfectant permeated the room, but hiding just below it was the unmistakable odor of old urinals. The dingy gray walls were spotted with graffiti. Above an old cast iron radiator was a double-hung window that had been painted over. Wedge pushed the lower sash up as hard as he could, but it wouldn't budge. He grabbed the upper sash. Using all his strength, he tried to pull it down, but it was frozen in place. Sweat trickled down the side of his face.

"Calm down," he said to himself out loud. "This guy's a drug dealer, and he's got a gun—a big gun—but there are customers out front. He won't try anything here." He took three deep breaths, splashed cold water on his face and used some paper towels to dry off. The muscles in his back were knotted up and going into spasms. If I keep cool, I can talk my way out of this.

Joubert was waiting for him as he stepped back out into the hall, but Mack had returned to his place behind the bar. "Are you all right?" he asked.

"I'm just a little nervous," Wedge said. He could feel cold sweat running down his armpits.

"Relax. Here, finish your drink in the office." Joubert handed his glass back to him.

Wedge followed him into a medium-sized room set up as an office at one end with a sitting area at the other end. Joubert sat down on a brown leather sofa, propped his feet on the coffee table, and motioned Wedge over to a wooden chair to his right.

"Is this your office?" Wedge asked.

"No. Mack is a friend of mine. He lets me use it when the owner is not here. So, tell me about yourself. How long have you been married?"

"Just over two years."

"And your wife does not know?"

"No, and I don't want her to . . . well, at least not until I'm certain. What I mean is . . . when I met Dale, I like, acted on an impulse, but now I want to see him again and try to figure this out. You know, try to figure out what I want."

"What do you do for a living?"

"I, ah . . . sell cellular telephone service," Wedge said. He finished his drink in one long gulp and set the glass on the coffee table. "Could I have another drink?"

"Selling cellular telephones, is it a difficult job?"

"It's all on commission, so you have to hustle, but I do pretty well."

"It probably wears you out by the end of the day." Joubert swung his feet off the table and pulled out a small, neatly folded piece of paper from his jacket pocket.

Wedge watched intently as Joubert reached into another pocket and withdrew a small black plastic box. He placed the box on the coffee table and spread out its contents. He emptied white powder out of the paper bindle onto a mirror and began scraping it into three neat little rows with a razor blade, he looked up at Wedge and asked, "Do you do coke?"

"Once in a while. Not very often."

"Here, would you like a line?" Joubert asked. He held out a small gold-colored metal tube.

"No. One line would only be a tease, and I don't have much money with me." The tension in his back started to relax just a little, but he still felt hot.

"Well, if you change your mind, I have more." Joubert leaned forward to snort the three lines of cocaine. His jacket gapped open exposing the butt of his pistol again. The muscles in the small of Wedge's back cramped and caused his whole body to quiver. Joubert was too busy to notice. He wiped his nose with the back of his hand. A trace of white powder clung to the small ulcerations on the septum of his nose.

Wedge noticed the heavy odor of musk oil. His mind searched for an excuse, any excuse to get out of the building, out into the open. "Look, there's an ATM just up the street. I could like, go get some money. It would only take me a few minutes."

"An excellent idea," Joubert said. "Dale wants to party tonight. You should come with me, after you stop at the ATM."

Wedge bolted up and headed for the door. Joubert followed him through the building out onto the sidewalk. The cool night air refreshed Wedge and cleared his head. He glanced back and saw McGuire fall into step twenty yards behind them as they walked up Lighthouse Avenue to a convenience store a few blocks away. Wedge tried to think about what he would do once he was in the store, but his mind kept flashing back to the gun stuck in Joubert's waistband. Inside the store he looked around and saw the ATM against the wall to their left.

The store clerk eyed them suspiciously for a minute before turning his attention back to the magazine he was reading. Wedge took his bankcard out of his wallet and fed it into the machine. He punched in his PIN and hit the transaction button, but instead of money, the machine spit out his card. He tried again with the same result. There was something he wasn't doing right, but his mind couldn't figure out what it was.

"*Zut alor*," Joubert cursed and pushed him aside. "Give me your number. I will do it for you."

Wedge saw McGuire motioning to him, but didn't react fast enough.

Joubert suddenly turned on him. "The name on his card is Wedgwood, not Wedgeport." Joubert saw McGuire standing by the door fifteen feet away with his gun drawn.

"*Merde*, what is this?" He pulled Wedge in front of him and drew his pistol.

"Hold it right there," McGuire commanded.

"Back off, or he loses a kidney."

McGuire stepped away from the door. Wedge felt Joubert grab the back of his belt and prod him forward with the revolver. They moved slowly to the door in chain step. McGuire retreated to the middle of the store. Joubert pivoted Wedge around, keeping Wedge between him and McGuire as he backed up to the door. He let go of Wedge's belt, reached behind him with his free hand, and groped for the door.

The door suddenly burst open and slammed up against Joubert, pushing him into Wedge and sending them both sprawling across the floor. The revolver clattered across the linoleum tile to within a yard of McGuire's feet.

Two motley looking bikers, complete with leather vests, strands of heavy metal chain, untrimmed beards, and tattoos, stumbled into the store almost stepping on Joubert and Wedge.

"Watch where you're stepping!" Joubert said.

"What the fuck are you doing crawling around on the floor? Look Snort, these two bastards are so stoned they can't even walk." The bikers staggered past them to the beer cooler.

McGuire holstered his weapon and stuck Joubert's pistol into his waistband. He helped Joubert to his feet, cuffed his hands behind his back, and patted him down. "Keep him here until I come back with the car. Knock him down and sit on him if you have to."

Wedge sat quietly next to Joubert in the back seat of the car as McGuire drove it into the sally port of the police station. Once inside, the garage door closed behind them. They took Joubert into the detention area and placed him in one of the holding cells. It was a ten-by-ten concrete cubicle painted a repulsive shade of medium blue. A metal cot with a thin mattress was pushed up against one of the side walls, and at the center of the back wall was a stainless steel toilet without a seat or lid.

McGuire pointed down a hallway to the right. "Go through that door, past the desk clerk's area, and on back to my office. I'll meet you there in a few minutes. I have to move the car."

Wedge was aiming a dart at a wanted poster when McGuire walked into the office. "Why did you have your gun drawn when you came into the store?" Wedge said.

"Because you told me he had a big gun."

"When did I tell you that?"

"Right after you handed him your drink and went into the bathroom."

"But. . . ." Wedge wrinkled his brow, then reached into his jacket pocket and pulled out a small metal container, the size of a cigarette pack, with a short length of wire attached to it. "Oh yeah, that's right, I sort of forgot about this." He held the Fargo unit in front of him for a moment before laying it on McGuire's desk. "So like, what do we do with Joubert now that we've got him?"

"We'll use him to get Ellis."

"How're we going to do that?" Wedge took aim again and launched his dart. It missed the wanted poster and stuck into a training bulletin next to it.

"Joubert's been busted twice for selling cocaine. In fact he's out on parole right now from his last conviction." McGuire took off his jacket and hung it up on the coat rack. "We've got him for parole violation, possession of cocaine with the intent to sell, carrying a concealed weapon, and assault with a deadly weapon. He's gotten off pretty light in the past, but this time the court can give him four years plus three years for each of his priors. I think he'll be willing to make a deal."

"What kind of deal?"

"We'll offer to let him go if he'll make a controlled sale of cocaine to Ellis at Ellis's apartment. That way we can bust

Ellis and search his apartment. Come on, let's have a little chat with Louie." McGuire stepped out of his office and headed down the hall. Wedge followed him reluctantly.

McGuire unlocked the cell door and stepped in. "Well, Louie, have you made yourself comfortable? This is your third stay with us, isn't it?"

"*Daissez-vous.* Fuck you, McGuire. I have nothing to say." Joubert sat on his cot.

"My friend here is a federal agent. He's convinced me we should try to help you." McGuire leaned against the wall across from Joubert.

"Well, you can tell your asshole friend, I do not need your fucking help. I will make bail and be out of here in a few of hours. This is a humbug. You have no case on me. When I saw you, I did not know you were a policeman. I thought you were going to rob me. I was only protecting myself."

"Sure. Big man like you won't have any trouble making bail, but what about later? You might get a judge to believe you were confused when you pulled the gun, but how are you going to explain having the gun and the cocaine in the first place? You'll probably be going away for three years just on the parole violation. If this new offense sticks, it'll be your third, and there's no way you'll get off with less than three years, probably more like ten."

Wedge stood in the open doorway, feeling a little queasy, unable to cross over the threshold into the cell.

McGuire continued, "I understand there's a real problem with AIDS in our prison system these days, but why suffer the inconvenience of being out of circulation and risk getting AIDS when it's not necessary. We're not interested in your suppliers or anyone that might get nasty. We just want one of your customers and some questions answered." McGuire paused for a moment. "Do you want to do a deal or not?"

"What is the deal?"

"You give us Dale, a few answers, and you go free."

"What do I have to do?"

"We can talk about it in the interview room."

The three men seated themselves around the gray metal table in the interview room before McGuire started to speak. "Where do you plan to see Dale?"

"I am to meet him at his apartment at nine."

"How much does he want?"

Joubert hesitated for a moment before answering. "He telephoned me yesterday. He asked to buy two grams—some for tonight, some for later."

"Good." McGuire glanced at his watch. It was 8:13 P.M. "I'll let you call him in a while to confirm your meeting."

"How does this work?" Joubert asked.

"You'll go to Dale's apartment and sell him the coke. You'll be wearing a wire. We'll be outside listening. When the transaction's completed, we come in and arrest Dale."

"What about me? I do not want it getting around to my friends that I—"

McGuire cut him off, "Don't worry, we'll arrest you too. Now, tell me about your conversation with my brother last Thursday."

"Your brother . . . of course . . . he was interested in Dale also. He came to the Gilded Cage asking questions. Too many questions."

"What did you tell him?"

"I told him to suck eggs." Joubert grinned.

"Where were you at eight last Sunday?"

"Sunday . . . Sunday . . . . Yes, I remember, I was with Dale at his apartment that evening."

"Anyone else there?" asked McGuire.

"Yeah, Dale's young friend, Tim."

"Tim who?"

"Tim . . . just Tim . . . a kid."

While McGuire put Joubert back in his cell, Wedge went outside for a little fresh air. McGuire had the Fargo unit taken apart on his desk, and he was fiddling with the small transmitter when Wedge came in.

"Between his bad breath and his cheap cologne," Wedge said, "I almost got ill in there. What are you doing?"

"I'm putting a fresh battery in this thing, so we can hear what goes on when Louie's in Dale's apartment." McGuire reassembled the device.

Wedge found a chair and slumped into it. "Keith, we need to talk."

"Yeah, what about?"

"Look, I was feeling ill earlier, but it wasn't just because of Joubert's cologne," Wedge said. "I was scared stiff from the minute I saw Joubert's gun at the Gilded Cage until he fell on top of me at the store. I was so scared I couldn't think straight. I was totally useless. When he stuck the gun in my back, I almost pissed in my pants." Wedge looked up momentarily and paused. "I don't think I can help you tonight with Ellis. Right now I feel completely wiped out."

"That's just the adrenaline wearing off."

"Yeah, well I feel like shit."

"You know, a couple of years ago one of our patrolmen, Monk Mosley, was checking out some strange noises coming from under a house that was being renovated. He was on his hands and knees in a tight crawl space when he came face to face with a fully-grown mountain lion. Not only did he soil his trousers, by the time he scrambled out of the crawl space opening, he tore the hell out of his uniform and had dozens of splinters the size of toothpicks imbedded in his skin. I never thought any less of Monk for it.

"When you feel really threatened—in fear for your life— your body releases a lot of adrenaline to give you extra strength, but if you can't fight or run, the adrenaline does really strange things to your body and your brain. There's nothing you can do about it; you just learn to deal with it. You did okay out there. You'll be fine."

"I don't know, Keith."

"Look, I'm going to get us some help. You won't need to be involved in Dale's arrest, but I'll need you afterward. I had the desk clerk radio Sergeant O'Donnell. He should be here pretty soon. When he comes in leave the talking to me. Just stand there and look federal."

"Sure, no problem." Wedge wiped his hands slowly down his face. "Joubert gave up Dale pretty easy, didn't he?"

"You think a low-life slimeball like Joubert gives a shit about what happens to one of his customers, especially if he can avoid a prison sentence?" McGuire looked over toward the door and smiled broadly as Sergeant O'Donnell walked into his office.

"Jesus McGuire, don't you ever go home?" O'Donnell said.

"Frank, I'd like you to meet Special Agent Wedgwood with the Defense Investigative Service. We've been working together for a week on a case. We just busted Louie Joubert. He's locked up in one of the holding cells. But Louie's not the one we're really after, he's only a middle man."

"So, what do you want from me?" O'Donnell rested his forearms on top of the leather gear attached to his utility belt.

"I wouldn't ask if it wasn't important. We've spent a lot of time on this case." McGuire leaned back into his chair and laced his fingers behind his head. "We want to use Joubert to do a buy-bust on the guy we're really after, and we need a uniformed officer to help make the arrest."

"When?"

"At nine."

"Can't do it. I'm one man short as it is, and it's Saturday night."

"It won't take more than 40 minutes."

"No." O'Donnell scratched the back of his head. "I'll tell you what, if you can delay it till ten when I get off shift, I'll help you myself."

"Thanks Frank. You're a real credit to the force."

"Save the bullshit for someone else, McGuire. You'll owe me for this one . . . in addition to that other favor I did for you."

"What other favor?"

"Bruce."

As soon as O'Donnell left, Wedge, who had been standing by silently trying to look like a federal agent, asked, "So, what's the deal?"

"O'Donnell will help me with the bust, then transport Joubert back to the station. You'll come in after the arrests have been made and help me search Ellis's apartment."

# CHAPTER SIXTEEN

SATURDAY 10:15 P.M., 17 NOVEMBER 1990

Wedge and McGuire watched from McGuire's car as Joubert walked up to Ellis's apartment. McGuire turned up the volume on his portable radio and heard Joubert knocking on the apartment door. They sat in the car with their attention glued to Ellis's apartment door. O'Donnell was parked down the street about a block away in his patrol unit.

"He just made the sale," McGuire said in a hushed voice. "When we get to the apartment, close the door behind you, and stay out of the way while O'Donnell and I make the arrest."

Wedge nodded.

"Okay, let's go."

As he walked toward Ellis's apartment Wedge looked down the street and saw O'Donnell moving briskly in their direction.

McGuire and O'Donnell positioned themselves on either side of the apartment door. McGuire knocked. When the door opened, O'Donnell moved into the doorway with his gun leveled at Ellis and used it to motion Ellis back into the apartment. Ellis with his mouth gaping open and his eyeglasses sliding down his nose raised his hands and began backpedaling into the living room.

"Police! Don't make any sudden movements, place your hands on top of your head, get down on your knees in the center of the room. Do it now!" O'Donnell ordered.

As the two men kneeled down, O'Donnell got in front of them and McGuire moved around behind them. "Now, cross your ankles," O'Donnell barked. "You're under arrest for possession and sale of cocaine."

McGuire knelt behind Ellis. He grabbed Ellis's left wrist and started to bring it down behind him. "No. Leave your right hand on top of your head until I bring it down for you," McGuire said. Ellis was trembling. With Ellis's left hand positioned between his shoulder blades, McGuire clamped the handcuff on his left wrist, reached up, grabbed Ellis's right wrist, pulled it around, and secured the cuff around it.

McGuire moved over to Joubert and looked up at O'Donnell. O'Donnell already had a pair of cuffs in his free hand and pitched them over to McGuire. McGuire repeated the process with Joubert, then helped him to his feet and patted him down. He found ten, twenty-dollar bills in Joubert's jacket pocket. "Okay, you can sit down over there on the couch." He patted down Ellis, found a wallet, and threw it onto the coffee table. McGuire guided Ellis over to the couch and set him down next to Joubert.

There were eight, quarter-gram bindles of coke lying on top of the coffee table. He examined the contents of one of the bindles. O'Donnell holstered his pistol and began reading from his rights advisement card.

When O'Donnell finished reading, McGuire picked up Ellis's wallet and read from his military ID card, "Ellis, Dale C.; Lieutenant Commander, U.S. Navy; 012-37-1117; six foot-two inches; 175 pounds; blonde hair; blue eyes; born 17 November 1957." He put the ID card away and set the wallet back on the coffee table. "Well, Commander Ellis, I'm Sergeant McGuire and it appears you've become an unfortunate victim of our efforts to put Mr. Joubert out of business.

What a shame. And on your birthday too. Do you mind if we look around a little?"

Ellis looked over at Joubert before answering. Joubert nodded his head and Ellis said, "Yes . . . I mean no . . . go ahead."

"Sergeant O'Donnell, why don't you take Mr. Joubert to the station in your unit and book him? We'll be along in a few minutes," McGuire said.

O'Donnell hustled Joubert out of the apartment. McGuire walked over, locked the door, and fastened the security chain. "I'm sure you wouldn't try to leave. We just don't want any unexpected visitors barging in. You're not expecting any more visitors, are you?"

"No . . . no, I'm not." His eyeglasses sat crooked on his face, but with his hands cuffed behind him, he couldn't straighten them.

"Good. Now, I'd like you to stay seated until we're finished." McGuire pulled a pair of leather gloves out of his jacket pocket and slipped them on. "Wedge, let's start in the bedroom."

"Why the gloves?" Wedge asked as he rummaged around in a chest of drawers.

"Didn't they teach you anything at your school? This guy's a homosexual drug user." McGuire slid open a closet door and started patting down coat pockets. "You want to accidentally prick your hand on a hypodermic needle?"

Wedge jerked his hands out of the drawer. McGuire found a pair of brown leather gloves in the pocket of an overcoat and threw them to Wedge. Wedge turned the gloves inside out, then back again, before squeezing his hands into them.

"Well, look what I found," McGuire said. In his hands he had a half-dozen Polaroid pictures of Ellis engaged in a variety of sex acts with a teenage boy. "We'll just save these for later," he said and slipped them into his jacket pocket.

"What for? Do you like, keep a scrapbook or something?" Wedge asked.

"No," he said, "but these are special. I'll finish up in here. Why don't you check out the bathroom."

The bathroom was immaculately clean. It was neither feminine nor masculine in appearance. Except for the extra large tubes of K-Y Jelly and the economy size box of condoms, nothing in the medicine cabinet seemed out of the ordinary. He lifted the lid of the toilet tank and peered inside. Nothing. The toilet paper dispenser caught his eye. There was nothing unusual about it, but recalling the videotape of the restroom at Lovers' Point, he removed the roll of toilet paper from the dispenser and examined the roller. It looked like a normal spring-loaded chrome-plated roller. It was just slightly larger in diameter than others he had seen. He gently pulled the roller apart and something fell to the floor. Wedge knelt down and picked up a small packet sealed in waxed paper. He carefully tore open the end of the packet, exposing a 16-millimeter film cartridge.

"Keith, look what I found," he whispered as he came back into the bedroom. McGuire was looking through the view-finder of a Minox camera.

McGuire stuck out his hand and accepted the waxed paper packet from Wedge. "Good job. That should do it. We can get a search warrant later and come back for a more thorough look. Come on," he said, "let's take him back to the station."

Ellis continued to tremble during the ride to the station and all through the booking procedure. Between his shaking and profuse sweating, McGuire had a hard time rolling his fingerprints. In the interview room McGuire again advised Ellis of his rights. Wedge sat off to the side, out of Ellis's line of sight. If Ellis had used any deodorant, it had worn off hours ago.

"Is it okay if I call you Dale?" McGuire asked.

Ellis nodded.

"Dale, you've gotten yourself into a serious mess, and I want to help you resolve it. You must've been under a lot of stress trying to hide your lifestyle from the Navy. It's not your fault the Navy takes such an uncompromising attitude towards gays. If you were a civilian, you wouldn't have had to conceal anything and you probably wouldn't have turned to cocaine to escape the stress. Those are minor problems and we can help you deal with them, but you have to help yourself too by cooperating with us. I know you didn't get involved in the other problem on your own."

Ellis tightly crossed his legs and folded his arms over his chest. "I don't know what you're talking about. I—"

McGuire stopped him before he could continue. "Come on, Dale. It's over. It's time to face up to things and try to help your government and your country minimize the damage that's occurred. Mr. Wedgwood here is a Special Agent with the Defense Investigative Service. We have a videotape of you servicing a dead drop at Lovers' Point. We also found your Minox camera and a 16-millimeter film cartridge. We haven't processed it yet, but we both know what's on it, don't we?"

Behind his sagging glasses Ellis's eyes were damp. He seemed barely able to maintain his composure. McGuire pushed a box of tissues over to him. Ellis uncrossed his legs and dropped his hands into his lap.

McGuire let the full impact of what he had said sink in before he continued. "I know you're basically a good person who's gotten himself into a jam by making some mistakes. I can help you correct some of those mistakes now. Why don't you tell me about your contact?"

Ellis stared down at his hand and his shoulders drooped. "I don't know who he is."

McGuire looked over at Wedge and gave him a faint nod. Ellis had just resigned and admitted defeat. "What do you know?" asked McGuire.

"I just drop the film at the restroom. Someone picks it up. I never see him." Ellis used a tissue to blot the moisture from under his glasses.

"But you go back to the restroom afterwards, don't you?" McGuire asked.

"Just to retrieve the toilet paper holder. There's usually some instructions left in it—sometimes money."

"How did all this start?"

"Last December I met a guy at a bar and we became friends, good friends. He sold insurance. He asked for some information about my coworkers in San Diego, so he could try to sell them some insurance. I gave him a copy of my unit roster with names and addresses on it. I did it as a favor to him, but he wanted to pay me for it. He told me the money was from his insurance company—expense money. All he needed was a signature on a receipt to account for it, so I took it and signed his receipt." Ellis's voice lost its emotional timbre and acquired the detached quality of a court recorder reading back testimony. "Later he introduced me to his boss. His boss was totally different—obnoxious, vulgar, and demanding. He wanted sensitive Navy documents. I refused, but he had pictures of me handing an envelope to my friend and of me accepting the money. He also had pictures of my friend and I . . . being intimate. He threatened to send the pictures to NIS and tell them about my use of coke."

"Go on."

Ellis grabbed another tissue and blew his nose before continuing. "In the beginning I tried to pass him unclassified documents I had stamped Secret, but he knew they were phony. I was due for a transfer, so I pulled some strings to speed it up. I left San Diego in July without him knowing I had transferred to Monterey. I thought I could get away from him. It didn't work. One day in August just after President Bush announced we were sending troops to Saudi Arabia, I was jogging on the Recreation Trail and he was sitting on a bench next to the trail waiting for me. He handed me a large envelope. In it were some written instructions, the Minox camera, and one of the photographs of my friend and me. I never saw him again."

"What were the written instructions?"

"It specified the type of information they wanted—about ship movements to the Persian Gulf. I had to give it to them. I didn't have any choice. There were also instructions on loading and unloading dead drops."

"When are you supposed to make your next delivery?"

"On Monday. Since I started using the dead drop at Lovers' Point, it's been on Monday and Wednesday evenings. I make my drop at 5:45 and my pick up at 6:15."

"What's the procedure?"

"I go into the first stall in the restroom and switch my toilet paper roller for the one that's there. I go outside and stick a piece of green plastic tape seven feet up on the lamp post near the women's entrance. I jog to the golf course, then turn around and go back. If there's a piece of blue plastic tape on the lamp post where I left the green one, I take it down, go in the restroom, and switch the toilet paper rollers again."

"What else?"

"There's a lot more if things go wrong. There're alternate locations and drop backs and a complicated system involving flowers in case of emergencies. I've got it all written down in my safe deposit box." Ellis stopped to clean his glasses with a tissue.

"How do you know Louie Joubert?" McGuire asked.

"I connected with him at the Gilded Cage shortly after I transferred here."

"Does he have anything to do with this?"

"No. He's just a friend I party with sometimes. Once in a while I buy coke from him."

"How about Howard McGuire?"

"Who's Howard McGuire?"

"You've never met anyone named Howard McGuire?"

Ellis shook his head. "No, you're the only McGuire I know. What's going to happen to me?" he asked.

"We're going to hold you here for awhile," McGuire said. "Later you'll be taken to the county jail, be sure to tell them you're gay. You don't want to be thrown in with the straight prisoners. They might get nasty with you. Oh yeah, it would be better if you didn't say anything about this to the people at the jail. If you're asked, just tell them about the cocaine. We'll have to discuss your case with the Naval Investigative Service. They may be willing to make a deal with you, if you continue to cooperate." McGuire paused and looked over at Wedge. "Mr. Wedgwood do you have anything you want ask?"

"Just a couple of questions." Wedge pulled his chair around so he faced Ellis. "How do you initiate contact with them?"

"I haven't had to, but I have an address in San Francisco I can have flowers sent to. There are different flower arrangements for different messages. I can only send simple messages and only when it's an emergency."

"What kind of messages?"

"Like, if I'm sick and can't make a drop, or if I need to meet someone in person immediately." Ellis was sitting up straight now and he was starting to gesture with his hands as he talked. "In the case of a meeting, someone is suppose to telephone me and use a prearranged code to indicate the time and place of the meeting."

"What are your instructions if there's an emergency?" Wedge asked. "Say someone found out about you and threatened to tell the Navy."

"I'd stall the person, then use the flowers to arrange a personal meeting and let them deal with it. It would be as much their problem as mine and they're better suited to handle it."

"Oh," McGuire said almost as an afterthought, "Dale, where were you last Sunday night?"

"Last Sunday, I was at my apartment."

"Who was with you?"

"Louie."

"Anyone else?"

"No. Just Louie."

McGuire finished the interview by obtaining names and descriptions of the two men in San Diego. Neither of them resembled Howard or Karasov.

McGuire sat behind his desk throwing darts at the wanted poster on the bulletin board.

"How were you able to keep yourself from spitting on him?" Wedge asked.

"Just because I think he's a gutless traitor doesn't give me the right to treat him like one. Everyone deserves to hold on to every last scrap of dignity they have. It's not my place to take it away from them." McGuire fired another dart at the poster. The point of the dart buried itself deep into the bulletin board. "Besides, it always works to my advantage to treat them well. I may not like doing it, but then, I do a lot of things I don't like."

"When are you going to tell NIS about Ellis?" Wedge pulled up a chair and sat in it backwards with his arms draped over the back of the chair.

"Soon, but there're still a few things we need to do before we let them come in and muck things up." McGuire lighted a cigarette.

"Well, when you do tell NIS, I'd appreciate it if you'd like, leave my name out of it."

"Why?"

"They're gonna be miffed that they weren't notified immediately." Wedge got up and began pacing around the room. "They can't do much to you, but they can get me in a lot of trouble."

"We just made a big case for them. If they want my cooperation in quashing the drug bust, they won't raise any stink." McGuire winced as he landed a dart in the fugitive's right eye.

"All the same, try to keep my name out of it."

"Look," McGuire said, "you're not the only one who's stuck his neck out on this case. Upham knows about you. He knows I've been doing things behind his back. He just doesn't know what I've been doing. But he knew enough to go to Captain Headley, and Headley convinced the Chief I shouldn't be in charge of the investigation. Headley wanted the Chief to take me off the case entirely."

"When did that happen?"

"Yesterday after lunch. The Chief called me into his office and officially put Upham in charge. He also warned me about withholding information from Upham." McGuire pulled the darts out of the wanted poster and returned to his desk.

"Did you tell Upham what we had planned for tonight?"

"How could I without telling him about Eugene Leach or the video tape? If I told him about that, he'd have had me thrown off the case in a heartbeat."

"But you haven't done anything wrong."

"The hell I haven't." McGuire's voice grew louder. "I've intentionally withheld information from Upham. As soon as he hears about these two arrests, he'll go straight to the Chief. I'll be taken off the case and placed on suspension."

"Don't get mad at me," Wedge said.

"Well, damn it, everything we've done so far seems to benefit the Department of Defense, but we still don't know shit about Howard's shooting and we don't have much time left." McGuire lighted another cigarette from the butt of the one he was smoking.

"Why didn't you tell me about all this earlier?"

"I didn't want you getting cold feet. None of it matters anymore. I'm going ahead with this regardless of what the Chief does." McGuire paused. "I was hoping Ellis was our man or at least he would lead us to him."

"What about Pavlenko?"

"I was thinking about him." McGuire again took aim at the wanted poster. "We could load the dead drop on Monday—one roll of film. We'll arrest Pavlenko as he comes out of the restroom. Hell, he's the only suspect we haven't questioned. At this point, I don't think Ellis or Joubert had anything to do with Howard's shooting, and I haven't gotten hold of Leach to have him look at the photograph of Karasov yet." He let a dart fly. It bounced off the bulletin board and fell to the floor.

"I don't know, Keith. Couldn't we turn the whole thing over to NIS right now? They can coordinate with the FBI and arrest Pavlenko. All we need is a couple of hours of interview time with him."

"Do you think the FBI will let us get within a mile of Pavlenko once he's been arrested for espionage? We don't have anything that links Pavlenko to Howard's shooting. Without some hard evidence we can hardly force the issue."

"Okay, relax, I'm still on your side."

"If it were just the local FBI guys, they might give us a shot at him, but you know how their headquarters types like to come in and take control of high visibility cases."

"What are we going to do about Ellis?" Wedge asked.

"I need to get him out of here before he attracts too much attention. McGuire glanced at his watch and said, "It's one-fifty now. I'll take him over to the county jail for booking. I've got a friend in the Sheriff's Office who can make sure Ellis's arraignment is delayed until Wednesday morning. That should give us enough time."

"Okay then, we can try the dead drop on Monday."

Sunday afternoon Keith and Alycia walked from his apartment to the Fishwife Restaurant and had a late lunch. Afterward they strolled down to Asilomar Beach. They wound their way leisurely on the twisted path along the shoreline toward Point Pinos Lighthouse.

"Hardly any at all returned this year," she said absently.

"What?" McGuire asked. A wind blew in off the ocean, and the rocks were washed white with surf. They had to raise their voices to be heard over the roar of the ocean.

"Monarchs." Alycia was in her element. She had a beach dweller's careless sun-streaked hair that danced with each gust of wind. Tall and lean, she was outdoorsy without looking athletic.

"Where did they go?"

"North, silly—Washington, Oregon, Idaho, Northern California." Under her green hooded parka shell she wore a rose colored turtleneck sweater, and jeans. "We have great hopes for the Dively property, and we should be able to do more at Washington Park," she remarked as she stood out on a rock facing the sea.

"What are you talking about?" McGuire studied her face. Her lips were too thick, her eyebrows too straight, and her chin too small for her to be beautiful. Her eyes were large and almost the color of wood smoke. They combined with her sad smile and high cheekbones to make her face somewhat haunting.

"Butterfly habitat. You really don't know much about the monarchs, do you?"

"No, I guess not." McGuire wondered how she would look with a little makeup.

"We need to spend more time getting to know about each other's interests," she said.

"I know I've been kind of busy lately, but I've got some compensatory time built up." McGuire searched for an excuse to postpone matters. "Maybe, when Noguchi gets back from Saudi Arabia, I could ask for some time off."

"Could you? You know my birthday's in January." She stepped up to him and grasped both his hands in hers.

"Oh?"

"Well, it is. My mother wants to give me a vacation in Mexico." She bounced slightly on her toes like a young girl. "I'd love to go, if you could come with me."

"It's nice of you to offer, but I'm sure I'd be in the way while the two of you are trying to do mother-daughter stuff." McGuire flipped up the collar of his jacket against the wind.

"She's not going, silly. She wants to treat you and me to a two-week vacation in Puerto Vallarta or Mazatlan. I think I'd rather go to the Yucatan and spend some time exploring Mayan ruins."

"Oh."

"You don't sound very interested, Keith."

"It sounds great. Just you and me for two whole weeks. In January, huh?" The wind sprinkled them with salt spray. McGuire looked up at seagulls effortlessly hovering overhead.

"It doesn't have to be January; we could go in December. And it doesn't have to be just two weeks. We can stretch it out to three weeks, if we stay away from the tourist hotels."

"I'd really like to, but I don't know how long of an absence my boss'll approve. Don't start planning anything till I have a chance to talk to Captain Headley. Things are a little rocky at the department right now. There's also the promotion board in January. I'm not sure I can take the time off."

"I saw just the thing at Eddie Bauer yesterday," she said. "It's an olive drab three-quarter length traveler's vest. It'll be perfect for hiking around. It's got a dozen pockets on the front to carry just about everything."

He drove her out to her mother's mansion in Pebble Beach and dropped her off. As he wove his way along the narrow tree-lined roads back to Pacific Grove, he thought about her and the possibility of a more permanent relationship. He had been married twice. Both marriages lasted about seven years; both sort of withered on the vine instead of maturing and blossoming; and both ended because he allowed his work to take priority over his home life.

He disliked being alone, but now he was coping better than he did after his first divorce, and he wasn't as anxious to jump into an exclusive relationship. He realized he needed to change his expectations regarding relationships, and he needed to develop other aspects of his personal life. If Howard got better, he would take up fishing again, so they could do something together. When Noguchi returned, he would accept one of his frequent dinner invitations. McGuire smiled as he pulled into his carport. Who knows, he might even join the Friends of the Monarch.

# CHAPTER SEVENTEEN

MONDAY 8:35 A.M., 19 NOVEMBER 1990

Martha Pembroke stormed into his office clutching the files in front of her. "Wedge, I wanna talk about these cases you dumped on me," she said. She wore a lavender polyester pants suit with puckered seams from repeated washings. She sat in front of Wedge's desk without waiting for a reply and began spreading out the case files on his desk.

Well, don't even say hello, how are you, or are you busy, Wedge thought. Just barge in here yelling and plop your fat ass down in a chair. "Sure, I've got a few minutes before my next appointment," he said and put away the papers he was reviewing.

"Half of these cases you gave me on Friday have multiple issues. What did you do, cherry pick the easy ones and pass all your dirty cases to me?" she said.

Wedge leaned back in his chair and shook his head slowly. "Actually, I like, tried to give you the less complicated ones. What you have are fairly easy cases for DLI." He opened a desk drawer pulled out a stack of case folders. "Look, these are some of the cases I kept. This guy's been fired from like, six jobs and has eight delinquent credit accounts. This one's alleged to have stolen $15,000 from a prior employer. Here's a lieutenant colonel who just got out of a residential treatment program for alcoholics." Wedge flipped through the case files.

"I also have two Russian émigrés, a skinhead, and a weenie waver." Wedge noted with satisfaction that Martha's pudgy face had turned bright red. "If you like, I'll trade any of these cases for the ones I gave you." Otherwise, Wedge thought, shut the fuck up and get out of my office.

"That won't be necessary," she replied brusquely. "Do you have a contact list with names and locations of the unit commanders and the language department chairpersons?"

"No," Wedge lied, "but I've got a map of the Presidio with all the buildings on it and an organization chart. If you want, I'll copy them for you. It's a small base. You'll find your way around in no time at all." And I hope to God you don't try to throw your weight around and screw up our relationship with the staff and faculty. Pembroke had a reputation for being a little badge heavy.

"I guess that'll have to do. Which of these offices will I be using?"

"The one in the back. Here, I'll show you," he said and got up to lead the way. The office was situated just beyond the door at the end of the hallway and immediately to the right of the auditorium stage. It looked as if it had once been used as a dressing room or perhaps to store props for theatrical performances. The office contained a telephone, two desks, a bookcase, and a typewriter. There were no window coverings and the walls were bare. Wedge had used the room for a few months. When Steve retired, he moved into Steve's office next to Howard's in the main hallway.

"Make yourself at home. I know it's not much, but it's only temporary."

"This is not acceptable," she said. "I prefer to use Howard's office."

"Well, you'll have to talk to Butler about that. I don't have the key to Howard's office," Wedge lied again.

"I'm a GS-11, journeyman investigator, and I'm not going to be shoved away into a storage room in the back of this building."

"Hey, I used this office for like, almost four months." Wedge bit his tongue. No sense in arguing with her. Let Butler handle it. That's what he gets paid for. "I've got a Subject Interview in ten minutes," he said and quickly left.

McGuire briefly explained to Wedge how the small radio worked as they sat in McGuire's unmarked car in front of the Tinnery Restaurant across from Lovers' Point Park. They could see the public restroom clearly from their position. The sun was down already and it was getting dark.

"Use the earphone," McGuire said. "That way no one will hear the squelch when you key the mike. When you're sure he's made the switch, key the mike twice. You don't need to say anything; I'll hear you. We're set to the tactical frequency. There won't be anyone else using it. Here, I brought some green tape." McGuire handed him the small roll of plastic tape.

"How do you think Howard was able to like, set up his camcorder inside the restroom without being noticed?" Wedge asked.

"I'm not sure. Every night at about ten o'clock, a patrolman locks the place up. It's unlocked at about six in morning. Sometimes they even check it periodically during the night. My best guess is Howard went there late at night and picked the lock. Have you been in the restroom?"

"No, and I'll probably avoid the place in the future."

"Well, you can't see it from here, but the restrooms don't have regular doors. They have metal gates in place of doors. I figure Howard bought a padlock identical to the one on the gate. After he picked the lock and entered the restroom, he put his lock on the gate, so anyone who came by while he was in there would see that the restroom was secured. When he finished, he took his lock off and replaced it with the original lock. That would give him as much time as he needed to set up his camcorder. He probably hooked it up to some sort of timer, then came back the next night to removed it."

"Clever."

McGuire hated surveillances, particularly stationary surveillances. This one wouldn't be too bad because they were only dealing with a short period of time. Stakeouts could last hours and sometimes days. On a major surveillance you worked on shifts with other cops. You might spend three or four days diligently watching, only to find out all the excitement happened on someone else's shift. Moving surveillances were better, but you never had enough men or the right equipment to do the job properly.

Reaching for his thermos of coffee, he recalled the first rule of surveillance—always take comfort items. He poured the coffee and kept glancing up, never looking away from the general direction of the beige building for more than a couple of seconds at a time. There were still a number of people walking around the park. Hopefully Pavlenko would come on his bicycle making him easier to spot. McGuire settled back into a comfortable position sipping his coffee. He rolled down his window just a little to prevent the windshield from steaming up.

The park at Lovers' Point covered a few acres of priceless shoreline on Oceanview Boulevard. Situated on the leeward side of the point was a small beach covered with fine white sand where people swam without wetsuits only on the warmest days, because the water temperature stayed generally in the fifties. The point itself was one of those magnificent large rock outcroppings that created spectacular vertical towers of frothing white water whenever a strong wind would whip up some large waves. It was also the southwestern terminus of the fifteen-mile long Monterey Bay Recreational Trail. The park was lined by a row of large gnarled cypress trees. The public restroom, a small beige cinder block building with brown trim, sat just behind the trees. Beyond the building was an expanse of well-kept grass lawn, a concrete path, some benches, and a rock and mortar seawall.

McGuire could clearly see the men's entrance to the small beige building. The nearest lamppost to the building was at least fifteen yards away, but a small light over the doorway illuminated the entrance area. During the thirty minutes they had been sitting there, two-thirds of the cars parked nearby had left, and the foot traffic had decreased by half. It had also changed from twilight to darkness.

Wedge looked at his watch; it was almost 5:40 P.M. He looked over at McGuire and said, "Okay, I guess it's show time."

McGuire smiled. "If you meet anyone interesting in there, get their phone number for Eugene. We owe him a favor."

"I'm locking myself in a stall until you come and get me out of there," Wedge said and stepped out of the car. His light jacket didn't offer much protection against the wind coming off the ocean. He had a small strip of green tape in his left hand as he approached the lamppost. Without looking around or breaking his stride, Wedge stuck the tape to the post and continued on to the men's entrance on the other side of the building. It was empty. He went into the first stall and bolted the door. For a moment he stood there dumfounded. There was no toilet paper. Christ, I should have brought some, he thought.

Hurriedly, he went into the other stall to find what he needed. As he was removing the toilet paper, he heard someone enter the restroom. He quickly closed the stall door and looked at his watch. It was only 5:47. It couldn't be him already. Wedge bent down and peered under the stall door. All he could see was brown trouser legs from the knee down, brown socks, and brown loafers. Standing motionless in the stall, he felt the uncomfortable pounding of his heart subsided a little. It wasn't Pavlenko. Pavlenko would be dressed as a bicyclist wearing athletic shoes of some type, and he wouldn't be standing in front of a urinal.

He looked at his watch again and followed the sweep of the second hand. Finally he heard the flush of a urinal and footsteps. It was 5:52. Holding the roll of toilet paper inside his jacket, he darted out of one stall and into the other. It took him a good half-minute of fumbling around before he was able to set his roller and the toilet paper into the holder properly. He stood perfectly still for a moment and listened for any noise, then made another mad dash back to the other stall. He glanced at his watch again. It was 5:54. He wanted to sit for a while and let his heart slow down, but the toilet seat was wet and now there was no toilet paper in his stall to wipe it off. He pulled a handkerchief out of his hip pocket and used it to clean the seat and sat down. For a moment he stared at the stained handkerchief in his hand. He shook his head in disgust and dropped it on the floor behind him.

Time passed more slowly. Sitting there waiting, Wedge's mind played out different scenarios of how it all would end. For a moment he envisioned himself receiving a commendation from the Director of DIS for catching a spy. Then his mind turned to other possible outcomes. What if DIS takes a dim view of his activities, even if he and McGuire are successful? What if something goes wrong and the whole thing blows up in his face? He saw himself standing at attention, flanked by Clayton Butler and Miles Quinlan. In front of him the director of the agency ceremoniously dropped Wedge's credentials into a paper shredder.

Aleks Pavlenko switched on his headlight and looked at his watch again as he passed under a street lamp. It was 5:45 P.M. The sun had been down for over forty minutes. He had just passed Fisherman's Wharf and was back on the bike path. Right on schedule, he thought. At the Coast Guard pier he glanced over his shoulder. He could see a number of walkers and joggers on the trail but only one other bicyclist. The other cyclist was gaining on him rapidly. He made a mental note of the cars on Cannery Row and on Foam Avenue. The other cyclist passed Pavlenko as he crossed Reeside Avenue. For the next half mile the recreational trail ran parallel to Cannery Row on what used to be the Southern Pacific Railroad tracks. It was now paved over, but still bordered by old warehouses. Some of the warehouses had been renovated and now housed restaurants and stores for the tourists. You couldn't see the parallel streets from this section of the trail.

The foot traffic on the trail became heavier, and Pavlenko slowly wove his bicycle between the pedestrians. He looked directly at as many faces as he could. Once he passed the Aquarium he was able to increase his speed. From the Aquarium to Lovers' Point was usually the most scenic part of the trail, but now it was too dark to see the rocky shoreline. Pavlenko had taken up bicycling four months ago. He hadn't ridden a bike since he was a teenager. It had taken him a while before he got over his initial wobbliness and felt confident in his riding ability. It was 6:01 P.M., when he pulled up next to the lamppost near the public restrooms at Lovers' Point.

The green tape was clearly visible. He leaned his bicycle against the lamppost, took off his helmet and ran his fingers through his short matted sandy hair. Kneeling down he pretended to tighten his shoelaces and looked over at a gray Volvo station wagon parked nearby. Its radio antenna was raised. Pavlenko slowly pushed his bicycle over to a water fountain, took a sip of water, then remounted and rode back in the direction he came from. Within a minute the gray station wagon pulled out of the parking lot and drove away.

Pavlenko left the bike path just east of the Naval Post-graduate School and headed south on Casa Verde Way. From there he wove around randomly turning at each intersection until he was certain no one was following. Finally he turned onto Virgin Avenue and pulled up to his house. He wheeled the bicycle through the back door of the garage and rested it against a workbench in front of the gray Volvo station wagon.

His was a yellow three-bedroom ranch-style house on the west side of Virgin Avenue. It was a quiet street. Across from his house was a small park on the edge of Laguna Grande Park where the city limits of Monterey and Seaside met. In the daytime you could barely see the small Russian Orthodox Church on the other side of the narrow lake. They had chosen the house because it would have been very difficult for anyone to establish a surveillance on it without being easily detected. It was also convenient to Fort Ord, the Presidio, and the Naval Postgraduate School.

"Okay, Wedge," McGuire announced as he entered the restroom. "You can come out now."

Wedge emerged from the stall with a baffled look on his face. "What the hell happened? Didn't he show up?"

"I'll tell you in the car. Grab the roller and let's get out of here."

Wedge climbed into the car and looked at McGuire.

"He made it right up to the lamp post, fiddled with his shoes, drank some water, then rode away," McGuire said. "I don't think he saw me, but something spooked him."

"I'm sure I put the tape in the right place."

"I saw it, it was okay."

"What do you think he'll do now?"

"Damned if I know." McGuire started up the engine. "I guess it depends on why he didn't go in. He wouldn't have come, if he didn't think everything was all right. So it must have been something he saw or heard when he got here."

# CHAPTER EIGHTEEN

MONDAY 6:30 P.M., 19 NOVEMBER 1990

Aleks Pavlenko strode into the kitchen from the garage. "What went wrong?" he asked.

"I don't know," Zhanna replied. "I didn't see your contact. I'm sure he didn't enter the restroom."

Aleks checked his watch against the kitchen clock. "The green tape was in the proper position. He must have been there. Are you sure he didn't go in?  Did you get there in time?"

Zhanna busied herself preparing dinner. "Yes, I'm sure. He didn't go in or come out. I'm positive he wasn't there. Perhaps you forgot to take down the green tape from the last time."

"Did you see anyone go in the restroom before I got there?"

"Two men went in and one man came out."

"Did you recognize either of them?"

"No," Zhanna retorted.

"Was there anyone standing around nearby?" Aleks asked tersely.

"There was one man sitting in a dark blue car, five cars over from me, but I couldn't see him very well because of the other cars. A young couple with a child was over by the rocks, but they weren't paying any attention to the restroom. What's so important about this dead drop that I have to cover it?"

"That's my business."

"Well, what are you going to do about it?"

"Whatever I choose to do, I'll work out on my own." The trouble was Aleks didn't know what to do. He should have changed the dead drop site two weeks ago before he met with Kropotkin. He didn't want to go running to him again unless he was certain the operation was in danger. Kropotkin had already implied that Aleks was loosing his nerve. "I'll be in the study. Call me when dinner's ready."

Things had been tolerable for Zhanna until August. Since then, she had become increasing unhappy with her situation. She didn't mind doing all the housework and cooking while she had been unemployed. She had hoped that once she got her job back at DLI, Aleks would help around the house a little.

Shortly after she lost her job two years ago, they had asked Kropotkin for permission to have a second child, but the answer was no. Kropotkin insisted it would not be feasible for them to have another child when their income was reduced. People would question how they could afford a child at a time like that. As it was, the KGB had to supplement their income in order for them to survive financially. That alone strained their cover story. At the time she accepted his decision without complaint, but she felt with the loss of her job, it was an ideal time to be pregnant. She wouldn't have contact with any students and her pregnancy wouldn't interfere with her mission.

Her job was to identify students who were weak and easily influenced, then to cultivate a relationship with them to learn as much as she could about their weakness and how to exploit it. Her targets were invariably eighteen to twenty-two year old boys who were pimple-faced and socially awkward.

Life in America changed her. She felt she and Alex were equal partners. She resented having to work full-time as a teacher and as a mother, carry a full operational load, and do all the housework, shopping and cooking.

Since returning to work, Zhanna had not been required to spot and assess any new students. When Aleks was given the task of servicing the new agent, he handed over to her the job of supporting an émigré network at DLI. The network consisted of a dozen instructors, each acting independently without any knowledge of the others. Each collected biographical data on the students and wrote assessments of their personalities. They also reported on the activities of their colleagues, as well as other Russian émigrés in the Monterey area. These instructors were not trained intelligence officers, but rather ordinary émigrés who were coerced into working for the KGB.

She suspected there were other professional KGB officers at DLI, like Aleks and herself, but she didn't know who they were. If they existed, their activities were totally separate and compartmented from hers. It was just as well. She had enough work of her own and had no desire to know what others might be doing. Between the émigrés and the recent special tasking to report on Sergei Karasov, the new instructor, she often found herself correcting student papers late into the night.

Aleks had an emergency meeting with Kropotkin a week ago and Zhanna had argued with him for two hours before he left for the meeting. She had wanted him to ask Kropotkin again for permission to have another child now that she was employed. Aleks had disagreed. The meeting was to discuss emergency operational matters. Nevertheless, Zhanna had pleaded and cried until he agreed to broach the subject with Kropotkin. When Aleks returned from the meeting with Kropotkin, he was short-tempered and ill at ease.

Kropotkin had berated Aleks for even thinking of having another child. It became one of many criticisms Kropotkin heaped upon him during the meeting. There had even been veiled threats of sending them both back to Moscow. Aleks told Zhanna only the main points of his meeting with Kropotkin. He passed on most of Kropotkin's criticisms and his order for Aleks to turn over to Zhanna the task of reporting on Karasov. He also gave her special instructions regarding Karasov, which were for her eyes only. The nature of these instructions and the fact they were passed to her by microdot left no doubt that Karasov's activities were of extreme importance to the Centre. The instructions ordered her to use all available resource to closely monitor Karasov's movements and report immediately on any unusual activity.

Dinner passed with hardly a word between them. When he finished eating, Aleks returned to the den, leaving Zhanna to clean off the table and wash the dishes.

In the two years Kropotkin had been their control, Aleks had only had three PMs—personal meetings—with him. The one on 11 November in Tijuana was the first emergency meeting. The previous one in Mexico City in July and the one a year prior to that were both routine PMs at which Kropotkin gave Aleks new tasking. Routine PMs occurred outside the United States every year or so. At the July meeting Kropotkin had been full of praise for Aleks and Zhanna. Aleks learned of his promotion to major. He was told of the confidence his superiors had in both him and Zhanna and the great responsibility they were being entrusted with. It was the typical bullshit a control used before piling on more work.

Lieutenant Colonel Viktor Semenovich Kropotkin was a *Chekist* from the old school. As the KGB Residency Line N officer at the Soviet Embassy in Mexico City, he was responsible for the support of "illegal" agents. But his only real concern was his own career. He had survived several purges during his years in the KGB and always profited by the failures of his superiors and the successes of his subordinates. His one and only real concern was getting his *papaha*, the big hat worn by full colonels and generals.

At the July meeting Kropotkin had told Aleks that the new agent he would service was critical to the security of the motherland and the ultimate defeat of the main enemy. The agent's code name was Dora. It was a great responsibility; however, it would not require much work. The agent had access to valuable information, but would only need to be serviced every three months once he was activated. With Zhanna back at work, she could relieve Aleks of a few mundane tasks. During the meeting, Aleks also passed on routine information he had picked up concerning Karasov who had been hired as an instructor the month before.

Kropotkin's prediction lasted less than a month. In early August Aleks received new instructions by way of coded message over Radio Moscow's overseas broadcast. It was his routine method of receiving instructions. Three nights a week Aleks tuned in his Sony ICF-2010 to Radio Moscow at 1:00 A.M. and recorded the program as he listened attentively for any coded instruction intended for him. That night the instructions came in two parts. He didn't finish the decoding until 3:00 A.M. Dora had been activated and instructed to begin reporting immediately. Information was to be passed twice a week by dead drop until further notice. Moscow Center also required additional information on Sergei Ivanovich Karasov as soon as possible.

After early August, Aleks started receiving a steady stream of instructions—some pertaining to Dora, others requesting even more information about Karasov. The pace of his activities had become frantic. It was unheard of to service a dead drop twice a week. It posed too great a risk to the security of the operation.

When Zhanna was rehired, she was required to complete new security forms and it was discovered that Aleks needed to complete new security forms also. The clerk at the security office did not know why the forms were required, so Aleks attributed it to some routine administrative requirement. At the time Aleks was so busy with other matters, he put it out of his mind until late August when he and Zhanna were informed DIS was conducting background investigations on them. It caught him totally by surprise. Having been a DLI employee for five years, he had relaxed his guard somewhat, thinking the Government had completed its security checks on him and Zhanna long ago, and they had successfully avoided detection.

His interview with DIS went poorly. He grossly underestimated the ability of the young man who conducted the interrogation and had not prepared properly for it. Had it occurred five years earlier, when he and Zhanna were first hired by DLI, they could have breezed through it. Back then they had rehearsed their legends repeatedly in anticipation of an in-depth interview, but now they had forgotten many of the details of their legends. They also relied heavily on Kropotkin's and his predecessor's assurances that DIS was an incompetent organization, staffed by poorly trained inexperienced investigators.

Aleks chose not to call a crash meeting with Kropotkin after his interview with DIS in September. He didn't want to tell Kropotkin about his miserable performance in the interview, nor did he want to alarm him unnecessarily. But then, almost two weeks ago on 7 November when Aleks was servicing the dead drop at Lovers' Point, Zhanna thought she saw Howard McGuire, the DIS agent who conducted her interview, sitting in a parked car nearby. It wasn't McGuire's red Porsche or his government car, but the man inside looked somewhat like McGuire. The incident unnerved him and he immediately activated the emergency contact procedure for a crash meeting.

The meeting had taken place in a sleazy apartment building in Tijuana on Sunday, 11 November. At first Kropotkin had listened attentively to Aleks's concerns, but then he began to berate Aleks for poor operational security. "Why have you not changed dead drop sites more frequently?"

Aleks Pavlenko sat at attention. "There has not been time. I have identified two other locations, but you have not given me approval on them yet."

"You should have submitted them earlier. And this request by Zhanna about a baby—what are you thinking of at a time like this?" Kropotkin ran his stubby fingers over his bald head as if smoothing down some invisible hair.

"She is thirty years old," Pavlenko protested. "She is a woman. She wants a playmate for Natasha. She—"

Kropotkin silenced him with a wave of his hand. "Now is out of the question! Tell her to be patient. As to this other matter, who was the DIS investigator?"

"His name is Howard McGuire. He—"

"Before, you said his name was Wedgwood," Kropotkin interrupted.

"Gordon Wedgwood was the young investigator who conducted my interview. An older man, Howard McGuire, interviewed Zhanna. It was McGuire that Zhanna may have seen at the dead drop site."

"You are loosing your grip, Sasha, and Zhanna's imagination is playing tricks on her. I have it on good authority that DIS does not conduct surveillances." Kropotkin flared his nostril. His thick eyebrows nearly came together forming one long bushy furrow protruding from his otherwise large flat forehead. "If Zhanna saw McGuire, then it was only a coincidence and you are blowing it out of proportion."

"Of course, you are more knowledgeable of these things, Comrade Colonel," Aleks replied. "I may be over reacting. I have been under considerable pressure because of the investigation and operational requirements."

"What of Sergei Karasov?" Kropotkin's voice became friendlier.

"There is nothing new. Why the special interest in him?"

"It is a request from my old friend Colonel Cherniavsky. When you return to Monterey, I want Zhanna to report on his activities. You already have enough to do. Here take this postcard. Write a note on it and address it to Zhanna, but do not mail it; hand carry it back to Zhanna. Under the postage stamp is a microdot with instructions for her eyes only. Do you understand?"

"Yes, Comrade Colonel," Pavlenko replied.

"Do not worry about DIS. They are amateurs. Even the FBI is no longer a real threat. If DIS makes additional inquiries, contact me and let me know, but do not panic. We have ways of knowing. . . ." Kropotkin stopped and changed the subject. "There is someone I want you to meet. He has been patiently waiting in the next room for us to finish our business."

Kropotkin called someone on the telephone and spoke briefly. A minute later he answered a knock at the door and admitted a tall distinguished looking man about sixty with silver-gray hair and a long thin face.

"Major General Vasilyev may I present Major Aleksandr Timofeevich Lopatin." Aleks Pavlenko snapped to attention. It had been a long time since he last heard his real name spoken out loud.

"Relax Major Lopatin. I have been looking forward to meeting you." Aleks accepted Vasilyev's outstretched hand and grasped it firmly. Vasilyev as the head of Directorate S of the First Chief Directorate was directly responsible for all "illegals" like Aleks and was Kropotkin's boss at Moscow Centre. "I commend you on the excellent job you are doing in forwarding Dora's reports to the Centre."

"Thank you, Comrade Major General."

Kropotkin stepped closer and placed his hand on Alek's shoulder. "Sasha, there are *zakuski* and vodka in the kitchen. You will also find glasses, plates, and a serving tray in there. Please bring them out for our distinguished guest."

Pavlenko went into the kitchen and began arranging the hors d'oeuvres on a large plate and pouring the vodka. He strained to hear the conversation in the living room.

"Viktor Semenovich, I was listening from the other room. Why do you use a microdot to pass instructions to Zhanna?" Vasilyev asked.

"Her mission is an important one," Kropotkin said, "but it will seem even more critical and will make Zhanna feel even more important when her instructions arrive by means of such secret tradecraft. Because of it she will pursue her task with greater vigor. It is a little motivational technique I learned when I was younger."

"By the way, Major Lopatin had good reason to be concerned about his security. And you, Viktor Semenovich, should be more careful. Our successes against the DIS should not be made known to field operatives, certainly not one who is operating as an illegal in enemy territory."

"It was a slip. I will be more careful. But why do you say Aleks has reason for concern?"

"Howard McGuire is known to our counterintelligence people in Directorate K. I have seen his *spravka*. It is one of their thicker files. He has been a formidable adversary. Because of him two agents at DLI have been neutralized and one case officer in Japan is dead."

"He has not uncovered any of my assets at DLI," Kropotkin said.

"No, none of yours, Viktor Semenovich, but two belonging to our former sister services—the Polish SB and East German Stasi."

"Why was I not told of this before, comrade Major General?"

"At the Centre we have to be selective about what information we disseminated out to the field, even information furnished by our former socialist partners," Vasilyev said.

"If this McGuire tripped up two agents, they must have been bumbling fools. I know about DIS. I've read dozens of case studies where they failed to detect some of our worst errors."

"Our trade is practiced by strong-minded individualists. The reputation of an agency is secondary," Vasilyev said. "Your primary adversaries are men not organizations. But you need not concern yourself with McGuire in the future . . . ."

The two men became silent when Aleks entered the room with a large tray of cold food and vodka. He set the tray on the coffee table and offered glasses to Vasilyev and Kropotkin. Grabbing a glass for himself, Aleks lifted it to eye level and looked straight at Vasilyev. "*Budte zdorovy*," he toasted and emptied the glass in one swallow.

Aleks ate the herring. He never developed a fondness for the salted cucumbers his older comrades always had with their vodka. After an hour of small talk and several more toasts, Kropotkin brought the meeting to a close. "Sasha, you have a long drive ahead of you. You should leave before it becomes too late."

"Tomorrow is a worker's holiday, the American Veteran's Day. I have the day off. I will take the trolley back to San Diego and spend the night there before driving to Monterey."

Aleks was still sitting in the study when he heard Zhanna's voice call to him from across the hall. She had just put their daughter in bed, and it was now time for him to read her a story.

# CHAPTER NINETEEN

TUESDAY 1:55 P.M., 20 NOVEMBER 1990

McGuire drove past the familiar battered green Toyota sitting in front of the building and parked his car out of sight on the south side of the Tin Barn.

He entered the DIS office and saw Wedge behind his desk anxiously shuffling through a file of papers. Eugene Leach was seated across from Wedge working a toothpick around in his mouth. Leach stood up as McGuire approached him. Wedge looked up at McGuire, rolled his eyes, and shook his head.

"Keith, I've been trying to get hold of you since Sunday," Leach said.

"Yeah. Well, I've been trying to get hold of you since Friday. Where the hell have you been?"

Leach pursed his lips and sat back down. "Bruce asked me to thank you for getting the charge reduced to disorderly conduct."

"I did it as a favor to you, not for Bruce."

"I understand . . . and I have something for you. I was at the Gilded Cage on Sunday, and Mack, the bartender, tells me Louie got arrested Saturday night for carrying a concealed weapon. He also says Louie's friend Dale got busted for dope. They're both in jail. Some other friends tell me Dale's a Lieutenant Commander in the Navy working at Fleet

Numerical." Leach then read from a small notepad. "Lieutenant Commander Dale Carston Ellis; security clearance: Top Secret, issued by the Navy, 13 September 1986; address: 1045 Sloat Avenue, Apartment 6, Monterey."

McGuire exchanged glances with Wedge, who had looked up from his files.

"Where're you getting this information?" McGuire stepped toward Leach and tried to look at what he had written down. Leach rocked back in his chair and pressed the notepad close to his chest as if shielding a poker hand.

"I've got my sources. There's more if you want it. I know where he's been to school, where he's been assigned, date and place of birth, blood type . . . ."

McGuire stepped back and folded his arms across his chest. "Which one of your navy friends has access to Dale's personnel file?"

"You want the information or not?" Leach asked.

"You've already told me everything I need to know about Dale." McGuire laid the ID photo of Karasov on the desk in front of Leach. "Have you seen this guy before?"

"He's the one who was with Howard at the Tavern."

"You're sure?"

"Yeah, that's him."

McGuire pocketed the photo and looked at his watch. "I don't mean to give you the bum's rush, but we're expecting someone any minute now and you shouldn't be seen with us." He took one step toward the door, then waited for Leach.

"Whose reputation are you worried about, mine or yours?" A large smile spread across Leach's face. He slowly got up and ambled to the door.

"Thanks Eugene, I appreciate your efforts . . . and I'll remember them," McGuire said as he patted him on the back.

As soon as Leach was halfway down the hall, McGuire turned back to Wedge and whispered, "Is everything on track?"

"I telephoned Pavlenko this morning and arranged for him to come over. As long as Pembroke doesn't barge in, we're set."

"I hope Leach doesn't bump into Pavlenko on the way out."

Wedge put his papers back into the file folder and put it away. "It's only two-ten," he said. "Pavlenko won't be here until exactly two-fifteen, not a minute earlier or a minute later. You can like, set your watch by this guy. By the way, have you run any checks on Karasov?"

"Yeah, but I haven't turned up anything yet. I haven't been able to contact this guy I know at the FBI Identification Division. He's been out the past couple of days. I'll call him again as soon as I get a chance." McGuire looked around the office. "Is there an ashtray somewhere?"

"Sorry, you can't smoke in here—government regulations."

"What did Howard do?"

"He went outside and smoked on the back stairs."

McGuire put his cigarettes away. "Well anyway, it's obvious now that Karasov lied about his friend Charles Howell and meeting him at the American Tin Cannery. The address he gave for Howell doesn't exist and if it did, it would be a hundred feet under water."

"What do you mean?"

"Karasov told me Howell was moving to 5210 Pacheco Street in San Francisco."

"So?"

"Pacheco Street runs east to west and only goes up to the 4400 block, beyond that is the Pacific Ocean," McGuire said.

"Oh."

"How did Pavlenko sound on the phone?"

"A little shaky. He had a lot of questions about why and how long," Wedge said. "I just told him I needed him to like, clarify a few matters."

Heels with taps clicked against the linoleum tile and echoed up the hallway. "That's probably him now." Wedge looked up at the wall clock as he moved toward the door. It was 2:14 P.M.

McGuire sauntered over to the window and turned his back to the door.

"Hello Mr. Pavlenko." Wedge stood in the doorway and greeted him with a handshake. "Please come in."

"Will this take long?"

"We'll try to be as brief as possible," Wedge said.

McGuire turned from the window and studied Aleksandr Pavlenko as Wedge went through the introductions. Pavlenko's gray windbreaker jacket hung limply over his slender frame. Under the jacket he had on a white button-down shirt and a pair of shapeless khaki slacks. Below that was a pair of highly polished brown Oxfords.

"Sergeant McGuire asked for my assistance in arranging an interview with you," Wedge said. "He's conducting an investigation into the robbery and attempted murder of Howard McGuire. Why don't you have a seat?"

Pavlenko's face became flushed, and the veins in his neck bulged. He turned to Wedge and objected, "I don't understand. What has this to do with me?"

"Sit down and relax Mr. Pavlenko," McGuire interceded. "On a major case like this it's necessary to question everyone who's had contact with the victim."

Wedge had already seated himself behind his desk and Pavlenko took the chair directly in front of Wedge where Leach had sat only five minutes earlier. McGuire leaned against the credenza with his back to the window, looking at Pavlenko.

"What questions?" Pavlenko asked.

"Well, for starters, where were you on Sunday the eleventh?" McGuire said.

"Do you mean the Sunday prior to this past Sunday?" Pavlenko's eyelids blinked rapidly, and he licked his lips.

"Yes, Sunday before Veteran's Day, the night Howard McGuire was shot."

"I didn't know about it," Pavlenko said. "Should I have?"

He's stalling, McGuire thought. He's not sure how to answer. "It was in the newspaper. Howard McGuire was fairly well known at DLI. There must have been some talk about it here among the staff," McGuire said. "You obviously knew who he was from your recent contact with him."

"I don't recall seeing it in the paper or hearing about it." Pavlenko shrugged his shoulders and leaned back in his chair.

"Where were you that evening?" McGuire asked again.

"I believe I spent the evening at home with my wife." Pavlenko shifted his eyes to Wedge then back to McGuire.

"Are you sure?"

"Yes, quite sure." Pavlenko nodded his head for emphasis. "Is it something I must prove?"

"Did you have any visitors that evening?"

"No."

"How did you spend the evening?" McGuire slowly moved toward the door, positioning Pavlenko between him and Wedge, so Pavlenko couldn't watch both of them at the same time.

"How did I spend the evening?" Pavlenko responded. "You expect me to remember what I did on a specific evening ten days ago?"

McGuire glanced down at Pavlenko's shoes, then looked him straight in the eyes and said nothing.

Finally, Pavlenko averted his eyes and continued. "I'm not sure. We didn't do anything special. I believe we just watched television."

"What about Tuesday, the thirteenth?" McGuire noticed moisture appeared on Pavlenko's forehead and temples. His legs were crossed and his arms tightly folded across his chest. Pavlenko must have realized the significance of the posture he had assumed and shifted in his seat slightly. He eased his left hand down onto his thigh, draped his right arm on top of Wedge's desk, and uncrossed his legs.

"I don't remember."

"Have you ever been to Howard McGuire's house?" McGuire continued.

"Have I been to Howard McGuire's house?" His voice became raspy. "No, I don't even know where he lives. Why should I?"

"What size shoes do you wear?"

Pavlenko stared down at his shoes, then back up at McGuire. His eyebrows raised and his mouth opened slightly. "You want to know my shoe size?"

Pavlenko sat up in his chair, held his fist over his mouth and belched. "I have stomach problems. Too much acid." He reached into the right pocket of his jacket.

Without taking his eyes off of Pavlenko, McGuire pulled back the right side of his sports coat exposing his Browning Hi Power.

Pavlenko forced a nervous chuckle and kept his hand inside his jacket pocket. "I have some medicine I take." He withdrew his hand slowly, holding a small plastic container of pills between his fingertips.

"I'd like you to hand the pills over to Mr. Wedgwood." McGuire let his coat fall forward and cover his pistol.

Wedge opened the small plastic container and examined one of the small orange diamond-shaped pills. "It says 'Zantac 150' on one side and 'Glaxo' on the other."

"Okay, you can give him the pills back."

Pavlenko held the container up in front of him. "May I take one of these now?"

"Later. Right now I want to know about your shoe size."

Pavlenko sneered and said, "My shoes are size nine. What other clothing size would you like to know about?"

"What brand of shoes are you wearing?"

"They're Florsheims."

"Mr. Pavlenko," McGuire said, "you're under arrest for burglary."

Pavlenko's whole body stiffened, and he jerked himself up right. "Burglary? What burglary?"

"We'll talk about it down at the station. You'll have to come with me." McGuire walked over to Pavlenko.

"This is absurd. I demand to know what burglary I'm accused of."

"The burglary of Howard McGuire's home on thirteen November. Now, if you'll come with me, you'll have ample opportunity to straighten this all out at the station." He grabbed Pavlenko's left arm and guided him out of the office.

"I need to contact my wife. She is expecting me back by four-thirty."

"You can do that from the station."

McGuire walked Pavlenko out of the building and around to his car with Wedge following close behind. McGuire patted him down, cuffed him, and put him into the back seat. Wedge got into the front seat, but kept an eye on Pavlenko.

After McGuire completed the booking procedure, Pavlenko again asked to telephone his wife. McGuire made the phone call for him and told her he was being questioned regarding a police matter and would personally call her at home in a few hours.

McGuire instructed Wedge to place McGuire's briefcase on the table in the interview room, then go into the observation room, turn off the lights, and turn on the tape recorder. McGuire took Pavlenko into the interview room. He advised Pavlenko of his rights and told him the questioning would cover the burglary, as well as the robbery and shooting.

"I have done nothing wrong. I have no need for a lawyer," Pavlenko declared.

McGuire decided to lead with the less serious of the two crimes. He pulled two, eight-by-ten photographs out of the briefcase. "Mr. Pavlenko, here's a photograph of a shoe print found just outside Howard McGuire's kitchen window. Here is a close up of the imprint made by the heel. See the Florsheim logo and outline of the tap." Pavlenko nodded an acknowledgement. "Now, look at the heel of your own right shoe. They match, don't they?" McGuire didn't wait for a reaction. Without skipping a beat, he asked, "Why didn't you tell me the truth about being at his house?"

Pavlenko tucked his legs back under his chair and rested the weight of his legs on the balls of his feet. "It's true," he said. "I lied. I was there last Tuesday. But I didn't go there to take anything of value. This is hard for me to talk about. My wife had an affair with Howard McGuire. When she saw in the newspaper that he had been shot and might not survive, she panicked. He took intimate photographs of her. She was afraid if he died, someone would find the photographs and she would be identified. She confessed this to me on Monday night. I didn't know anything about it before that."

McGuire looked at him askance. He knew something wasn't right. The admission had come too quickly. "Go on," he prompted.

"At first I was outraged, but then she told me he had made promises to her. Mr. Wedgwood can tell you our security interviews did not go well. We carelessly made a number of innocent mistakes about small details of our lives in the Soviet Union. Howard McGuire convinced Zhanna his report could be written to make us look suspicious and possibly result in the loss of our jobs. But if she were nice to him, he could write the report differently." Pavlenko sat back in his chair, stretched his legs out in front of him into a normal position, and continued with his smooth articulate narration, occasionally gesturing with his hands and smiling for emphasis.

"After having been out of work for so long," Pavlenko said, "she was very scared by the prospect of both of us losing our jobs. So she agreed to see him. Once or twice a week they met at his house while I was out bicycling. I have a set routine. Twice a week I ride for about two hours. It was just enough time for their rendezvous."

McGuire caught himself clenching his fists and forced himself to relax his hands. He could see the photographs of Zhanna in his mind and could feel himself losing control of the interview. Settle down, he told himself. You've got what you need to regain control. Let him go on for a little longer.

"I wanted to report him to his superiors," Pavlenko said, "but then, after I thought about all the possible consequences, I couldn't go through with it. It would be my wife's word against the reputation of a government investigator. My wife's reputation would still be ruined. I decided to try to retrieve the photographs myself before someone else found them. I wasn't successful. Someone came to the house while I was looking for them."

McGuire studied Aleksandr Pavlenko carefully. This was not the same man who less than an hour ago had stumbled ineptly in Howard's office. Now he was poised, confident, sincere, and convincing. McGuire said, "You realize in addition to admitting to breaking and entering, you've given yourself a motive for shooting Howard McGuire."

"What I've told you is the truth. I didn't shoot Howard McGuire. I was at home watching television when it happened. I didn't even know about his affair with my wife until after he was shot."

"You actually had two motives for shooting Howard McGuire." McGuire paused for effect. "Yes, you had a second motive. Howard McGuire had built up a fairly impressive dossier on you. A dossier complete with a video tape of you servicing a dead drop and receiving classified defense information from a Navy officer, Dale Ellis." McGuire reached into the briefcase and threw the 16-millimeter film cartridge still partially encased in its torn wax paper wrapper onto the table. Then he produced the videocassette, toilet paper roller, and a copy of a handwritten statement. He placed these things next to the film cartridge on the table. The toilet paper roller was in a clear plastic bag with an evidence label on it.

Pavlenko quickly read the first few sentences of the statement without touching it. "That's right, Mr. Pavlenko," McGuire said, "Commander Ellis has already made a complete confession. We not only have a video tape of you servicing the dead drop, we also have your fingerprints on the concealment device—this toilet paper roller," McGuire lied. He hadn't been able to lift any identifiable prints, other than Ellis's, from the roller.

"You're not only going to be convicted of espionage, we're going to try you for attempted murder. If Howard McGuire dies, it'll be first degree murder. You'll spend the rest of your life in prison. Do you know what your life in prison will be like as a convicted spy and murderer? I'm not talking about one of those fancy federal penitentiaries. You'll go to a state prison and be thrown in with common murders and rapists who, despite their mistakes, are fiercely patriotic and will eat you alive. There'll be no chance of you ever being released in a spy swap." McGuire was laying it on as heavy as he could, making some of it up as he went along. He wanted Pavlenko to focus on the attempted murder charge.

"You have no evidence that I shot your brother, because I did not do it." Pavlenko's voice cracked.

McGuire noticed Pavlenko only denied the shooting, not the espionage. "I have enough evidence to convince a judge to hold you in jail without bail until your trial." McGuire relied on Pavlenko's ignorance of the criminal justice system. "And you've probably heard how slow our courts are. You could be in jail for months before there's a trial. Do you have any idea how the other inmates are going to treat you in there? I'm sure you've heard about the gang rapes and the stabbings in jail."

Pavlenko shifted his weight in his chair and fidgeted with the zipper of his jacket. Pavlenko's eyes had widened when McGuire mentioned gang rapes.

"This . . . this is absurd. I had nothing to do with Howard McGuire's shooting," Pavlenko stammered as he pointed to his chest for emphasis.

"Do you deny you've been involved in espionage against the United States?" Keep him off balance and keep him talking.

"I've never stolen any secrets. I'm not a spy."

"What about this video tape of you switching toilet paper rollers at Lovers' Point. Rollers that contained money, espionage instructions, and 16 millimeter film cartridges of classified documents?"

"I don't know what is in the packets. The packets I remove from the rollers are all sealed in wax paper. I've never opened them. I send and receive these things by mail. I just act as a deliveryman. That's as far as they will trust a Jew."

"Who are they?"

Aleks Pavlenko took a deep breath and spoke slower. "I'm not sure. Probably KGB. Before we left the Soviet Union, I was directed to report to a special room near the office where the exit visas are issued. The man in the room told me that if I wanted our exit visas approved, I would have to agree to perform small services for them after I reached the United States. I agreed. I would have agreed to anything to get our exit visas. I thought once I was out of the Soviet Union, they would have no way of forcing me to cooperate with them."

Pavlenko's eyes wandered around the room and settled on the large mirror surface of the observation window. He leaned forward and squinted trying to see what was on the other side. "I was wrong. Last summer I received an envelope in the mail. There was no return address. In the envelope were a letter and a copy of the written agreement I had signed. The letter said if I did not comply with their instructions, a copy of the written agreement would be sent to the FBI and I would be fired from my job. The letter also said if I tried to get the FBI to help me, my parents' pensions would be cut off and they would become destitute, declared social parasites, and sent to the gulag."

Pavlenko paused, looked closely at McGuire face, and continued, "There was nothing else I could do. Later more letters came. The letters told me I would not have to do anything illegal—just pick up and deliver small sealed packets at certain locations. The letters assured me there was nothing illegal in the packets." Pavlenko belched and swallowed a few times, then grimaced.

"What else did they have you do?" McGuire asked.

Pavlenko shrugged. "Nothing important. Just low-level things."

"Like what?"

"They wanted to know which of my colleagues were pro-Soviet, which were anti-Soviet, names and addresses of new instructors, that sort of thing. Nothing of military significance. You see, they only had me do small things—nothing important. I never worked for them willingly. I was never trained to do any of this. I didn't know my activities had been discovered. You must believe me. I had nothing to do with the shooting of Howard McGuire. Perhaps I can do something to prove my innocence. As long as it wouldn't jeopardize the safety of my parents, I might be of some value to your government."

McGuire stirred in his chair. It sounded like a ploy to stall for time, but it was one he could use to his advantage. "I'm inclined to believe you, but I'll need more than just your assurances. A lie detector test would prove you had nothing to do with the shooting. Are you willing to take one?"

"Yes. I no longer have anything to hide. Does it take long?"

"Two or three hours, if all goes well."

"I suppose it will take some time to arrange."

"I'll have to call and see." McGuire turned to the mirror and said to Wedge, "I'll be back in a minute."

McGuire went to his office and telephoned Manny Garcia at his home. Garcia was an investigator at Monterey Police Department and the only local polygraph examiner. Like McGuire, he was a bachelor who loved his work and was always ready to help out another department. Garcia agreed to come over in an hour.

McGuire went back to the interview room. "Okay," he said, "we're set for six tonight. You'll have to wait in the holding cell. When it's over you'll have to spend the night here."

"I'd like to phone my wife and let her know I won't be coming home tonight," said Pavlenko.

"Sure. You can use the phone by the holding cell, but keep it brief." McGuire stood by with his finger on the hook switch and watched as Pavlenko keyed in his home phone number. Aleksandr Pavlenko spoke slowly in English and explained he would not return home, but would telephone her in the morning with more information.

# CHAPTER TWENTY

Wedge helped himself to some coffee from the break room and was sitting in McGuire's chair with his feet propped up on his desk when McGuire came in.

McGuire stared at Wedge's shoes, then at Wedge. "Mind if I pull up a chair?" he asked.

"No. Go right ahead," Wedge said. "Make yourself at home."

McGuire reached over and grabbed Wedge's coffee cup, cradled it in his hands and took a sip. Making a sour expression, he returned the cup to the desk. "You always put that much sugar in your coffee?"

"Only when the coffee's four hours old."

McGuire pulled up a chair and said, "How about some pizza?"

"Sounds good to me."

"I'll pay if you'll go get it."

"I don't mind getting it, but I'll pay for half."

"No, let me get this. I want two large combo's—one for us and one for Garcia and Pavlenko." McGuire thumbed through the bills in his wallet and found two twenties. "Oh yeah, and pick up a six-pack of coke. Garcia doesn't drink coffee."

"Do you think Pavlenko can handle pizza with his stomach?" Wedge got up and grabbed his jacket from the coat rack.

"If he needs to, he can take some more Zantac." McGuire handed Wedge the money and his car keys. "Take my personal car. It's the green Chevy Blazer parked across the street by the bank."

McGuire and Garcia were talking in the interview room when Wedge returned. After the introductions were made, Garcia continued setting up his machine.

"Manny, when you're through fondling your machine, join us in my office," McGuire said. "Some of this pizza's for you."

"Why not in the break room?" Wedge asked. Garcia smiled as if anticipating McGuire's response.

"Because if we eat it in the break room, we'll be lucky to get one slice each. The patrol guys have some sort of radar when it comes to food. It's a wonder they haven't already started pulling into the station." McGuire opened the interview room door and stuck his head out to see if anyone was nearby. He motioned for Wedge to go ahead of him. "Quick, go straight to my office." They almost made it to McGuire's office undetected.

A deep booming voice called out from the break room, "Hey, is that pizza I smell?"

"Sorry Monk, it's for a prisoner." McGuire quickly closed his office door behind him.

A few minutes later Garcia slipped into the office quietly.

"So, how's the polygraph business been?" McGuire said.

"Slow. I haven't run an exam in three weeks, but my other work's keeping me fairly busy. I want you to know, I don't come out at night on short notice like this for everyone. But for you, and since it concerns your brother, I made an exception."

"What bullshit. I bribe him with pizza and coke, and he thinks he's doing me a favor. He won't admit it, but he enjoys polygraph exams more than sex. Sometimes when he's alone at night, he puts those pneumatic tubes around his chest. I won't tell you where he hooks up the blood pressure cuff and the finger plates."

Garcia smiled and shot back, "You've been peeking through my bedroom window again, haven't you?"

"Yeah, and I've been thinking about writing an article for the *Lawman* to go with the photos I want to send them."

"Speaking of photos . . . Wedge, you should ask Keith to show you the pictures he took of his anatomically correct Ken and Barbie dolls getting it on." Garcia punctuated his sentence with a loud belch.

When they finished eating, McGuire and Garcia went over the test questions. "So what's the plan?" McGuire asked.

"I'll run two charts for starters," Garcia said, "a 'stim' test and one set of questions. We'll play it by ear after that."

The stimulation test was used to get a baseline and to show the subject how well the machine worked. Pavlenko chose a number between 93 and 97 and was instructed to answer "no" to all the questions. Garcia wrote the numbers 99 to 91 on a large sheet of paper using a felt-tipped pen and taped the paper to the wall in front of Pavlenko. Garcia then asked Pavlenko if he had chosen the number 99, if he had chosen the number 98, and so on. The polygraph chart showed clearly which number Pavlenko had chosen. Properly administered, the stim test could make a believer out of anyone who was skeptical about the accuracy of the polygraph.

McGuire and Wedge sat in the observation room and watched as Garcia reviewed the actual test questions with Pavlenko before they began the exam. After he finished the test, Garcia deflated the blood pressure cuff on Pavlenko's arm, but left it, the pneumatic tubes, and fingerplates in place. He told Pavlenko to relax for a few minutes and motioned McGuire to meet him out in the hallway.

"I'm not sure," Garcia whispered and held the chart paper in front of him. "Here, look at this. He did okay when I asked if he shot Howard and if he knew who shot Howard, but he nailed the question about him being at home on Sunday night. I'll run another chart to validate this one."

McGuire nodded.

Garcia ran another test, but rearranged the order of the questions. In fifteen minutes he was out in the hallway again with McGuire. "He's clean," Garcia said. "I'm sure of it, but he's lying like hell about where he was on Sunday night. Probably out with some hooker doing something his wife won't do for him, and he doesn't want to admit it."

"Can you clear it up?"

"Is it important?"

McGuire shook his head and answered, "I don't know, maybe."

"I don't like to use the machine for fishing expeditions, but I'll see what I can do."

Garcia pulled a chair around and set it a few inches in front of Pavlenko. He sat with his knees spread apart trapping Pavlenko's legs between them. "We've got a small problem Aleks. You haven't been totally truthful with me."

Pavlenko sat quietly gripping the arms of the special chair they had brought in for him.

"You weren't at home on Sunday evening, were you? Now, why would you not tell the truth about that?"

"Your machine is mistaken. I was at home."

"Look at these charts. Here's the question about the number you chose, ninety-six, and here is where I asked if you were at home on Sunday evening. See how on both charts this line goes up and cuts across all the other lines."

"I must have twitched or swallowed or something. I did not lie. There must be some other reason for it," Pavlenko said.

"There's no other reason. You just didn't tell the truth. Where were you on Sunday evening?"

The questions and denials continued for twenty minutes. Garcia suggested every possible embarrassing excuse for

Pavlenko's absence from his house that night, but Pavlenko didn't grab at any of them and stubbornly held to his story.

Finally Garcia gave up. "Okay Aleks, I'd like to run one more test, but this time we're going to do what's called a Searching Peak of Tension Test. The questions will be about different locations on a map. Is that okay with you?"

Aleks nodded.

Garcia drew the outline of North America on a large sheet of paper. He then drew three horizontal lines and two vertical lines that divided the drawing into twelve sections and numbered each of the sections. After taping the paper to the wall, he connected Pavlenko to the machine and began again. He intoned his questions in a low voice, slowly and deliberately. "The test is about to begin." Long pause. "Were you in section one that Sunday night?" Long pause. "Were you in section two that Sunday night?" Garcia went on to ask Pavlenko about the twelve sections and any area outside the drawing. Finally, Garcia unhooked Pavlenko and stepped into the hall.

"Look Keith, I don't know the details of this case. You're going to have to take over from here." Garcia had about six feet of chart paper in his hands. "According to these charts—"

"You don't have to show me," McGuire said. "Just tell me."

Garcia rolled his chart paper up into a tube. "I think Pavlenko was in Mexico on Sunday night. I could probably pinpoint the location for you, but it would take time."

"Thanks Manny. You've been a great help. I need to talk to Wedge for a minute while you pack your things up, okay?"

"Sure. Take your time. I'll sit with Pavlenko until you come back. I need to explain the results of the test to him."

McGuire and Wedge huddled in the office, and McGuire repeated what Garcia had just told him.

"He went to Mexico to meet his control," Wedge said excitedly.

"His what?" McGuire lighted a cigarette.

"His control." Wedge gestured with his hands for emphasis. "The guy that like, gives him his orders."

McGuire shook his head. "What makes you say that?"

"Because Steve told me Mexico is one of their favorite places for PMs—personal meetings," Wedge said.

"Okay, but why wouldn't he just tell us he went there? He already admitted to providing the KGB information."

"Because going to Mexico for PMs wasn't part of his story. Remember, he only sends and receives things through the mail. Besides, he already told us he went on vacation to Mexico for a week this past July."

"When did he tell us that?"

"Not you and me. Howard and me. During our interviews with them, they like, told us about their vacations each summer to Mexico. He's gone every July since 1987. Zhanna and the baby went with him in '87 and '88. He went alone in '89 because they couldn't all afford to go, and he claimed he really needed two weeks off from teaching. And he went alone this past July, because she had just been rehired at DLI and didn't have any vacation time accrued."

"So if he went to Mexico in July to meet his control, why would he go again on eleven November?"

"I don't know." Wedge began pacing around the office.

McGuire looked around for his ashtray. "I still don't see what the big deal is about Mexico. He could've told us anything—that he went down there for prostitutes or that he likes the donkey shows."

"Because what he's been telling us is that he's a low-level recruited agent with no intelligence training who was blackmailed last summer into cooperating with them. During their interviews in September, we came across enough discrepancies in their personal histories to pretty much prove they were using a cover story. Recruited agents don't need cover stories, and the ones at DLI don't have PMs with their control in Mexico." Wedge stopped abruptly and glared at McGuire. "Are you paying attention to me?"

"Yeah, I'm listening," McGuire said, hunched over his lower desk drawer.

"Well, stop looking for your stupid ashtray. Here, use this." Wedge grabbed a small glass bowl full of paper clips, dumped the clips out on Noguchi's desk, and handed it to him. McGuire ground his cigarette out in it and placed it on his desk.

"Remember what Steve Wepsala said? If the KGB wants to personally meet with their recruited émigrés, they do it in Moscow where they have total control of the situation," Wedge said. "Pavlenko's a support agent, an illegal, who wants us to think he's more of a victim than a spy. Steve said illegals have multiple cover stories. He called it 'cover within a cover.' Pavlenko even used the term 'low-level.' I don't think a émigré would use a term like that."

"Okay, so what the hell are you going to do about it?" McGuire said.

"Well, we can pass it on to the Bureau when we turn Pavlenko over to them," Wedge said. "What do you think we should do?"

"I don't know!" McGuire raised his voice in frustration. "I'm not sure this trip to Mexico is going to lead us anywhere, but we damn well better do something. The bottom line is Pavlenko didn't shoot Howard, but if he's still holding something back, I want to find out what it is. It might lead us somewhere. Right now aside from Karasov, we're fresh out of leads, and we're running out of time fast."

Wedge looked at him and shook his head.

"Look," McGuire said, "you know a lot more about this intelligence stuff than I do. Maybe you should take a crack at questioning Pavlenko. You might be able to get a lot more out of him."

"I don't know hardly enough," Wedge said. "This is like, way out of my league."

"Think about it, Wedge. I'll be back in a few minutes. Manny's waiting for me in the interview room. As soon as I put Pavlenko away, I want to try to get a definite reading on Karasov."

After locking up Pavlenko, McGuire went back to thank Garcia. On his way out Garcia said, "I don't know why he won't admit he was in Mexico, but I'm not sure it matters. He definitely doesn't know who shot your brother."

# CHAPTER TWENTY-ONE

TUESDAY 8:30 P.M., 20 NOVEMBER 1990

McGuire pulled a card from his Rolodex file and dialed the number for the FBI Identification Division. If he was lucky, he would catch his friend on the swing shift.

"Identification Division, Bunney." A man's voice answered.

"This is Sergeant McGuire with Pacific Grove PD. Is Ralph Hastings there."

"No, sorry. He won't be back till next Monday."

"Oh." McGuire let out a sigh and sunk down in his chair.

"Is there something I can help you with?"

McGuire sat up as his mind raced for a suitable reason to justify asking for a fingerprint search on a priority basis. He'd have to lie to the technician on the phone. "I've got a suspect in custody who doesn't have any identification. I have reason to believe he's not giving us his real name and I'm worried about him making bail and splitting."

"No problem. Fax me his prints, I should be able to check 'em and call you back."

Before faxing Karasov's fingerprint card, McGuire altered it to appear as if the fingerprints had been taken that evening at the station.

Twenty minutes later the technician called back. "The prints on your fax copy aren't clear enough for me to classify.

Is there someone at your end who can classify them?" he asked.

"Yeah, I can do it," McGuire said. "I'll call you back in a few minutes."

About half an hour after he passed the information on to the technician, he received another phone call. "Hey partner, you're in luck. There were only four cards with that classification. I have them here in front of me. None of the physical descriptions really seem to match, but let's check 'em out a little closer. Look at the ulnar loop on the left middle finger on your card. What's the ridge count?" he asked.

"Eleven."

McGuire could hear the phone being set down on. Then there was silence. About a minute later he pick up the phone again. "Well, that eliminates three of the cards. Look at the right index finger. What kind of pattern is that?"

"It's a central pocket whorl," McGuire replied.

"Then we don't have a match for you."

"Thanks. I appreciate you doing this." McGuire looked puzzled as he hung up.

"Well, what did he say?" Wedge asked.

"No match."

"That's impossible. They must have a card on file for him. DLI sent in fingerprint cards with their Request for Investigation and INS would have submitted a set when he applied for permanent resident status."

"I know."

Wedge threw his arms up in the air. "Well, that about does it." He grabbed his sports coat off the rack.

"Where do you think you're going?"

"Home."

"Hang your coat back up and go make some more coffee, while I go roust Mr. Karasov."

Wedge looked at his watch. "Keith, it's like, almost ten o'clock. Shit, I've got to call Katherine."

"I'll be back in about thirty minutes." McGuire grabbed his coat and headed for the door.

Wedge reached for the telephone and began keying in his home number. Just as the answering machine message came on, he heard the sound of squealing tires and a car racing away. He had forgotten the Crown Victoria came with a V8. His own Plymouth Reliant was equipped with a gutless four-cylinder engine that would barely make it up Carmel Hill.

While Wedge made coffee, Sergeant O'Donnell and a few police officers came into the break room for shift change. Wedge went out to the front desk to talk with Kenneth Graves while the coffee brewed. It was just past ten o'clock. "So did you see in the paper today where Iraq is going to like, send 250,000 more troops to Kuwait?" Wedge said.

"How many troops do they have there now?" Graves asked.

"About two hundred thousand."

"Oh, and how many troops do we have there?"

"None in Kuwait," said Wedge, "but we have two hundred and thirty thousand in Saudi Arabia just across the border and another two hundred thousand on the way. The military comes up with neat names, don't they? Operation Desert Shield. Operation Imminent Thunder."

"What's the second one?"

"That was the large training exercise U.S. and Saudi forces started on Sunday—the mock invasion near the Kuwaiti border."

"I haven't been following that stuff very close," said Graves.

"Well who do you think's going to take the Redskins—Cowboys game on Thursday?"

"I'm not into football either."

Wedge proceeded to mention Michael Milken, Margaret Thatcher, Charles Keating, and Alan Cranston, but drew a blank stare from Graves.

The lobby door creaked as it opened. Wedge turned to see a tall thin man about thirty years old with a wild look in his eyes striding toward the counter. His black hair stuck out in all directions and he wore a dark brown raincoat buttoned up to his neck. His hands were concealed in his pockets. Wedge stepped back from the counter out of arms reach and eyed the man suspiciously.

"Sorry I'm late," the man said. "I overslept. I just threw on my clothes and came straight over." He unbuttoned his raincoat revealing his light blue uniform shirt and police clerk's badge.

Graves released the electric door latch and the man came in and walked around into the desk clerks' area. Graves introduced him as Thomas Skallerup, the night shift clerk.

"If you don't mind too much," Skallerup asked, "could you standby for just a couple more minutes while I splash some water on my face and run a comb through my hair?" He began moving in the direction of the restroom before Graves even answered.

Wedge went back to McGuire's office, so he wouldn't be in the way during their shift change routine. Shortly after he settled in comfortably behind McGuire's desk, he heard Skallerup's voice page him over the PA system. "Agent Wedgwood report to the interview room."

McGuire met him outside the closed door of the interview room. "Karasov wasn't in a very cooperative mood, so I arrested his ass for being an illegal alien. It's a bullshit charge, but I don't care. I don't have anything else to hold him on."

Wedge shrugged. "Okay. You want my help?"

"I'd like you to slip into the observation room," McGuire replied. "Try to go in at the same time I open the door to the interview room. It'll be enough of a distraction, so he won't notice any light coming through the one-way glass." McGuire opened the interview room door and Wedge quietly slipped into the observation room.

In semi-darkness Wedge climbed onto the barstool next to the observation window. Through the window he had an elevated view of the entire interview room. On his right a cassette tape recorder sat on a small table. He turned the lever to the record position and a little red light came on. The sound of McGuire clearing his throat came through the cassette recorder's speaker and the needles of the VU meters bounced.

He turned his attention to the interview room and saw a rather large man seated in a straight back wooden chair at the side of the small metal table. McGuire settled into a black swivel chair behind the table. He pulled a manila file folder from the table's center drawer. From Wedge's vantage point he could see the right side of the Karasov's body including a full profile of his face. McGuire sat facing Karasov and rocked back in his chair.

"Mr. Karasov, since our last meeting, I've been checking on everyone who's even remotely connected with last Sunday's shooting. In your case some anomalies have surfaced that require explanation."

"Excuse me. What are anomalies?" Karasov asked.

"Irregularities, discrepancies," McGuire said.

"I am suspect?"

"I don't have any definite suspects, Mr. Karasov. I'm in the process of identifying possible suspects. Your answers to my questions may determine whether or not you become a suspect. I'm sure you can see it's in your best interest to cooperate in this matter."

"But I am under arrest."

"Yes, you're under arrest. And you'll remain under arrest until you prove to me you're Sergei Karasov and you're legally in this country."

McGuire asked Karasov series of unimportant questions regarding residence, occupation, and age. Karasov replied without hesitation or noticeable reaction to the questions.

McGuire's voice was low and monotonous and there was an uncomfortable silence before he asked each question.

"When was the first time you saw Howard McGuire?" McGuire said.

Karasov's eyes glanced up and to the left just before answering the question. "When he was carried away to the ambulance."

"Why did you go to the American Tin Cannery on Sunday evening?"

"To do shopping." Karasov's eyes again glanced up and to the left before answering.

McGuire stood and walked around the table behind Karasov. Karasov stayed seated, but craned his head around to watch him. McGuire paused for a moment directly behind Karasov and said nothing. Karasov sat quietly with his hands laced together in his lap. The long silence was even beginning to make Wedge feel uncomfortable.

McGuire walked back around in front of Karasov, leaned forward grasping both arms of Karasov's chair, and got his face close to Karasov's. Seconds passed before McGuire spoke. "Now, you've become a suspect."

McGuire took one step back, but remained standing in front of Karasov. "Your real name isn't Sergei Karasov. You know Howard McGuire. You didn't go to the American Tin Cannery to shop. You went there on Sunday night specifically to meet him at the Tavern On The Bay. You also went out to the parking lot ahead of Howard McGuire and shot him when he came out to his car."

"*Idi Na' huy,*" Karasov snarled. He quickly softened his tone of voice. "You are mistaken."

McGuire reached for the file folder on the table and withdrew the written statement attached to Howard's DIS report on Karasov. He put it down on the table in front of Karasov. Wedge watched Karasov swallow twice as he stared at his name on the document.

"This document shows you were interviewed by Howard McGuire over a two day period in August, that you made a written statement, and that you reviewed and signed the statement in Howard McGuire's presence. How do you explain this?"

Karasov began flipping through the pages of the statement faster than he could possibly read it. A look of total disbelief spread over his face. "I can not explain. This document is about me, but I was never interviewed by Howard McGuire. I do not know how. . . ." Karasov stopped abruptly when he reached the last page. Moisture beaded above his upper lip and around his temples. He stared at the signature near the bottom of the page. After scrutinizing the signature for several seconds, he lifted his head, narrowed his eyes, and glared at McGuire. The muscles in his neck bulged and the expression on his face changed to anger. "It is a cheap trick, a provocation! This looks like my signature, but I did not sign it. You are no better than a *Chekist*."

"And you, Mr. Karasov, or what ever your real name is, you've become trapped by your own lies. A witness saw you with Howard McGuire at the Tavern on Sunday right before the shooting." McGuire's voice became increasingly accusative and loud as he continued. "There is no Sergei Karasov, nor is there a Charles Howell, the man you claim to have bumped into that night. Charles Howell does not exist. There's no record of him in the State of California and there's no 5210 Pacheco Street in San Francisco. As for Sergei Karasov . . . well, you know what we found when we conducted checks on that name."

McGuire pulled a photo of Howard out of his shirt pocket and threw it in front of Karasov. "This is the man you met at the Tavern On The Bay. Howard Charles McGuire. The same man you shot in the parking lot of the American Tin Cannery."

Karasov looked to his right, stared hard at the large mirror surface of the observation window, then looked back at McGuire. He slumped slightly in his chair, his shoulders dropped down, and he shook his head slowly. "Turn off your recording machine and have the person on other side of glass come here," he said. "Have him switch on light in room, so I can see it is empty."

McGuire looked at the one-way glass and nodded his head. Wedge turned on the lights in the observation room, turn off the tape recorder, and walk out of the room. When Wedge entered the interview room, Karasov came to his feet and addressed McGuire.

"Before I begin, I must know who this man is."

"His name is Gordon Wedgwood. He is an investigator with the U.S. Department of Defense."

Karasov said, "Mr. Wedgwood, your identification papers please." Wedge pulled out his badge and credentials and held them in front of Karasov.

Karasov returned to his chair and began speaking in a low voice. "I know your brother as Charles Howell, not Howard McGuire. I knew Charles Howell is not his real name, but not until Wednesday when you came to see me, did I suspect Charles Howell might be Howard McGuire. Your brother knew me as Lieutenant Colonel Stanislav Zagorsky of the KGB's First Chief Directorate. Sergei Karasov is the name your government gives to me when I come to America."

McGuire and Wedge listened intently to the story offered by Karasov.

In 1982 shortly after he had made an offer of service to the CIA in Tokyo, he met the man calling himself Charles Howell. From then until 1985 Charles had been his primary contact, his case officer. Karasov had been in charge of the KGB Residency's PR Line at the Soviet Embassy in Tokyo. The PR Line encompassed political, economic, and strategic military intelligence, as well as active measures. His specialty was active measures: agitation, propaganda, disinformation, and agents of influence.

In late October 1985 Karasov noticed the Embassy Security Officer began showing unusual interest in him. In early December his wife and daughter were granted leave to go back to Moscow on vacation to visit family. While they were gone, he detected he was under surveillance. These events and others that followed convinced him the KGB knew or suspected him of being a traitor. On the night of 24 December, Charles helped smuggle him out of Japan to Pusan, Korea where he was formally granted asylum by the U.S. Government.

Karasov continued to see Charles for about two weeks at a U.S. Army base in Pusan. Just before he left for America, Charles had come to see him and told him he had been reassigned. Others had handled his debriefing and eventual resettlement in America.

"I never saw him again," Karasov said, "until we passed each other in the hallway near my office at DLI almost two weeks ago. On Sunday he telephoned and asked me to meet him at the Tavern at 6:00 P.M. I thought he had instructions for me from CIA, but we only talked about old times. About 7:30 P.M. he said I should leave first. I go and do some window shopping in the mall. Then I go to my car and meet you. I did not know it was Charles who was shot. I did not see the family resemblance until you came to my apartment. Then I suspected Charles Howell was Howard McGuire. I said nothing because I worry about my cover. I do not want to move and start another life. I think CIA will not give me much help. I am no use to them any more, and I think they will be happy if I did not exist."

"Why?" Wedge asked.

Karasov briefly related the series of events that brought him to Monterey. He had spent two restless years bouncing around from one apartment to another in Washington while his CIA inquisitors had drained him of every ounce of worthwhile information he possessed. To prepare him for a life of obscurity, they had him attend a barber's school.

When they were satisfied he had revealed everything of value, the Agency set him up in a barbershop in a small town in northern Illinois. Meaningful work had to engage the mind as well as the hands, and even though he tried hard to succeed in his new occupation, eventually his business failed. His request to move and attempt some other work was not well received by the Agency. When it was obvious he could not even make enough money to feed himself, they had grudgingly secured a position for him at the DLI.

"They did not want me to come to DLI because there are too many Russian émigrés and because of the security investigation. But I had no other skills and it is a place where they have influence. I filled out all security forms as they instructed, and I turned them in, but there was no investigation."

"If you were never interviewed by my brother, what about the signed statement?" McGuire asked.

"There was no statement, no interview, no investigation. CIA handled all of it."

"Mr. Karasov," Wedge asked, "why would they be concerned about other Russian émigrés?"

"They worry my presence here might be reported to KGB and my true identity uncovered. To KGB, all Russian émigrés are *nashi*. *Nashi* means ours. KGB thinks it can control all émigrés and make them report on one another. KGB never forgives or forgets anyone who betrays them. They will never stop looking for me, and if they find me, they will kidnap or kill me." Karasov shook his head. "I should have called CIA when you come to my apartment, but I like it here, and I do not want to ask CIA for help, unless I am certain there is danger."

"What else did you talk about with my brother on Sunday?"

"He asked about some old operations where we used flowers for communication and public restrooms for dead drop sites."

"Anything else?" McGuire asked.

"Just talk about old days."

"How can you prove your past association with my brother?"

"I have codename that can be given to someone at special 800 telephone number in emergency. I do not want to use it, but if necessary, I will give it to you."

"Write it all down."

Wedge motioned to McGuire to step out of the room.

"Make yourself comfortable, Mr. Karasov; you're going to be here for a while. Would you like some coffee?" McGuire said.

"No." Karasov handed him a piece of paper with the information on it.

In the hallway Wedge started to speak, but McGuire cut him off. "Not here. Let's go to my office." McGuire locked the interview room from the outside, then stepped into the observation room, pocketed the cassette tape, and turned off the lights.

"You believe all that stuff Karasov told you?" Wedge asked.

"I'm not sure. He sounds pretty convincing, particularly the parts about him and Howard in Japan and the CIA fixing his security investigation. That could explain Howard's reports. On the other hand, if Karasov's lying, then Howard was into some deep shit. We better hold onto him until we check out the telephone number."

# CHAPTER TWENTY-TWO

TUESDAY 10:45 P.M., 20 NOVEMBER 1990

A woman's voice answered the telephone, "Liaison Support and Coordination Office."

"Mr. Kopecki, please," McGuire said.

"There's no one here by that name, but if you'll leave your name, number, and a message, someone will get back to you," the voice replied.

"I'm Sergeant McGuire, Pacific Grove Police Department. My number is 408-555-5154. I'm calling about Tiny Dancer." As soon as McGuire used the codename Karasov had given him, the line went dead. McGuire replaced the receiver, turned to Wedge, and shook his head. "There's no one there by that name, but someone's going to call me back."

Both men stood staring at the phone, waiting for it to ring. McGuire looked up first. "What about Steve Wepsala?"

"What about him?"

"He could clear up a few points for us with Pavlenko. Wepsala knows how they operate, and he has the experience. He'd know how to squeeze more information out of him."

"If Steve could get Pavlenko to admit he's a trained intelligence officer, not some poor émigré . . . . I think I owe Howard that much. After all, that's what he started out to prove with the surveillance."

"Okay, so call Wepsala and get him over here," McGuire said. "We've got the time. There's no need to contact the FBI for a while, if Wepsala's willing to help."

"Wait a minute. I can't do that," Wedge said. "Steve Wepsala's retired. I'd really be stepping out of line, if I revealed any official information to him."

"You can get him to do it in-the-blind," McGuire said.

"What do you mean?"

"You don't have to tell Wepsala who it is you're interviewing. Just give him a general scenario of what's going on, but leave out the names. He can monitor the audio portion of the interview and feed questions into you by radio. That way he won't know who you're talking to in the interview room."

"He'll know who it is. Hell, we already told him about Pavlenko the other night at the hospital."

"So the damage is already done."

"I guess you're right. Shit, I've already like, bent every rule in the book. One more infraction isn't going to make matters any worse."

McGuire stood by as Wedge keyed in Wepsala's number. "Hello, Mrs. Wepsala? This is Gordon Wedgwood. I used to work with your husband at DIS . . . . Good things I hope . . . . I'm sorry to bother you this late at night, but it's very important I speak to Steve . . . . Oh, when will he be back in town? . . . . No, no message. I'll call tomorrow after he returns . . . . Thank you and I apologize again for calling so late at night." Just as he replaced the receiver in its cradle the telephone rang.

McGuire quickly picked it up. "Investigations, McGuire." He motioned Wedge to pick up the phone on Noguchi's desk and listen in.

"Sergeant McGuire. This is Mr. Kopecki. I understand you called about Tiny Dancer. What can I do for you?"

"Are you CIA?" McGuire said.

"Is there a problem?"

"If you're not CIA," he said, "then there's a big problem. So, am I speaking to the CIA or not?"

The voice paused before answering. "What did he tell you?"

"Look, it's late and I'm tired, so don't play games with me. Just answer my question."

"If I said the answer is yes, can we get to the problem?"

"Like I said, there's no problem if you're CIA." McGuire drummed the eraser end of a pencil against his desktop. "Except right now, as far as I'm concerned, you're just a voice on the telephone beating around the bush and unless you can prove you're CIA, Tiny Dancer's going to jail for being an illegal alien."

"What do you mean, illegal alien? He has a perfectly valid green card." The voice at the other end of the phone became forceful and irate.

McGuire looked over at Wedge and rolled his eyes. "Oh, I don't doubt the green card is valid. The problem is, it's not his. He's admitted he's someone else—someone who doesn't have a green card."

"As far as the U.S. Government is concerned, he is who that green card says he is." The voice now had an angry tone.

"Prove it," McGuire said in a challenging tone. "Prove you're speaking for the U.S. Government."

"Do you know any federal agents that you trust?"

McGuire chuckled, "Is this a trick question?"

"Do you personally know any federal agents?"

"Yeah, I know a few." McGuire looked over at Wedge and pointed at him.

Wedge shook his head vigorously and mouthed the word, no.

"Give me the agent's name and who he's with," the voice said. "We'll contact him through channels, so he can vouch for Dancer, but he won't be told who Dancer is, only that he's legitimate. Will that satisfy you?"

"I guess it'll have to do."

"Someone will be down to see you on Friday and tidy up. This whole matter needs to be kept confidential."

"Let's see." McGuire paused and smiled broadly. "Who would I like to have roused out of bed? Of course, Walter Dombrowski. He's the Bureau's Foreign Counterintelligence specialist in Monterey. How long will it take." His smile disappeared as Neal Upham barged into his office. Upham started to speak, but McGuire raised his free hand, signaling him to stop.

"It's just past two A.M. here," Kopecki said. "A few hours, maybe longer. If there's a problem, I'll call you. How long will you be at this number?"

Keeping his hand raised toward Upham, McGuire answered, "You either get this cleared up by midnight my time or I take him over to the county jail and give the local media a news release identifying him, where he works, why he was arrested, and this comical story of his."

"But that's less than an hour from now. Don't jerk me around McGuire."

"I'm not jerking you around, pal. I'm just doing my job. Why don't you do yours," McGuire said and hung up.

"Who was that on the phone?" Upham demanded.

McGuire pointed at Wedge and said, "Can't you see I have a guest here, Neal. Are you trying to embarrass me in front of Special Agent Wedgwood by barging into my office, interrupting my telephone call, and using that tone of voice with me?"

"Which brings up another question—"

McGuire cut him off and turned to Wedge. "Would you excuse us for a few minutes Mr. Wedgwood. Sergeant Upham and I have a few things to straighten out. Why don't you have some more coffee in the break room."

As soon as Wedge closed the door behind him, Upham started in. "You had Manny Garcia over earlier polygraphing some Russian who's now locked up in one of our holding cells. You've got another Russian stashed in the interview room. A federal agent was just listening in on a telephone call you were having with someone who is going to contact the FBI. What in the hell do you think you're doing, and why wasn't I brought in on it?"

"This doesn't concern you, Neal." McGuire stared at the gold ring in Upham's left earlobe and shook his head in disgust.

Upham reached up to touch his earring, but stopped short and quickly dropped his hand to his side. "I'll be the judge of that," he said.

"It started out as a possible lead on the shooting, but we found out real quick neither of them had anything to do with it. Ask Manny. He'll tell you the same thing." McGuire kept eyeing Upham's earring and making faces. "Once we got into it with Pavlenko and Karasov—they're the two Russians—we realized they may be involved in a totally different problem related strictly to immigration and security matters, so I agreed to follow through and help Wedgwood."

"Oh, is that all there is to it?" Upham raised his eyebrows.

"That's it. Just a little assistance to a federal agency." McGuire wondered how long ago he had his ear pierced. This was the first time he had seen him wear an earring.

"Do you see a lobotomy scare on my forehead?" Upham said.

The more McGuire stared at his earring the redder Upham's face became. "I don't think you're that dumb, Neal," McGuire said. On the other hand, he thought, knowing how much Captain Headley hates earrings on men and knowing how much influence the Headley will have on the upcoming lieutenant's promotion board, maybe you are pretty fucking dumb.

"Well, you've got another think coming, asshole. I know all about Joubert's arrest and the buy/bust on Saturday. I also know about the surveillance you pulled at Lovers' Point on Monday. The Feds don't use local polygraph examiners, they always bring in their own, so don't give me that shit about just helping out. I don't know exactly what you're up to, but you're running around like you're on your own private crusade. You're dangerous, and I'm bringing this shit to a halt as soon as I can get in to see the Chief. By the time he's finished with you, you can forget about ever being a lieutenant. You may not be a sergeant for much longer."

"Do whatever you have to do, Neal," McGuire said. "But in the mean time get out of my face."

Upham drew himself up. "Oh, just for your edification, I recovered a pistol from under the Outrigger Restaurant. It's a Glock with a special barrel that's extended and threaded on the outside." He turned and walked out of the office.

A minute later Wedge stuck his head in the open doorway and asked, "Is it all clear now?"

"For the moment," McGuire said.

Wedge sauntered into the office and leaned against Noguchi's desk. They stood there in silence for a minute until Wedge ventured, "What's going to happen when Upham tells your chief about everything?"

"Oh, you heard."

"You guys were loud enough, I probably could have heard it from out on the street. So, what's going to happen?"

"I don't know. I've never stepped this far out of line before. Not even close to it. I'll worry about it when it happens." Wedge started to ask another question when the telephone rang. McGuire snatched the receiver out of its cradle.

"Investigations, McGuire."

"Keith, this is Walter Dombrowski. What the fuck is going on over there?" Again McGuire motioned Wedge to pick up the telephone on Noguchi's desk.

"I'm sure I don't know what you're talking about," McGuire said.

"Then why are you still in your office at midnight?"

"Because I'm a dedicated law enforcement officer selflessly doing my duty for the community I'm sworn to protect and to serve."

"How can you say that without bursting out laughing?"

McGuire smiled. "Because I'm a dedicated law enforcement officer selflessly—"

"Once was enough. I have a message for you from on high, and I don't fucking believe this, but it concerns a Tiny Dancer."

"What's the message?"

"'Back off'"

"Who did this message come from?" McGuire asked.

"God," Dombrowski said. "Keith, what the fuck's this about? Is there some mess I'm going to have to clean up in the morning?"

"Walt, don't ask me about Tiny Dancer. I can't talk about it, but there is a related matter we need to discuss in person, and I don't think it would be wise to wait until morning."

"What's it about?"

"It's important, it's time critical, and it's something you wouldn't want me to discuss on the phone."

"Okay, I'll be there in an hour."

"Is Evelyn Shuman still your counterpart at the Naval Investigative Service?"

"Yeah. Do you know her?"

"Not really, but I arrested her teenage son a while back, and she came down to the station to pick him up."

"What'd you bust him for?"

"You know juvenile matters are confidential," McGuire said in a facetious tone. "I don't have Shuman's number—"

Dombrowski interrupted, "Don't tell me this involves her."

"Walt, are you harboring some professional animosity?"

"She's a fucking ball-buster. Every case I've worked with her has turned into a giant turd, because of her lack of patience."

"Well, could you call her and bring her along with you? It'll save me time having to explain things twice."

"In that case I'll be about an hour and a half."

"Oh, and Walt."

"Yeah."

"Don't say anything about Tiny Dancer to Shuman."

"Okay, but whatever you've got better be good."

"See you then." McGuire grinned and hung up the phone.

Wedge asked, "Keith, what do you think of Karasov?"

"If Dombrowski says he's okay, that's good enough for me."

"No, I mean as a substitute for Steve Wepsala. Karasov's a former KGB officer; he'd know how to twist Pavlenko's tail."

"Good idea, but we'll have to act fast. We don't have much time. I want both of you out of here before Dombrowski and Shuman arrive," McGuire said.

# CHAPTER TWENTY-THREE

WEDNESDAY 12:10 A.M., 21 NOVEMBER 1990

It took some persuading and a promise of anonymity, but finally Karasov agreed. McGuire gave Wedge a small hand-held radio. Wedge clipped the radio to his belt and ran an earphone wire inside his jacket, so it came out at the back of the collar. The short length of wire from his jacket collar to his right ear was barely noticeable. Karasov grumbled while Wedge told him the bare essentials of the situation.

Wedge brought Karasov to the observation room. He drew the drapes across the window and motioned Karasov to a seat.

In a few minutes McGuire entered the observation room. "Okay, our guest is in the interview room. I've read him is Miranda rights again." McGuire handed Karasov a radio. "Here, push this button to speak. Mr. Wedgwood will be able to hear you."

Wedge left McGuire and Karasov and entered the interview room. He took a seat across the table from Pavlenko. Wedge started with some initial questions Karasov had prepared for him. "What is your control's name?"

"My control? What is a control?"

"The KGB officer who gives you instructions?"

"I don't know. I receive instructions by mail. They are never signed."

"Who was the KGB officer you saw in Mexico?"

"I don't know any KGB officer in Mexico."

"Then why were you in Mexico on Sunday?"

"I wasn't."

"You went to Mexico to meet your control. Who is he?"

Pavlenko stared back at him in silence. Wedge started getting instructions from Karasov. "Look, Aleks, the game's over," Wedge said. "It's time to put your cards on the table. We know you're not some hapless Jewish émigré; you're not even Jewish. You're a trained KGB officer who was dispatched to the U.S. as an illegal. There's not going to be any deal with the FBI, unless you're more forthcoming with information. Neither you nor your wife is U.S. citizen yet. We may not have enough to put you away in prison for very long, but we have enough to get you deported. How do you think you'll be received by your KGB bosses in Moscow when we send you back to them? They'll never trust you again. At best you will be given menial jobs, live in a one-room apartment, spend most of your lives standing in line with everyone else trying to buy the basic necessities, and never be allowed to leave the Soviet Union again. At worst you may spend several years in the Gulag . . . counting the trees as they say.

"Then there's your daughter. What kind of existence will she have? You've been in the West for four years. You've learned a lot about our system and probably some things you never knew about your own system. Things were different when you left the Soviet Union. Their ideological underpinnings have eroded away. Gorbachev wants a new union treaty to transform the country into a confederation of sovereign states. If Yeltsin gets his way, there will be no Communist Party in Russia. There will be food rationing in Russia this winter, because of seventy years of gross mismanagement by the Party. Gorbachev must visit other world leaders with his hand out begging for aid. Have you asked yourself what your daughter's life will be like?  Have you asked yourself why you still want to work for them?  You've done your best, but now it's over. You have to start thinking about your own welfare and the welfare of your wife and your daughter."

Wedge sat back and watched Pavlenko closely to gauge the impact of what he said. After the first several seconds passed, Wedge began to feel uncomfortable, but he knew the silence was even more uncomfortable for Pavlenko. Then he saw what he had been waiting for. Pavlenko's head bowed and his shoulders slumped slightly. Wedge let a more few seconds pass before he asked, "Who did you see in Mexico?"

Pavlenko looked up at Wedge. "Lieutenant Colonel Viktor Semenovich Kropotkin."

"What is his official cover?" Wedge began taking notes on a pad of yellow lined paper.

"He holds the position of Assistant Cultural Attaché at the Soviet Embassy in Mexico City. In fact he is the Line N officer for the KGB Rezidentura at the Embassy." Pavlenko placed his hands on the table and laced his fingers together.

"Where did the meeting take place?"

"In an old apartment building in Tijuana."

"Why did you meet with him?"

"I requested an emergency meeting, because I had reason to believe my security was in jeopardy. I complained about the risks that I faced servicing the dead drop so frequently during a time I was being investigated by DIS." Pavlenko covered his mouth and belched. He reached in his jacket pocket, withdrew his container of Zantac, and looked at Wedge.

Wedge nodded. "Who else was at the meeting?"

"No one."

"What instructions were you given?"

"To continue what I was doing," Pavlenko said and popped a Zantac pill into his mouth and swallowed it dry.

"What else?"

"To have Zhanna monitor and report on Sergei Karasov."

"Why is he interested in Karasov?" Wedge asked.

"I mentioned before that part of my tasking included reporting on Russian émigrés at the DLI."

"But why specific instructions about Karasov?"

"I don't know."

"When did you first report on Karasov?"

"Last summer, right after he arrived at DLI."

"Is Karasov of greater interest to them than the others?"

"Yes, I believe so."

"What information have you passed on concerning Karasov?"

"I gave them his address, a description of him with habits and mannerisms, a photograph, and his fingerprints."

"How were you able to get those things?"

"The photograph was easy. I went to the graduation ceremony of the class he had been teaching. Everyone was taking pictures of one another after the ceremony. I had my wife pose with a few of her students near Karasov and got him into the edge of the picture." Pavlenko slumped a little in his chair and seemed to relax. "The fingerprints were difficult. I was at my wife's office when she invited him in for tea. When he left, I placed the teacup he used into a plastic bag and mailed it to an address in San Francisco. His address was most difficult of all. He is a very secretive person. I tried many different things to learn where he lived. Finally I had to follow him after school."

"Who would want to know about Karasov?"

"Perhaps the Line EM Officer at the Embassy. He is in charge of émigré matters—no, now I remember, Kropotkin mentioned a Colonel Cherniavsky was interested in Karasov."

There was a long silence before Karasov fed in his next question. Karasov talked Wedge through the rest of the interrogation. Even after Pavlenko started talking freely, he didn't give up very much. There were about twelve recruited émigrés at the DLI that Pavlenko knew of. He knew them only by their code names and never had direct contact with them.

DLI was only an intermediate objective for Pavlenko. His ultimate goal was to gain employment at the Defense Nuclear Agency's On-Site Inspection Agency, which monitored compliance with the Intermediate Nuclear Forces Treaty between the U.S. and the U.S.S.R.

When Karasov indicated he had no more questions, Wedge asked a couple of is own. "Who's Colonel Cherniavsky?"

"I'm not sure. I recall hearing of a Colonel Cherniavsky during our training. I think he was the head of one of the sections of Directorate S of the First Chief Directorate, but that's all I remember. Zhanna and I were trained by ourselves. We never saw anyone else, except the instructors who came to us at the apartment we used in Moscow."

"Tell me about the photographs of Zhanna," Wedge said.

"Oh, did you find them?"

Wedge waited for the rest of Pavlenko's response.

"That was only for cover. I went to Howard McGuire's house that night because, despite what Kropotkin said, I was worried he might have surveillance photos of Dora and me. I took the photos of Zhanna and planted them there for two reasons. First, it would give me a cover story for being in the house if I was caught. Second, I was worried about our security investigation. By leaving the photos of Zhanna there and having them found by someone else, it would discredit Howard McGuire and his investigation of us. I finished searching the first floor and just went up to the second floor when I heard a car drive up. I dropped the photos next to a typewriter in the den and hid in the hall closet."

When Wedge finished, McGuire came in and helped take a short statement from Pavlenko, then led him back to his cell.

McGuire poured himself a cup of coffee as Karasov paced back and forth deep in thought. As soon as McGuire seated himself next to Wedge at the break room table, Karasov set his cup down and looked at the two men. "You should have told me."

"Told you what?" Wedge responded.

"You are already knowing KGB has special interest in me."

"He never mentioned your name before," Wedge said.

"Do you know who Colonel Cherniavsky is?" Karasov made his question sound more like an accusation. When neither Wedge nor McGuire replied, he answered the question himself. "He is head of Executive Action Section. He is in charge of *mokre dela*, wet affairs, assassinations."

"Are you saying they've identified you and intend to kill you?" McGuire said.

Karasov nodded. "Maybe they are already here."

"What do you mean?" McGuire asked.

"The night your brother was shot."

McGuire could see the scene clearly in his mind—the fog, glare of lights reflecting off the wet pavement, the emergency vehicles, the body on the ground, the placement of the two bullets, the blood obscuring half of his face. "Wait a minute. You think my brother was shot by a KGB assassin?"

"Possibly."

"I don't understand. I was told there's an unwritten rule against knocking off your opponent's intelligence officers."

"There is such a rule against—"

"Then why do you think my brother was—"

"Because your brother accidentally killed a KGB officer in Japan while helping me escape."

"But if it was an accident—"

"To them it makes no difference. Even if they thought it was accident, in their eyes it was your brother who violated the rule. Now it is . . . ah, *quid pro quo*, an eye for an eye." Karasov sat down across from McGuire and clasped both his hands around his coffee cup.

McGuire asked, "How did it happen?"

"As I told you before, in December 1985 while my wife and daughter were in Moscow visiting family, I detected a surveillance. For two months I had suspected something was wrong. Your brother and I studied it thoroughly," he said. "We knew it was not something we did, and we were certain it was not Edward Lee Howard, the CIA agent who had defected to Moscow three months earlier. Someone at CIA Headquarters in your brother's division had been careless or had sold out to KGB."

Early on Christmas Eve, around two-thirty, Karasov had returned to his apartment building and had found a Christian pamphlet in his mailbox. It was addressed to his neighbor, Anatoli Pronin, a nice young man who worked as a cipher clerk at the Residency.

Karasov and his wife had Pronin over to dinner on a few occasions and had become fond of him. Karasov didn't know if he was secretly a Christian or if the pamphlet was put in Karasov's mailbox as a test. Rules at the embassy were strict. It was his duty to immediately report the matter to the Security Officer. But if it was not a test, Pronin's career, his life would be ruined. If Karasov did not report it, and it was a test, he would be sent back to Moscow on next airplane.

Karasov said, "Without going up to my apartment, I turned around and went straight to a telephone booth three blocks away to call Charles . . . I mean your brother. We agreed it was time to activate the emergency plan."

From the telephone booth Karasov took a taxi to the Ginza district of Tokyo and walked around for thirty minutes trying to detect a surveillance. He then got on a subway and took the Hibiya Line to Ebisu Station.

"Charles watched me get off the subway at Ebisu and saw Vasili Stechkin following me as I walked to the platform for the J.N.R. Line," Karasov said. "Stechkin was young officer assigned to the Residency's KR Line—Counterintelligence and Security. I should have known they were on me from the moment I left my apartment building. I was moving fast, so I must have shaken off the others and only Stechkin was able to keep up with me."

Karasov continued, "Charles tried to delay Stechkin long enough for me to get away on next train, but there was scuffle, and Stechkin fell onto tracks in front of oncoming train. Charles just made it onto train with me."

They went south two stops and switched back to a subway and went to Mita station. From there they walked a hundred meters to Tamachi Station and took a local train into Tokyo Central Station where they caught a Bullet train to Shimono-seki. They arrived in Shimonoseki seven hours later. The next day they took a ferry across the Korea Strait to Pusan where Karasov was eventually granted asylum by United States. Two weeks later Karasov was flown to Washington.

Wedge asked, "Why didn't they just fly you out of one of the U.S. military airfields in Japan directly to America?"

Karasov took a sip of coffee and pondered the question for a moment before answering. "Your government did not want to be accused of kidnapping me. The plan was for me to slip out of Japan using my own resources without Charles or CIA breaking any Japanese laws. We expected KGB to cover major airports, but they would not expect me to take ferryboat to Korea. South Korea was much more cooperative about those kinds of things than Japan. Your bother was only to escort me to Pusan and vouch for me to U.S. authorities there."

"Is my brother wanted for murder in Japan?" McGuire asked.

"Fortunately, to average Japanese person all Caucasians look alike. Tokyo Metropolitan Police were never able to positively identify your brother. The CRO knew he was responsible for Stechkin's death, and they had him declared *persona non grata*. He can never go back to Japan."

"The crow?"

"The Central Research Office—their intelligence agency."

"If the KGB was to assassinate someone, how would they do it?" McGuire asked.

Karasov cleared his throat, swallowed, and took a deep breath. "It depends. Do they want to shut him up or to punish him? If they want to shut him up, they try to make death look natural or like accident. They killed Hungarian dissident using ampule of prussic acid that exploded in front of his face. Breathing prussic acid made his heart to stop. It looked like heart attack. If they want to punish and teach lesson, they use gun and make it look like robbery. They can deny involvement, but others will get clear message that KGB's enemies can be executed in any country, anywhere at all." Karasov looked up at McGuire. "I know what you are thinking and answer is yes, they shoot people in face. But usually that type of execution is only for people like me who have been convicted of treason and sentenced to death. It makes others think twice about betraying Soviet Union."

There was a long silence until Karasov pushed his chair away from the table and stood up. "I am at risk here. I must leave."

"Wait a minute," McGuire said. "When do you think they will try?"

"I must assume they are still here. By now they must know your brother is still alive. They may come after me first, then make another attempt on him, or perhaps him first, then me. They will try again as soon as they can. They will not wait any longer than they have to and take the chance I might disappear."

"It's been nine days. Why haven't they made another attempt before this?"

"Perhaps I have not given them opportunity, or perhaps there is problem concerning your brother."

"Like what?"

"A suitable method. If they want to finish the job on your brother, they are not going to walk into hospital and shoot him. They will do it quietly with poison or suffocation. It takes time for decision to be made and for assassin to get what he needs. Now, I must leave. Time is important."

"You keep saying they." McGuire pushed his chair back and stood up. "Will there be more than one?"

"Perhaps, but not more than two."

"I appreciate your help, but I need you to do one other thing for us." McGuire came around the table toward Karasov.

"If I can," Karasov said.

"I want you to delay your departure for a few hours. If you could go to work in the morning and tell your supervisor that a relative in Chicago died and you need the day off to pack and make travel arrangements. Tell him you're flying back to Chicago tomorrow night—I mean tonight, Wednesday night. Make no secret of it. I want your co-workers to hear about it. Perhaps one of them will report it. In fact, as soon as you get home, I would like you to use the name Karasov and make a flight reservation to Chicago. After you check out with your boss, return to your apartment and leave your car there. I'll meet you there at 9:30 am and take you wherever you want to go, but I'll need your apartment key."

Karasov nodded and the two men shook hands. "You are going to take my place and wait for them to try to kill me."

McGuire smiled. "No, Mr. Wedgwood's going to take your place. He's closer to your size."

Wedge sat up in his chair and stared at McGuire. "I'm going to do what?"

McGuire turned to Wedge and said, "There's nothing to worry about. I'll explain it to you in the morning, once I figure it all out myself. You'd better call your office in the morning and ask for the day off."

"You're serious about this, aren't you?"

"Trust me," McGuire said. "By morning I'll have a plan worked out that'll minimize any danger. Oh, and Wedge."

"Yeah."

"I need you to go to Community Hospital. I'll telephone a nurse I know and have her arrange to move Howard to another room. Her name's Gayle Fantes. She knows everyone there well enough to get things done informally until morning. Could you go there to make sure it gets done right away?  Oh, and I don't want any paperwork or records showing that he moved."

"Sure."

"Check in with the nurse in Garden North. I'll have Gayle call her, so she'll be expecting you. I'll be there first thing in the morning to clear things with the hospital administrator."

# CHAPTER TWENTY-FOUR

WEDNESDAY 1:45 A.M., 21 NOVEMBER 1990

Dombrowski and Shuman were seated across the table from McGuire in the break room. Only minutes earlier he had hustled Wedge and Karasov out of the station. Shuman was dressed in tennis shoes, gray sweat suit, blue nylon windbreaker and a baseball cap with the NIS emblem on it. Dombrowski wore a gray pin stripe suit and appeared to have just showered and shaved. He looked as though he expected a TV camera crew to show up at any moment. Judging from the scowl on Shuman's face, Dombrowski must have dropped by her house and roused her out of bed without calling first.

McGuire slowly spun his tale about Howard's investigation and about his own recent activities involving Joubert, Ellis and Pavlenko, leaving out little bits and pieces as he went along. He failed to mention anything about Wedge, Karasov, and the KGB hitmen. Dombrowski sipped his coffee and listened attentively without interrupting. Shuman sat with her arms folded staring at her untouched coffee cup. When he finished, Dombrowski and Shuman both tried to speak at once.

"Walt, where're your manners. Ladies first," McGuire said, nodding at Shuman.

Shuman gave them both a dirty look. "Where's Ellis now?"

"He's in county jail. He'll be arraigned in Monterey Muni Court this morning on a drug charge."

"When did you arrest him?"

"Late Saturday night."

"That was three days ago!" Shuman exploded. "I should've been notified immediately. Ellis is my jurisdiction. You had no authority to—"

McGuire folded his arms across his chest and rocked back in his chair. "Relax Evelyn. No harm done. Considering the evidence I'm sitting on, you're going to want my full cooperation in this matter."

"You withhold evidence from me, you shitbird, and I'll have you up on federal charges. I'll—"

Dombrowski waved his hands in front of Shuman to get her attention. "Whoa, Evelyn, give the man a chance." He turned to McGuire and said, "You'll have to excuse Evelyn. She's a former Marine. What evidence do you have?"

McGuire opened his briefcase and pulled out the written statements. One by one he placed the plastic bags containing the toilet paper roller, the partially wrapped 16-millimeter film cartridge, and the Minox camera on the table.

No one spoke. Shuman's lips moved rapidly as she read each word of Ellis's statement. Dombrowski read a few lines of Pavlenko's statement, examined the film cartridge, then went back to the statement. Shuman looked up from the papers in her hand. "I want custody of Ellis right away."

"Well then," McGuire said, "I guess you'll need me to quash the drug charge?"

"What is it you want, Keith?" Dombrowski asked.

McGuire leaned forward placing his elbows on the table causing it to shake and Shuman's coffee to slop out of her cup. "I want the FBI and NIS to give credit for this case to the Defense Investigative Service. I want letters of commendation for Gordon Wedgwood and my brother, signed by your directors and I want them by close of business today. The media doesn't have to know about it, but it has to be done through channels."

"Come on, Keith, we can't get that out here to the West Coast in one day," Dombrowski said. "We'll need more time."

"Okay, but they have to be signed and the DIS Regional Director in San Francisco has to be notified and sent a fax copy by the end of the day."

"I'd like to know what in the hell DIS, your brother and Wedgwood have to do with this," Shuman demanded.

"Pavlenko was their case," McGuire said. "In fact they tried to get Walt to take the case a couple of months ago."

Dombrowski stared at the half-empty coffee cup cradled between his two hands.

"But Walt was too busy with other things. He declined to take jurisdiction." McGuire paused. "Of course, there's no need for anyone else to ever know that."

Shuman looked at Dombrowski and smirked. "That's why you're being so agreeable. Well, no one offered me a shot at the case two months ago. I sure the hell wouldn't have turned it down."

"Because the only work you have is taking stolen bicycle reports at the Naval Postgraduate School," Dombrowski muttered.

"What was that?"

"Look," McGuire intervened, "can we get back to the situation at hand?"

"Was Wedgwood in on Ellis's arrest?" Shuman demanded. "Because if he was, you can forget any letter of commendation from us. I'll have his fucking badge for violating the 'Delimitations Agreement.'"

"Evelyn, do you want the transfer of jurisdiction on this case to be quick and smooth, or do you want it to be plagued by the usual bureaucratic snafu's? Think about how your superiors are going to view any protracted delays in getting their hands on Ellis. It'll reflect on you and your liaison with us locals." McGuire stood up and motioned toward the door. "Can I speak with you privately in my office?"

"What for?"

"It's about Ellis. It'll only take a minute."

She turned her head and looked at Dombrowski. "Walt, is this some trick the two of you worked out in advance?"

Dombrowski shrugged and shook his head.

Shuman followed McGuire into his office and closed the door. "Okay, what's so damn important?"

McGuire placed a Polaroid photo on his desk and stepped aside, so Shuman could examine it closely. As she bent over the desk, her mouth fell open, and a shocked expression froze on her face. "Timmy," she gasped.

"I wasn't sure if you knew. We found the pictures in Ellis's apartment. I could've had Ellis charged with sodomy with a minor, but I felt the drug offense was enough to hold him."

Shuman turned to face McGuire. "This photograph and my son have nothing to do with this case."

"Well, I didn't ask Ellis about him. Your son probably doesn't know anything about his activities. Anyway, I thought I would leave it up to you to sort it all out. I didn't want it to become known unnecessarily. The news media would have a field day with it."

"Who else knows?" The blood had drained from Shuman's face.

"No one . . . except Wedgwood," McGuire lied.

"You said pictures. Where are the others?" Shuman asked as she palmed the photo and put it in her jacket pocket.

"Wedge has them."

Shuman grimaced. "Look, McGuire, I'm going to play ball, because time is critical in an espionage case. These photos have nothing to do with it."

"We've kept Walt waiting long enough. You can tell him anything you like, later." McGuire led her back to the breakroom.

DLI's School of Russian Language was located along the south boundary of the Presidio. It occupied a dozen old buildings that originally housed a cavalry squadron stationed there before World War I.

Standing in orderly rows on either side of Evans Road, the beige and brown buildings were separated by large oak, cypress, and pine trees. A veranda ran the length of the eastside of each classroom building. The buildings were set on wooden posts anchored to exposed pier blocks, giving them a rickety appearance, but none had ever collapsed or suffered major damage from the areas occasional earthquakes.

Karasov pulled his car into one of the parking spaces near the office of Konstantin Yakovlevich Tsetlin, his department chairman. As Karasov entered Tsetlin's outer office, he could hear Tsetlin speaking to someone, but couldn't see who it was. He stood there and waited for a minute. Lada Kartseva walked out of the office and past him briskly without pausing to say hello. The door was left open, so he knocked gently on the doorframe and leaned forward enough to see Tsetlin sitting at his desk. "Konstantin Yakovlevich, may I speak to you?"

"Come in, Sergei Ivanovich. What is it?"

"I need today and Friday off. My cousin Yuri in Chicago died yesterday. My flight does not leave until tonight, but there are personal matters I must attend to before I can go."

"Of course, take as much time as you need. You should be with your family in Chicago as soon as possible. I will arrange for someone to take your classes." Tsetlin paused. "Two emergencies in one day and at a time when we are so short handed. But don't concern yourself, I will manage it."

"Is there some other problem?"

"The Pavlenkos did not show up this morning. I have called their home, but no one answers. I hope nothing bad has happened to them." When Karasov turned to leave, he saw Lada Kartseva standing in the doorway listening.

After Zhanna Pavlenko had received the phone call from Sergeant McGuire at three in the afternoon, she had begun packing a suitcase for herself and her daughter. After she received the telephone call from Aleks at five, she called the emergency number and told the person who answered that Aleks was in custody. She then burned documents in the fireplace and destroyed other evidence of their operations. By nine o'clock she had the Volvo station wagon in the garage packed and ready to go. By midnight she was securely ensconced in a safehouse near San Francisco with her daughter.

She worried about Aleks, but there was nothing she could do for him. The questioning began as soon as her daughter was put to bed in another room. There wasn't much she could tell them. Yes, she had followed her emergency procedures exactly. No, except that Aleks had been arrested, she didn't know how badly the operation had been compromised. Had Dora been arrested? She didn't know. No, she was certain she hadn't been followed. Karasov? No, she had no idea of Karasov's status.

For now she would have to wait. In a few hours she would use her escape passport and fly with Natasha and their escort to Mexico City. From there they could take an Aeroflot flight to Moscow. Before leaving, she would call the newspaper in Monterey and place an advertisement. It would simply read, "House-sitting situation needed. Inquire at 555-3123." The number did not exist, but the members of the network would know to submit reports to an alternate address until further notice.

# CHAPTER TWENTY-FIVE

WEDNESDAY 8:30 A.M., 21 NOVEMBER 1990

Captain Headley came out of his office and stopped McGuire in the hallway. "Keith, the Chief wants to see you, now."

"I need some coffee. Can this wait a few minutes?"

"No. He's waiting for you in his office."

"At least let me take off my overcoat," McGuire said as he continued down the hall to his office.

"Make it snappy."

When he came back out of his office, Headley was still standing in the hall waiting for him. Headley led the way past Lois, the Chief's secretary. Lois glanced up at McGuire, rolled her eyes and shook her head. When you were summoned to the Chief's office, it was for one of two reasons. The signal she had just given him made it clear he was not going to receive a commendation.

As he followed Headley into the office, he saw Upham standing over in the far corner of the room staring at an oil painting of the Point Pinos Lighthouse. The Chief sat behind his oversized mahogany desk chewing viciously on the stem of an unlit pipe.

"Morning, Chief," McGuire said as he made a move to sit down in one of the uneasy chairs.

"No one gave you permission to sit," the Chief said.

McGuire saw Upham turn and grin at the sound of the Chief's gravelly voice.

"Stand up straight and get your hands out of your pockets when I'm talking to you." The Chief, a former Marine, expected all subordinates to be in awe of his authority. He rarely came out of his office and never socialized with the men. He purposely distanced himself from everyone except Headley, his assistant and personal henchman.

McGuire stood in front of the Chief's desk with his arms at his sides and his fists tightly clinched. He knew what was coming. There wasn't anything he could say that would change it. He was wrong. He would accept whatever punishment the Chief imposed. The punishment wasn't important. At this moment there was only one thing that was important to him.

"Upham tells me you intentionally withheld information from him concerning your brother. Is that right?" the Chief asked.

McGuire took a deep breath and stood mute.

"Did you purposely exclude him from certain investigative actions, including three separate arrests?"

McGuire's jaw tightened, but he still did not answer.

"Did you involve other agencies in this investigation without consulting him and hide evidence of a related burglary?"

McGuire glared in the direction of Upham who was now facing him, but intently examining the backs of his hands.

"Damn it, McGuire answer me. That's an order!" the Chief said.

"Yes."

"Yes, what?"

"Yes, I did!"

"Don't take that tone with me."

McGuire quickly turned his head toward Upham a second time. The Chief stopped abruptly and turned to look in the same direction. Seeing Upham he snapped, "Sergeant Upham, you can leave now."

After Upham closed the door behind him, the Chief resumed, "McGuire, I'm taking you off this case and . . . I'm suspending you for two weeks without pay for gross violations of department policy." The Chief paused and stared at McGuire, as if looking for some sign of contrition. "Is there anything you have to say for yourself?"

"No." There was nothing to say, nothing that would make a damn bit of difference to him or that he would ever understand.

Wedge rubbed the sleep out of his eyes and rolled over to look at the alarm clock on the nightstand. It was five past eight. He bolted out of bed and frantically searched for his robe and slippers before remembering he was going to take the day off from work. Katherine was getting ready to leave as he came into the kitchen. "Why'd you let me sleep so late?"

"After being out so late last night, doing who knows what, you needed a little extra rest." There was a slight quiver in her voice.

Uh oh, he thought. This didn't sound good. "I'm sorry I was out late, but I couldn't like, quit in the middle of things." He walked toward her with his arms out stretched, expecting his morning hug.

"You don't have to explain your actions to me. I'm only your wife, not your boss." She turned away from him and marched to the closet by the front door.

Whoa, am I in deep shit, he thought. He stood there with a hangdog look, an unshaven face, and the hair of a wild man. "I called last night at ten and left a message. Where were you?"

"I was in the shower when you called."

"It was work, hon; I had to be there."

"Then why didn't you answer the phone when I called your office?" Her voice lacked its usual warmth.

"Because I wasn't at the office."

"Then where were you?" She got her coat and scarf from the closet.

"I was at Pacific Grove Police Department until one; then I went to the hospital and didn't get out of there until two," Wedge said in his most sorrowful voice.

"And what were you doing there until two in the morning when visiting hours end at eight?" She stood at the front door, one hand on the doorknob, waiting for an answer.

"I'm sorry hon, but I'm not allowed to talk about it."

"Well, that's convenient!" She slammed the door behind her.

In the kitchen there was a note next to the coffeepot. "You'll be home at a decent hour tonight, won't you? Remember, we have to be at my parents' house by two tomorrow." Shit, he had completely forgotten the date. Tomorrow was Thanksgiving. The note went on "There's a baby shower for Mary Iverson this evening. I'll be back by 8:30. See you tonight. There's beef stew in the refrigerator." The usual "Love, Kathy" was noticeably missing.

Wedge called Butler and after an appropriate amount of whining, Butler okayed his request to take a day of annual leave. There was plenty of time before his ten o'clock meeting with McGuire. He could have a leisurely breakfast, read a couple sections of the paper, and try his new immersible electric shaver in the shower. The phone rang at nine-thirty as he finished getting dressed. It was McGuire.

"There's been a change of plans," McGuire said. "We're not meeting at the station. Meet me at eleven at a place called Custom Products in Sand City." McGuire gave him the address and directions to get there. "I'm leaving now. Karasov wants me to take him to the airport to rent a car." His speech was clipped and abrupt.

"Why the change?"

"The Chief suspended me this morning."

"What for?"

"You were there when Upham came in last night. He went straight to Captain Headley this morning and together they went to see the Chief. I'm off the case. I got a two week unpaid vacation."

Wedge exhaled loudly and said, "So we're out of it."

"I didn't say that! I'm going through with what we've got planned. I'm going after whoever shot my brother."

"You still want to go through with this?" Wedge asked. "Why not just let the FBI handle it?"

"Look, if you don't want to help, just say so. I'll do it on my own."

"Take it easy. I didn't say that. So like, why are we meeting at Custom Products?"

"I don't have time to explain right now. I'm meeting Karasov in ten minutes. Be there at eleven." McGuire rang off.

Keith sounded really pissed off, Wedge thought. Perhaps he's taking this more personally than I thought. Wedge went into the kitchen for another cup of coffee when the phone rang again. This time it was Steve Wepsala.

Wedge drove up to Custom Products and saw McGuire standing in front of the building with a gray suitcase in his hand.

"Come inside," McGuire said. "I want you to meet the owner, Matt Rice."

"So what does Custom Products make?" Wedge asked.

"You'll see."

They entered through a large garage door in the front of the building. Three cars with various body panels removed were in different stages of assembly. A small, makeshift office constructed of plywood occupied a back corner of the open work area.

"Matt, I'd like you to meet Gordon Wedgwood. Wedge this is Matthew Rice. He owns the place."

Wedge shook hands and looked around. Next to Rice's gray metal desk stood a large double-door safe. Through the open doors of the safe Wedge saw an assortment of pistols, rifles and shotguns. They were obviously not hunting weapons.

"The weapons are for testing my product," Rice said. He was a short man with broad shoulders and massive forearms.

"Matt's in the business of modifying vehicles for important people—people who worry about their personal safety," McGuire said. "Don't ask who his clients are. He won't tell you."

"What brings you here today," Rice said.

"I'm here to collect on that favor you owe me. I need some lightweight armor installed in this suitcase," McGuire said and handed Rice the suitcase.

"I can handle that." Rice set the suitcase on his desk. "What do you want it to stop?"

"As much as possible without going over thirty pounds."

Rice opened the suitcase. "We can use that new ceramic and Kevlar armor you helped us test at the police firing range last month. That'll stop anything up to a three-oh-eight. Anything gonna be in the suitcase?"

"No, just the armor."

"You're going to use it as a shield, huh?"

"No." McGuire pointed at Wedge. "He is."

Wedge's mouth gaped open. McGuire smiled in response to his wide-eyed stare.

"You're not as dumb as you look, Keith." Rice chuckled and examined the inside of the suitcase. "In that case I can pad it out with cotton. I think we can keep it under twenty-five pounds. When do you need it?"

"Today. As early as possible."

"You don't ask for much, do you. When you're done with it, I'll want the ceramic tiles back. They're not cheap." Rice closed the lid and snap the latches shut.

"Sure. Hopefully you'll get them back undamaged. Oh, would you happen to have a vest we can borrow that'll fit Wedge."

Wedge was still in a state of shock as he followed McGuire and Rice over to a row of battered old wall lockers. Countless questions assaulted his brain, each one seeking ascendancy over the other. Wedge knew this was not the time to blurt them all out, so his mind began to organize, then prioritize the questions.

Rice searched through a couple of wall lockers before he found what he was looking for. He brought out what looked like something a baseball catcher would wear, except it was light gray. It had a front and back, and the side panels went up high into the armpits. It even had a protrusion at the bottom front to protect the groin area.

Rice handed the vest to Wedge. "Here, try this on."

Wedge's thoughts were elsewhere. He allowed Rice to help him don the vest. It was a good fit, a little snug, but once he got it on under his jacket it would be less constricting. Finally a question escaped his lips. "What's this made of?"

"Spun Kevlar with a nylon cover," Rice said. "It'll stop a forty-four magnum from a pistol, but it won't do much good against a medium bore rifle. Come back at three and I'll have the suitcase ready."

McGuire followed Wedge over to his house in Seaside. Wedge picked up his raincoat and got into McGuire's car. After McGuire explained his plan, Wedge battered him with a multitude of questions. None of McGuire's answers seemed to mollify him.

"So that's your plan, huh," Wedge said. "Well, I'm not very impressed with it."

"The simpler, the better."

"Tell me again how you're going to get this guy before he shoots at me," Wedge said.

"Trust me," McGuire said. "I'll have you covered."

"You and who else?" Wedge reached over and changed the radio station from classical to light rock.

"Who else did you have in mind?" McGuire eased his way into the southbound traffic on Highway 1.

"Your whole fucking police department or at least the entire SWAT Team."

McGuire changed the radio back to the classical station. "Under the circumstances I don't think the Chief would approve it." Just beyond the Monterey Beach Hotel he took the Del Monte Boulevard exit.

"Well, I was just hoping there'd be a lot more guys on our side." Wedge started to reach for the radio again. McGuire glared at him. Wedge hesitated and pulled his hand back. Instead, he stacked his arms across his chest and fell silent.

McGuire glanced over his left shoulder, tapped his brakes, and merged into the traffic on Del Monte. "Look, Karasov said there'd only be one man, two at the most."

"Yeah, just one or two trained KGB assassins." Wedge paused. "What's the worst that could happen to me if I take a round square in the chest?"

"It'll knock the wind out of you and give you a bruise, maybe break a rib . . . if he uses a pistol," McGuire said.

"And if he uses a rifle?"

"That's why we're getting the suitcase." Because of the heavy lunchtime traffic, McGuire couldn't take his eyes off the road for more than a second at a time. He was having trouble trying to read Wedge's facial expressions. McGuire was counting on Wedge to do something a veteran police officer would balk at. Was he expecting too much? He was confident in his own ability to handle the situation, but if Wedge panicked or froze. . . . There was no choice. It had to be Wedge.

"If he uses a rifle, he could sit off at a distance and go for a head shot," Wedge objected.

"Don't worry, Wedge. I'm not going to have you expose yourself until they're out in the open. When they show themselves, I'll draw their fire. They'll be so busy with me they won't get a good shot at you." McGuire flashed his most sincere smile at him. Come on Wedge, don't flake out on me, he thought. I need you with me on this. "If they get any rounds off at all, they'll probably be fired at me, not you. You'll be protected by the best ballistic armor available."

"Oh, well, silly me to worry when you're taking all the risks. What am I getting myself all worked up for. We don't know for sure Karasov is right about his assassin theory."

"I thought you heard what Upham said last night."

"I did . . . well . . . most of it."

"He found the gun. It has a threaded muzzle."

"Yeah, so?"

"I checked out Upham's report after you left. The pistol was a Glock Model 19. It's a nine-millimeter, the same as the weapon that shot Howard. This one has a special barrel that sticks out a half inch beyond the slide and is threaded on the end. The threads are metric. Upham may be an ass, but he's thorough."

"So, what does that mean?"

"It means the gun was modified to accept a suppressor, probably a foreign-made suppressor."

"Oh, you mean a silencer."

McGuire nodded, and Wedge fell silent again.

When they arrived at Karasov's apartment, McGuire laid out a Smith and Wesson Model 39 with an extra seven round magazine and a Motorola Expo radio on the kitchen table. "The pistol and radio are for you. I'll pick up some food on the way back. What do you want?"

"That's right, condemned men get to choose their last meal. Get me a large barbecued beef sandwich, some baked beans, coleslaw, apple pie and a large coke." Wedge hefted the pistol and examined the button and levers. He pressed a button with his thumb and ejected the magazine onto the floor. One bullet dislodged from the magazine and rolled under the table. His face turned bright red.

McGuire stopped at the door, shook his head, and looked back at Wedge. "Try the vest on under your raincoat. And every once in a while walk past the living room window. If someone is watching, we want them to think Karasov's still here. I'll be back around three-thirty."

"What if someone comes to the door?"

"Don't answer it. I'll call you on the radio just before I come up, so leave it turned on. I've set it to the tactical frequency, so there shouldn't be any traffic on it."

For two hours Wedge paced around Karasov's apartment picking up and examining stray bits of statuary, books, and photographs. He occasionally peeked out the living room window, checked the radio to make sure it was still working, and looked at his watch to see how much time had passed since he last peeked out the window and checked the radio. I should have brought a book, he thought. Anything to take my mind off of this.

It was a little before 3:30 P.M. when Wedge finally heard the radio crackle. "Wedge, you there?"

"Yeah, I'm here. Where are you?"

"I'm parked in the shopping center, one street over on Forest Avenue. I'll come in from the back side of the apartment. Have the door open for me."

McGuire had the suitcase in one hand and a grocery bag in his other arm. He had changed out of his sports coat and tie and was now wearing blue jeans, a blue crew neck sweater, a leather flight jacket, and brown crepe sole shoes.

"It's about time you got back. I was starting to get weak from hunger," Wedge said and started emptying the contents of the grocery bag onto the dining room table.

"What a wussy."

"I haven't eaten since nine this morning. I checked out Karasov's refrigerator. He must be a vegetarian or something." Wedge had eaten half of his sandwich by the time McGuire sat down to join him. As Wedge tore another large bit out of his sandwich, barbecue sauce dripped onto the light gray Kevlar vest. He quickly tried to wipe it off with a paper napkin, but only managed to smear the blood red sauce into a large round stain over his heart.

McGuire shook his head. "That'll give the shooter something to aim at. You always eat like that?"

Wedge continued chewing for a minute, then washed it down with a large swallow of Coke. "Only when I'm hungry," he said. "What's all that other stuff for."

"We're going to be here for a while. I thought we might get hungry later."

"Oh. What about the empty jar?"

"That's for me. I'm going to be out in the car. I can't run up here every thirty minutes for a used coffee break."

"I forgot to mention," Wedge said, "Steve Wepsala called me this morning wanting to know if we needed any help. I told him we muddled through last night without him. While I had him on the phone, I asked him about Howard's financial situation." Wedge paused long enough to devour some baked beans. "He said, you would know about the inheritance from your parents—"

"But his half only came to about $22,000 after all the medical and legal expenses."

"He said Howard put all of it along with about $20,000 in personal saving into some mutual fund he had recommended. He said if Howard followed his advice and left it alone until he bought the townhouse last spring, his investment would have almost doubled."

"That accounts for about $80,000. What about the other $42,000?"

"Steve said Howard got about $35,000 in severance pay from the agency when he was fired. He's not sure how he invested it."

"Damn," McGuire said, "I could kick myself for not asking Wepsala earlier. It pisses me off to think I suffered through Upham's wild ass speculation about Howard's financial situation when I could have cut him off at the knees."

Wedge turned his attention to the apple pie.

# CHAPTER TWENTY-SIX

WEDNESDAY 6:00 P.M., 21 NOVEMBER 1990

Marat Nosenko watched his speedometer as he headed south on Highway 101. The indicator varied a little to either side of fifty-five. He didn't want to take any chance of being stopped. His contact in Oakland had given him a hypodermic syringe, a needle, and a small vial of clear liquid. The injection could be made to any vein or into an IV bag. It would cause death in a few hours.

His contact had also given him updated information on his other target, Sergei Ivanovich Karasov, also known as Stanislav Mikhailovich Zagorsky, a KGB defector. Zagorsky may have been alerted that the Centre had identified him. If so, he could go underground at any time and resurface elsewhere under a new identity. So, his orders were changed—first Zagorsky, then finish the job on Howard McGuire.

He had never known the traitor Zagorsky or McGuire, the CIA agent who killed Stechkin while helping Zagorsky defect, but he had known Vasili Petrovich Stechkin. They had played soccer together while they were both students in Moscow.

This was Nosenko's first job for the Executive Action Section. He was furious with himself for his failure to kill McGuire. Now he was being given a second chance. He wanted desperately to succeed, to advance his career, and to avenge his former friend.

Captain Marat Tarasovich Nosenko had come up the ranks the hard way. He was born in 1961, the son of a Ukrainian farmer from a collective outside Lubny, two hundred kilometers east of Kiev. His mother was a Tatar from the Crimea, one of the few whose family was allowed to return after being deported to Special Settlement camps in Uzbekistan in 1944.

Marat was conscripted into the army when he was eighteen. Because he had tested well, he was sent to a training division for six months to become a junior sergeant. He served a year in Afghanistan, then a year and a half in the long-range reconnaissance company of the 24th Samaro-Ulyanovsk "Iron" Mechanized Infantry Division of the 38th Army in the Carpathian Military District located in Lvov.

It was common knowledge among military officers that Tatars made the best sergeants, better than Russians who were too softhearted. Nosenko was no exception. He had no difficulty meting out punishment, no matter how severe.

In the army he saw the vast difference in status between officers and other ranks. He saw what separated them was higher education.

After he was demobilized, he applied to the Military Institute of Foreign Languages and to his surprise he was accepted. Ninety percent of the students admitted to the Institute were the sons of Soviet general officers. The other ten percent were the sons of colonels and majors, and occasionally the son of a factory worker or farmer. Five years of academic discipline were tough, but with graduation came a commission as a lieutenant and a university degree. As a graduate of the Institute his future in the military was assured. After a few years of service his entrance to a Military Academy for postgraduate work and eventual promotion to the highest ranks in the military would almost be guaranteed, or so he thought. He hadn't counted on the KGB.

The KGB took a certain number of graduates from the Institute every year. They mostly chose the sons of KGB generals, but they also looked for a few tough young officers for their *Spetsnaz* units. In secondary school Nosenko had excelled in soccer, so while attending the Institute he played with the Moscow Junior Dynamo soccer team. His athletic prowess and former military experience attracted the attention of the KGB.

Instead of an easy job as a staff officer at KGB headquarters or a choice foreign posting, Nosenko found himself at the KGB Balshikha complex undergoing military training that was far more difficult than anything he experienced in the army. KGB *Spetsnaz* units were trained in commando tactics, sabotage, espionage, and guerrilla warfare. Nosenko was trapped in an endless cycle of field training under extremely severe conditions.

His background made him different from the others in his unit. He was older than the other junior officers, and none of them had any real combat experience. The others resented his early promotion to Senior Lieutenant, because he had gotten it through his ruthless pursuit of tactical objectives during training exercises. When placed in charge of others, he drove them mercilessly, so his team always came in first.

After three long years in *Spetsnaz*, he was transferred to the 8th Department of Directorate S of the First Chief Directorate in Yasenevo just off the Moscow Ring Road.

Under different names the 8th Department had a long bloody history of peacetime kidnappings and assassinations on foreign soil, reaching back as early as 1926 as a section of the OGPU. During the Great Patriotic War, as part of the NKVD, it controlled partisan units involved in sabotage, espionage, guerrilla operations and assassinations behind German lines.

After the war as the *Spetsburo*, it used Russian officers to supervise killings and kidnappings conducted by "combat groups" of East German and Czech thugs. Their activities gained so much notoriety, the Politburo had to temporarily disband it 1953. Reorganizations and names changes continued until it was reconstituted within the First Chief Directorate and once again given responsibility for the direction of "combat groups," but instead of paid foreign thugs, they now had highly trained KGB *Spetsnaz* units and other professional assets. The task of peacetime assassinations and kidnapping was further delegated to the Executive Action Section within 8th Department. The section was commanded by Colonel Arkadi Petrovich Cherniavsky, who had once served with the wartime *Spetsburo*.

In this section Nosenko could work alone, demonstrate his individual talents, and earn the Order of the Red Banner. Such an achievement would insure his attendance at the Military Diplomatic Academy and his eventual posting to a Soviet Embassy in a western country where he could begin enjoying the good life.

Nosenko's rented car rode smoothly on the four-lane highway. He enjoyed driving on well maintained roads. The cloth upholstery of his car seat held him snugly and the quietness of the vehicle was relaxing. He needed to be in Monterey by 20:00 o'clock. His contact in Oakland had informed him that Karasov was booked on a flight at 22:30 o'clock that night out of Monterey. By the time he reached the city of Fremont the traffic had come almost to a complete halt. Even now ten kilometers south of San Jose, the traffic was still incredibly heavy. The announcer on a radio station had said something about "Get Away Wednesday" in reference to the traffic, but Nosenko didn't understand its significance. His English training at the Military Language Institute had been extensive, but nevertheless, he was not comfortable with it. Americans spoke so imprecisely and seemed to garble many of their words.

It was now the end of his third week in America. If things had gone as planned he would already be back on a ship, leisurely cruising down the East Coast and heading to Cuba for a little R&R before returning to Moscow.

He had arrived on a Soviet merchant vessel in the Port of Morehead City in North Carolina on 1 November and had passed through the cursory checks at the Harbormaster's Office without any problems. Ostensibly he was going on a day of shore leave while his ship took on provisions. Another man with Department 8, perhaps a sleeper agent returning to the USSR on leave, would get on the ship in his place.

He was glad to be on dry land again. A quick change of clothing, new identity papers, and he was on his way to Wilmington where he caught a flight to Atlanta, then on to San Francisco. He picked up a briefcase containing two pistols, a suppressor, and ammunition at a storage locker in the airport, then drove over to Highway 1 and down the coast in a rented Ford Taurus to Monterey. Along the way he made a short detour into the mountains to test fire the weapons—a Makarov and a Glock. He would have preferred to use only the Makarov, but he had been directed to use the Glock on first target. The Makarov chambered a slightly shorter and less powerful cartridge than the standard nine-millimeter parabellum used in the West. For the first target they wanted nothing that might suggest foreign involvement or that might link one killing to the other. For the second target they were not concerned about appearances, so the Makarov could be used on him. The Glock had been modified to accept the suppressor. At 19 centimeters long, it was designed to only eliminate most of the noise and flash.

Late on his second day in Monterey he located his first target. On Monday and Wednesday Howard McGuire left his house around 17:30 o'clock and drove down to Lovers' Point where he sat in his parked car for about an hour, then drove home. Other than that, he only left his town house to go to work. Each night from 17:00 to 23:00 o'clock, Nosenko sat in his car, parked a discreet distance away and waited for him. Targets were always more vulnerable at night.

During the days, he familiarized himself with the Monterey Peninsula and did some sightseeing. The beauty of the coastline was remarkable. So much different from the farming cooperative where he grew up. The Monterey Bay Aquarium fascinated him. It was unlike anything he had seen before.

His opportunity came on Sunday night. Nosenko followed Howard McGuire's car to the American Tin Cannery and waited for him in the parking lot.

It was almost 20:00 o'clock when he saw his target crossing the pedestrian bridge towards the parking lot. Leaving the key in the ignition, he quickly opened the car door to get out. The sound of a buzzer startled him. "*Chirt*," he cursed under his breath as he pulled the key out of the ignition, dropped it on the seat, and closed the car door. Regaining his composure, he walked casually toward McGuire's car.

Had McGuire been wearing a hat earlier? No, he decided, but the mist wasn't this thick earlier. Perhaps he had the hat in his coat pocket when he went in. His target turned and walked between the rust brown Volvo and the Porsche. Nosenko was certain it was his man. He was the same size and wore the same tan raincoat, but his face was obscured by the brim of his hat. The right side of Nosenko's raincoat was only draped over his shoulder. His left hand held the coat closed to conceal the gun he was holding along the right side of his body. He walked casually passed the rear of the red car and turned toward his target, who looked up at him as he raised his pistol to eye level. The target froze like an animal caught in the headlights of an oncoming car. He squeezed off the first round into the center of his chest. Even before the man's body recoiled from the impact, Nosenko fired another round to the head. The report of the weapon was muted, but audible to anyone nearby.

Two men in a truck stopped between him and his rented car, forcing Nosenko to head toward the concrete steps at the northwest corner of the lot. He walked briskly without looking back.

He discarded the weapon into the ocean near a restaurant on Cannery Row and went back to the American Tin Cannery parking lot. From behind the yellow police tape he watched as a large van from a television station arrived and the driver began setting up lights. A man who had been measuring and sketching the scene drove away while another in a white suit began talking with a television reporter. No one paid any attention to the Taurus parked about forty meters away from the Porsche.

Nosenko waited patiently until the television crew began putting their equipment away and a tow truck finished hooking up the Porsche to haul it away. He walked over to the Taurus and found the keys still sitting on the driver's seat as he got in. He started up the car and pulled out onto Eardley Avenue right behind the television station's van.

He could have left the car; they would never have been able to trace it back to him. But there was no sense in leaving it behind unnecessarily. At least this way, he wouldn't have to walk back to his motel, and he wouldn't have to rent another. It had taken him considerable time to figure out most of the car's knobs and switches that controlled the lights, heater, and windshield wipers. He didn't want to go through it again with a different car.

The excitement he experienced earlier was finally wearing off, and it was replaced by a strong sensation of hunger. He felt quite satisfied with his performance and decided to reward himself with an expensive dinner.

Nosenko slept in until 08:30 o'clock the next morning. After showering, he went out for a late breakfast. On the way into the restaurant, he noticed a newspaper rack and decided to check if there was any report on the previous night's shooting. He slowly read each article and had almost finished his breakfast before he made it to page three. There it was "Pacific Grove Man Shot and Robbed." Under the bold heading the article read, "Howard Charles McGuire, age 48, of Pacific Grove was shot at about 8:00 P.M. last night in the upper parking lot of the American Tin Cannery. Police suspect McGuire was the victim of an armed robbery, but declined to comment if any evidence was found indicating the identity of his assailant. . . . McGuire who suffered two gun shot wounds was taken to Community Hospital where officials say he is in critical condition."

Nosenko read the article a second time before setting the paper down. No, it must be a mistake. He was certain his target was dead. Without leaving a tip, he hurriedly paid for his breakfast and went back to his room.

*Pridurok*, you fool, he told himself. Cherniavsky will have your ass for this. Nosenko still had two weeks. He was scheduled to catch his ship in Boston on 26 November, but he also had a fallback rendezvous on 3 December in Norfolk. Norfolk would be trickier. The ship was picking up a load of wheat at the Cargill Grain Elevators. Security around Hampton Roads was much tighter than in Boston because of the extensive U.S. Naval facilities in the area.

The question was whether he would immediately go after his second target or wait until he obtained the means to dispose of his first target. His instructions prohibited him from contacting the KGB Rezidentura at the San Francisco consulate, except in an emergency—well, this was an emergency. They would have to determine other means for eliminating McGuire. Nosenko sent his emergency message to the accommodation address in San Francisco.

While waiting for a decision, he spent his time casing the hospital and making plans, but his target was moved to another area of the hospital before he received any instructions. He had just completed new plans when he received orders to meet a courier in Oakland who would give him the equipment he needed to finish his first assignment before attempting his second. But that was two days ago. Today there had been a change; his contact in Oakland had given him new orders. He had to hit the second target tonight.

As he drove past Fort Ord the lights of the peninsula came into view and his thoughts focused on the task ahead of him. Time was running out. He only had two hours left.

# CHAPTER TWENTY-SEVEN

"Standby, this could be it," McGuire said into the radio. "Yeah, it's gotta be. He just drove past me, and now he's turning around and heading back downhill. It's a dark blue Taurus." McGuire scrunched down in the driver's seat of his Chevy Blazer as the Taurus rolled silently past him. When he stuck his head back up, he saw it pull over to the curb and turn its headlights off. McGuire's car was pointed downhill about twenty yards up the street from Karasov's apartment. The Taurus was about fifty yards in front of him on the same side of the street.

"How many are there and what're they doing?" Wedge's voice cracked over the radio.

"It looks like only one man. I can't see what he's doing. The car in front of me's blocking my view."

"What do we do now?"

McGuire looked at his watch. It was 8:30 P.M. "Nothing. If he doesn't move and just sits in his car, we'll know for sure that it's him. At nine phone for the cab."

McGuire rolled his window down to prevent the windshield from fogging up. He wanted to drive the Blazer up to the Taurus and block it in, then use his shotgun to order him out of the car—handle it like a regular felony stop. But he had no evidence. He had nothing. No probable cause. No reasonable suspicion. Nothing. Until this guy did something, McGuire was powerless.

He wished O'Donnell were here with him. McGuire was confident in his own skills and training, but he really needed someone he could rely on to back him up. He had seen O'Donnell's cool, quick reactions under fire and trusted him more than any other man on the department.

McGuire worried about Wedge. Wedge had not shown his mettle in their two previous scuffles. It would be hard enough controlling the situation without additional back up; if Wedge panicked and did something unexpected, he could spook the assassin or endanger himself and they would lose their only chance to get him. They might lose more than that.

Wedge paced back and forth across Karasov's living room. Time passed slowly. He peeked out the window to try to get a look at the man in the blue Taurus.

McGuire's voice came over the radio. "Stay away from the window."

Wedge resumed his pacing. At exactly nine he telephoned for a taxi, then notified McGuire. He clipped the radio to his belt and went into the bathroom to empty his bladder again. When McGuire had told him there was only one man in the car, Wedge had felt the tightness in his back relax a little, but now his hand was a bit shaky as he pressed the lever on the toilet.

In the living room he loaded the pistol McGuire had given him and pocketed the extra magazine. He kept wiping his hands on the sides of his trousers as he paced around the living room, but it didn't do much good. He double-checked and triple-checked his vest and carefully readjusted its side panels and straps. The raincoat was a snug fit, but if he left it unbuttoned, it was okay. The room felt uncomfortably warm and stuffy, even though he had turned the heat off hours ago. His stomach felt queasy.

He went back to the window to watch for the cab. It was a starless overcast night, and a light drizzle made it difficult to see clearly out of the window. The street below him was dimly lit.

McGuire's voice came over the radio again, "Wedge, you there?"

"Yeah."

"Remember, walk slowly to the cab. If he starts shooting and you're close enough, get down behind the cab; otherwise, prone out behind the suitcase, so you're not in my line of fire. Oh yeah, and remember to turn out the lights when you leave the apartment. How long before the cab arrives?"

"It should be here now. If you have to like, use your shotgun, aim a little high. I'm not too thrilled about the possibility of getting a round of buckshot up my ass."

"Don't worry. There'll be less than twenty-five yards between us. There won't be much spread at that distance. Are you okay?"

"Yeah, fine." Wedge tried to conceal the nervousness in his voice.

"The cab's approaching now. Okay partner, this is where the nitty meets the gritty."

The cab honked twice as it pulled into the driveway of the apartment. It came to a stop, straddling the sidewalk. Damn it, McGuire muttered to himself. He grabbed the shotgun and positioned himself next to the passenger-side door. The man in the Taurus hadn't moved. McGuire looked over at the apartment and saw Wedge coming out with the suitcase in his right hand. If the cabby stays in his car, I can still get a clear shot over the hood of the cab. Please stay in your cab.

Wedge descended the stairs slowly to the driveway. There was only about thirty feet of open ground between the building and the front of the cab.

Just as Wedge walked out into the open, McGuire saw the door of the Taurus fly open and at the same moment he saw the interior light of the cab come on. He had intended to roll out of the passenger-side of his car and take up a prone position, but with the cab in his line-of-sight, he had to get out and stand erect. He could see the man walking briskly up the sidewalk towards Wedge.

"Stay in the cab!" McGuire yelled as he took aim over the hood of the taxi. Three shots rang out in rapid succession. Wedge fell to the ground. McGuire fired a round over the hood of the cab. Tires squealed as the cab backed out of the driveway. He racked another round into the shotgun as the gunman ran back to his car. McGuire fired at him, shattering the rear window of the Taurus. The gunman jumped into his car. McGuire sprinted toward the driveway where Wedge lay on the ground. "Are you hit?"

"No. I'm okay," he shouted from behind the suitcase.

McGuire spun around and raced back to his car. "Then, get on your feet," he yelled over his shoulder.

Wedge remained crouched behind the suitcase as McGuire's Blazer bounced over the curb next to him. The gunman's car screeched around the corner and headed north onto David Avenue. Wedge scrambled into McGuire's car as it lurched forward then sped down the street.

"Christ! Let me get the fucking door closed, will ya?" Wedge tried to lean out to grab the door handle, but was thrown back into his seat as McGuire made a hard right turn onto David Avenue. The door slammed shut by itself. "Did you hit him?"

"I don't think so." McGuire's hands were gripped tightly around the steering wheel as he floored the accelerator.

The Taurus slowed down as it crossed Forest Avenue about a hundred yards ahead of them. McGuire kept the accelerator pressed all the way down.

"Better fasten your seat belt," McGuire said.

"Keith, the light's red!"

McGuire swerved around a car in front of him and blew through the intersection barely missing a truck that turned left toward him from Forest Avenue. The rear of the Blazer skidded to the right. He spun the steering wheel to compensate for it just as they made it to the opposite side of the intersection.

The Taurus crested a high spot in the road and disappeared momentarily. When it came back into view, it was seventy yards ahead of them. David Avenue ran straight downhill to Cannery Row. The Taurus went airborne as it crossed Lyndon Street, then bottomed out leaving a trail of sparks flying behind it.

A young boy on a skateboard darted across the road in front of the Blazer.

"Look out!" Wedge shouted.

McGuire jumped on the brake pedal as hard as he could and the Blazer went into a four-wheel drift straight down the road with its tires screeching.

Wedge braced both his hands against the dashboard. "Can I call someone on the radio to head him off?"

"Won't do any good. It's on the wrong frequency." McGuire sounded his horn and kept it pressed down as he raced through the next intersection. Both cars were travelling over seventy. A traffic light two blocks ahead was green. The Taurus clipped the curb as it swerved around a car waiting to turn left at the middle of the next intersection.

"Don't change . . . don't change," Wedge prayed aloud to the traffic light. They nosed into the intersection just after the light turned red.

From ahead of them came the sound of car horns, screeching tires, and metal crashing against metal and glass. A station wagon had crossed in front of the Taurus, and the Taurus had smashed into its right rear corner and spun it around. Without slowing the Taurus cannonballed downhill toward Cannery Row.

McGuire pumped his brakes, but the momentum of his car caused it to skid on the wet pavement.

Just ahead the road turned sharply to the right. Unable to make the turn, the Taurus slammed over the curb. It leveled two large metal bollards that guarded the ticket area to the Monterey Bay Aquarium, then crashed into the building.

McGuire let off of the brake pedal as he turned his steering wheel hard to the right, but it had no effect. His car continued straight and followed the path of the Taurus.

"Brace yourself!" McGuire shouted and turned his wheels into the curb. He fell over on his right side against Wedge just before impact.

# CHAPTER TWENTY-EIGHT

WEDNESDAY 9:28 P.M., 21 NOVEMBER 1990

Nosenko staggered into the main hall of the Aquarium. Blood trickled down his arm and dripped onto the floor. Still stunned from the crash, he looked around and took his bearings. He had been here only a few days ago.

How many were there? Who were they—FBI, CIA, MI, local police? He had been hit by the first round. Luckily the bullet had passed cleanly through the muscle of his right forearm and didn't hit the bone. In his hasty retreat he had been unable to determine their number or disposition. But something was odd. Why would they have involved a civilian taxi cab driver? Why weren't roadblocks set up? Why was he chased by only one truck-like vehicle without any lights or siren?

He made his way to the second level of the Aquarium and looked for a good defensive position. Whoever was chasing him would be here any minute. He found a spot that over-looked the main hall and gave him a good view of the entrance to the Aquarium. His firearms training had regularly included practice using his left hand, but he never quite felt comfortable with it.

Wedge looked around, but couldn't see McGuire or the Taurus. He heard McGuire's voice was coming from around his feet, "You okay?" Wedge look down to see McGuire curled up on the floor.

"Yeah, I'm okay. How about you?"

"Help me up."

Wedge released his seat belt and climbed out the car. The front of the Blazer had ridden up onto the rear of the Taurus. He reached into the Blazer and pulled McGuire toward him.

The odor of engine oil leaking over a hot manifold assaulted their noses. Steam hissed and rose from the hood of both cars as they surveyed the scene.

"Did you see which way he went?" McGuire said.

"He may have gone through there into the building," Wedge said and pointed to the shattered window of the Aquarium Bookstore. The front of the Taurus was impaled into the wall beneath the window. McGuire climbed onto Taurus's hood and lowered himself into the Bookstore. Wedge stood there for a moment debating with himself, then hurried to catch up with McGuire.

A few display cases were overturned and books, pictures, and stuffed animals lay strewn about the floor. Broken glass crunched under his shoes. The room was in semi-darkness, but a half-open glass door at the other end of the room was visible.

Wedge took off his raincoat and followed McGuire's example by drawing his pistol and flipping the safety off.

The main hall of the Aquarium had a high ceiling with life-size replicas of sea mammals suspended overhead on wires. It was a massive structure of unfinished concrete, exposed wooden girders, and glass. As they stood there deciding which way to go, McGuire pointed to some blood on the floor by the door.

"Stay behind me and watch our rear," McGuire said and moved in the direction of the blood drops.

Nosenko peered over a waist high wall on the second level and watched two men enter the main hall from the bookstore.

He didn't want to shoot without knowing how many there were. He waited, but no one else appeared. Could there only be two? Amateurs, he thought. They must be fools to follow me into a dark building. The thought that he had been shot, chased off, and deterred from accomplishing his mission by two amateurs enraged him. He crawled to his right across the concrete floor to get into a better position, so he could engage both targets at the same time and quickly dispatch these two pests. As he started to rise, his knee bumped against his right forearm causing his whole body to shudder with pain.

McGuire looked up. A small red and white single-masted sailboat was suspended from the ceiling. It partially obscured the guardrail and half-wall of what looked like a mezzanine. Something moved behind the boat. Wedge scrambled into an information kiosk behind him. McGuire dove onto the floor and rolled next to the side of a column. Three shots rang out and reverberated in the large hall. McGuire pointed his gun in the general direction of the muzzle flashes and squeezed off three rounds, then rolled behind the column. Each shot sounded like cannon fire.

"He's behind the boat on the second floor. Cover me," McGuire called out. As Wedge began firing toward the boat, McGuire dashed forward, then dove across the smooth stone floor and under the boat. He sprang to his feet and pressed his back against a wall. Ahead and to his left was a wide tile staircase.

The clouds were clearing and moonlight filtered in through the large glass wall next to the staircase, casting shadows everywhere. The sides of the exhibit hall were still in darkness.

McGuire heard footsteps above him. He signaled Wedge to move forward along the opposite side of the hall. McGuire crept along his wall staying out of the dim light in the center of the hall until he was opposite the staircase. The staircase turned forty-five degrees at the first landing and disappeared to the left.

"Move over to the double doors where you can get a better look up the stairs," McGuire said in a hushed voice. "I can't see shit from over here."

McGuire watched Wedge shuffled along the wall until he got to a point where the hall turned right toward the staircase. He stuck his head out beyond the protection of the wall and looked up to the top of the stairs. Another shot ruptured the silence. A bullet ricocheted off the wall just above Wedge, and dusted his head with concrete fragments.

As the echoes subsided footsteps could be heard scampering up more stairs. McGuire made a mad dash for the bottom of the stairs as Wedge stepped out into the open just enough to fire twice toward the top of the stairs.

"Keith, is there any other way down?"

"I don't know."

"What's up there?"

"The upper half of that large aquarium in front of you," McGuire said and pointed at a massive concrete and glass structure to his left. There was more blood on the stairs in front of them. "He must have got hurt in the crash."

Wedge was on McGuire's left side as they made their way up the staircase slowly, quietly, one step at a time to the first landing. He concentrated on the area at the top of the stairs as they started toward the second landing. Wedge saw him, not at the head of the stairs, but higher, off to the right, behind a railing on the third level that looked down onto the entire stairwell. They were both completely exposed.

The gunman aimed down at them. Wedge hesitated, not knowing whether to stand and fire or yell a warning and dive for cover across the tile landing. Before he could yell or raise his weapon, McGuire pushed him out of the way. Two deafening shots exploded. From the corner of his eye he saw McGuire stagger back and fall. Wedge fired rapidly emptying his magazine at the small exposed section of the third floor and driving the gunman back out of view.

McGuire lay motionless on the landing. Wedge quickly dumped his empty magazine onto the floor and slammed the extra one into his automatic. He bounded up the steps two at a time. At the top he found another narrower set of stairs and continued his reckless pursuit, not knowing what he would do when he reached the top.

His mouth was hot and dry. A fire raged in his chest. His heart pounded violently. Sweat stung his eyes and blurred his vision. Six steps short of the third floor, he stopped and listened. He could hear nothing, but his own heart beat.

The vest he wore trapped his body heat, causing sweat to pour down his face. He wiped his shirtsleeve across his eyes to clear his vision and cautiously went up the last few steps.

To his right was a door leading to an observation deck. To his left he saw the top of the aquarium just beyond a pair of glass doors twenty feet away. The glass doors appeared to have been forced open and something on the floor near them glistened as the moon broke through the clouds.

I must have hit him at least once, he thought. Should I go back and see what I can do for Keith? He wanted to go back, but he went forward instead, crawling through the doors and a small puddle of blood.

The top of the aquarium was fifteen feet in front of him. Around the edge was safety cable held up by three-foot metal stanchions. A flat expanse of concrete roof extended around the water. From where he was, it looked like a kidney-shaped swimming pool. Across the water he could see a small corrugated-metal shed that housed the wave machine, which made the seaweed undulate. Beyond that was a larger utility building.

The water in the pool was choppy from the wind and sparkled in the moonlight. There was some movement near the shed. Wedge remained prone waiting for the gunman to show himself. Nothing happened. He lay there silently, trying to control his breathing. His hands were becoming numb from the tight grip he had on his pistol. Then he saw it. A figure ran from the shed to the utility building.

Wedge fired two rounds, then scrambled to his feet, but before he could take three steps toward the shed, he saw the muzzle flash and heard the shots. A bullet caught him in the right shoulder of the vest and spun him around. Another hit the heel of his shoe and knocked his feet out from under him. He fell hard onto his right side. His head made a cracking sound as it bounced off the concrete, and his pistol clattered across the tile rim of the pool and disappeared with a splash.

He lay there dazed, looking across the moonlit water as the figure of a man with a gun at his side appeared to move sluggishly around the edge of the pool toward him. With each step, the gunman became larger and more focused. Wedge rolled onto his back, grasped his right shoulder, and raised himself up at the waist. A sharp pain radiated from his shoulder to his right hand. Warm blood flowed freely behind his right ear, and his head pounded. The cold sea air helped clear his vision.

Nosenko stepped slowly, deliberately around the top edge of the aquarium as if in cadence with some unheard dirge. After missing his first chance, he had simply waited for them to come out into the open again. He had easily taken out the smaller man in the stairwell. Now he had done the same to the other man, almost. All there was left was to finish him off with a single shot to the head as you would a wounded animal. He felt only contempt for these men. They had interfered with his plans. They deserved to be eliminated. Nosenko stop ten feet in front of Wedge and stared down at him.

Wedge glared back at the gunman and uttered the only Russian insult he knew, "*Idi ti znaesh kuda?*"

Anger flashed across the gunman's face. With his left arm fully extended and locked, the he raised his pistol slowly until it was aimed directly at Wedge.

Two rapid shots rang out and mingled with the sound of shattering glass. The gunman lurched to his left clutching his chest and tripped over the safety cable into the pool.

Just beyond the glass doors, Wedge saw McGuire standing with his pistol dangling in his right hand. McGuire staggered through doors and out to the rim of the aquarium. "Are you all right?"

"Just bruised, I think," Wedge said and slowly rose to his feet. "I thought you bought it back on the staircase."

They looked over the edge of the water, but the body had disappeared.

McGuire reholstered his pistol. "I thought I did too." In the distance the sound of approaching sirens filled the air. "It hurt like hell. May have broken a couple of ribs. It totally knocked the wind out me. Took me two minutes to regain my breath. It still hurts to breathe."

Wedge stared at him in disbelief.

McGuire grimaced and lifted the front of his sweater just enough to reveal the shiny white cover of his Kevlar vest. "You didn't think I'd expose myself to gunfire without wearing one of these, did you? Mine's not as heavy-duty as yours, but it was enough to do the job."

They walked slowly down the stairs to the main hall on the ground floor and rested on the last two steps. They sat silently looking around for a while before Wedge said, "I'm glad we didn't like, bust the glass on one of these large aquariums. This place would be under a few feet of water."

"We got a small tank on the second floor. There's a lot of water and a bunch of anchovies flopping around up there."

Neither man spoke for a while until Wedge asked, "What are you going to do, Keith?"

"I'm going to have a lot of time on my hands after this. I guess I'll take up fishing and spend more time with my brother."

"No, I meant how are you going to handle the cops when they get here?"

"I'll think of something. I know most of their officers."

"Are we in Pacific Grove or Monterey?"

"At the moment we're just barely in Pacific Grove," McGuire said, "but the main entrance over there is in Monterey; so, we're in Monterey's jurisdiction. Just follow my lead. I'm going to tell them that you didn't know I was suspended and that I deputized you."

"Can you keep my name out of the newspaper?"

"Maybe."

"I'll have to telephone Butler tonight and tell him what happened. I'm sure he's like going to want a detailed report early tomorrow in person. And then there's Katherine."

"I can't help you there, Wedge."

"How about you? What do you think your Chief will do to you?"

"Don't worry about me."

# CHAPTER TWENTY-NINE

THURSDAY, 22 NOVEMBER 1990

The phone was ringing again. It was the third time in the past hour. Wedge stopped talking as Butler picked up the receiver of the STU III. Butler had just gotten off the phone with Evelyn Shuman. Right before that he had been speaking with Walter Dombrowski.

"Monterey Field Office, Butler."

"Clayton, this is Miles. Are you alone?" Quinlan's voice was loud enough for Wedge to hear him clearly.

"No, Wedgwood's here with me."

"Switch to secure mode." Quinlan paused. "Are you green?"

"Yes," Butler replied.

"What the hell's going on down there. I had to go to Treasure Island this morning to meet with the FBI and NIS. They seem to think we were involved in some major espionage case in Monterey. They had their big shots in from Washington. I was glad handed, slapped on the back, and shown copies of letters of commendation from their headquarters for Howard and Wedge. I felt like a bloody fool, dancing around their questions to hide my ignorance." Quinlan continued to speak loudly, and Wedge could hear every word.

"I told you as much as I knew last night. I was going to call you again as soon as I had all the details. I've been debriefing Wedgwood for the past hour, and I just got off of the phone with the local NIS and FBI people."

Butler then rehashed what he had been told by Wedge, Dombrowski, and Shuman.

"And you didn't know any of this earlier?" Quinlan said.

"No."

"Are you telling me you have agents running their own show down there?"

"Not with my approval, I assure you."

"How long has Wedge worked with Howard up at DLI?"

"Well, since he was hired, but not closely until Wepsala retired. No doubt he's picked up some bad habits from Howard. You know how difficult Howard—"

"I'm familiar with Howard's work," Quinlan said, cutting him off. "You know the Bureau and NIS think we did some sort of super bang-up job on this case."

"They were complimentary."

"Well, I don't see it that way. It seems to me two of your agents got way out of line. It also appears to me you're losing control of your office. Ordinarily I'd chop off a few heads because of something like this, but I won't. I won't because it would cause me too much embarrassment with the Bureau and NIS, not to mention our headquarters. I want a complete report from you no later than ten o'clock tomorrow. Do you understand?"

"Yessir."

"And you get that fool under control."

"Yessir."

"Do you realize it's Thanksgiving Day? I still have to telephone the Director, so he won't be blindsided tomorrow. Then I have a forty-five minute drive ahead of me just to get home."

"Yessir."

"And be careful of what you say to Wedgwood. The Director may want to pin a medal on him too. If you come down on him with both feet, you're going to look pretty stupid when he files a grievance."

"Yessir."

Wedge saw Butler grimace and slowly return the receiver to its cradle. Quinlan had hung up without saying goodbye.

Butler directed his attention to Wedge. "Tell me again how you got involved in this?"

Wedge shrugged, "Well—"

"Don't shrug your shoulders at me!"

Not knowing where to start, Wedge limited his response to the events of Wednesday night. "Keith McGuire asked me to give him a hand on his investigation of Howard's shooting. You approved my annual leave for Wednesday. I had some free time, so I helped him.  He needed someone as bait to flush out a suspect. I was the right size. Things didn't go exactly as planned."

"Go on."

"We expected the suspect to surrender to Keith once he was out in the open, but he tried to escape. Keith and I caught up with him at the Aquarium. The suspect was armed, and he shot at us, so Keith returned fire and killed him." Wedge was amazed at how simple it all sounded as he explained it to Butler.

"Were you armed?"

"Yeah. Keith gave me a gun, but only for my own self protection."

"You know you're forbidden to carry a weapon."

"I know DIS agents are prohibited from carrying firearms while on duty. But I wasn't on duty at the time. I was just assisting a peace officer. There's no violation of law in using appropriate equipment to like, provide that assistance." The more he talked the better it sounded, as long as Butler didn't know McGuire was on suspension.

"There's no excuse for not keeping me informed of your activities in this instance. Any time you engage in off-duty conduct that could result in adverse publicity for DIS, you are required to notify me in advance."

Wedge sat obediently with his head slightly bowed.

"And don't think I don't know about the rest of it—your other extracurricular activities with Howard's brother," Butler continued. "You're lucky everything turned out as it did. I'd say you were very lucky on this one. Quinlan can hardly ask for your head on a stick when the FBI and NIS want to pin a medal on you."

Wedge looked up. "What happened to Zhanna?"

"She and her daughter are back in Moscow by now. Dombrowski thinks she left the U.S. early Wednesday morning."

"I'm sorry I caused you embarrassment," Wedge intoned in his most contrite voice. "It won't happen again." After an appropriate interlude of silence, Wedge asked, "Is that all, boss?"

"Yes. You can go."

McGuire reported to the Chief's office as instructed. Lois greeted him again by rolling her eyes and shaking her head. "The Chief's expecting you. You can go right in."

McGuire hesitated at the open doorway, but the Chief immediately waved him in. "Close the door behind you and sit down." The Chief began even before McGuire had slipped into one of the uneasy chairs.

"McGuire, I've had it with you. You intentionally mishandled this investigation. You disobeyed a direct order at a time when you were on suspension. I won't tolerate that type of conduct—not from you or anyone. I'm prepared to seek more severe disciplinary action against you, including going to the City Manager and demanding you be terminated for cause." There was a long pause.

McGuire had expected the worst, including termination, but hearing the Chief say it made his heart sink. Once you were fired from a police department, your career in law enforcement was over. No one would ever hire you as a police officer.

"Ordinarily I would have no choice but to fire you. If I did anything less, the men would think I was going soft, and it would undermine my authority," the Chief continued. "But . . . I'm retiring in January. There's no question you deserve to be fired, but I have to assume some of the blame. I allowed you to remain on the investigation, even after Captain Headley advised me against it. You've invested fifteen years in this profession and I'm not going to be the one to flush your career down the toilet. I'll see to it you're given four additional weeks of suspension. You have three weeks of compensatory time on the books. I recommend you take it. I don't want to see you in the station again while I'm chief." The Chief swiveled his chair away and stared toward the painting of the Point Pinos Lighthouse in the far corner of the room.

McGuire took his cue and left the room quietly. As he passed the secretary's desk, McGuire stopped and smiled. "See you in two months, Lois."

# EPILOGUE

THURSDAY, 13 DECEMBER 1990

Keith McGuire walked over next to the hospital bed, smiling as he firmly took hold of his brother's right hand.

Howard looked up from the bed. "It's good to see you."

Without warning, tears began welling up in Keith's eyes. He released Howard's hand, turned away, and dabbed his eyes with a handkerchief before settling into an armchair next to the bed.

Howard spoke in a slow, tired voice. "Sorry I interrupted your vacation in Mexico. Had I known, I would've slept for a few more days."

Keith cleared his throat and spoke hoarsely. "It's a good thing you came around when you did. I don't think I could've survived an entire three weeks down there with Alycia. I can't tell you how grateful I was for the telephone call from your doctor."

"Why?" Howard pushed a button on the side of his bed. The top third of his bed began tilting up as a small motor hummed.

"Alycia was all hot on going to the Yucatan Peninsula and visiting Mayan ruins," Keith said. "Our accommodations were rustic. Actually, primitive would be more accurate. I didn't object to the lack of air conditioning in the hotel. I even got used to the temperature, humidity, mosquitoes, and geckos.

It was the hiking through miles of insect-infested jungles . . . but Alycia loved it, so I did my best to act enthusiastic."

"Well, I hope Alycia isn't too disappointed about having her vacation cut short."

"No. Not at all. When we heard you had regained consciousness, she insisted we fly back immediately. She wants to meet you."

"Why didn't she come here with you?"

"I wanted to see you alone first. She understands. She's really a considerate person. You'll like her." Keith lowered his voice. "Are you okay now? Are you feeling any pain?"

"Actually I'm pretty comfortable. A physical therapist is supposed to see me this afternoon for an evaluation. How about you? How have you been handling all this?"

"At first I couldn't really accept what had happened to you. I just kept denying to myself how serious your condition actually was. Then I started focusing on the gunman, and I could barely control the anger that was building up inside me. Later I convinced myself, if I could just catch the gunman everything would be all right, and you would get better. Of course, that didn't happen. You remained in your coma, and I got really depressed. Alycia helped me deal with it. It took a few days, but I was eventually able to accept things as they were." Keith paused. "God, to hear me tell it, I should be the one in the hospital bed connected to all the tubes."

"Don't be so hard on yourself."

"Who else has been by to see you?"

"Well, Steve and Wedge, of course, and some other people from work—Clayton Butler and Miles Quinlan," Howard said. "When I came out of it, the nurse asked if I wanted to notify anyone. I gave her your name and Steve's. Steve must have told everyone else, because there's been a steady stream of visitors since Tuesday. Steve's been by twice. I understand you've met a number of them."

"A few. How about Mrs. Thurgood?" Keith said casually.

Howard looked directly at his brother. "You know about her?"

"I, ah . . . bumped into her here at the hospital once too often. I sort of figured it out. Is it still a secret?"

"No, she finally agreed to come out into the open about us. We even began talking about our future together." Howard lapsed into silence.

Unable to think of anything to say, Keith nodded his head and said, "Good."

"Wedge told me all about what you two did . . . and the part you kept quiet about. Thanks."

"I understand you and Wedge got commendations."

"Wedge was a little disappointed about that."

"Why?"

"Oh, they did it up right," Howard said. "Quinlan and his counterparts from the FBI and NIS came down to make the presentations. His commendations were very impressive looking documents, praising his devotion to duty and investigative ability—definitely suitable for framing. Unfortunately he wasn't allowed to keep them or tell anyone about them, because they're classified."

A smile returned to Keith's face. "How's Wedge doing?"

"Steve had him and Katherine over for dinner a few nights ago. Steve tells me that basically Wedge is just happy to still have a job."

"Did he smooth things over with Katherine?" Keith asked.

"Apparently Wedge got Steve to tell a couple of war stories over dinner—war stories that involved staying out late and not being able to tell his wife about it."

"What about Butler? Was Wedge able to square things with him?"

Howard shook his head. "Wedge doesn't need to worry about him. Butler is a careerist. He'll go along with whatever his bosses tell him. Besides, he's been selected for a staff job back at headquarters in Washington. It'll be a promotion for him."

"Did you see the newspaper article about Pavlenko and Ellis?" Keith asked.

"Wedge brought me a copy of the paper."

"So you saw that bullshit story they made up about the arrest and all."

Howard nodded.

"You probably also noticed none of our names appeared anywhere in the article, and they made it look like it was strictly a joint FBI and NIS operation," Keith said.

Howard nodded again.

"In all fairness Howard, you should know I cut a deal with them. That was the agreement—no mention of our involvement to the media."

"It's exactly what I would've done under the circumstances."

"I understand three Russian instructors at DLI suddenly resigned and moved away," Keith said.

"Steve told me about that. One of them was a woman we both had our eye on for a long time—Lada Kartseva. Has anyone heard from Stan . . . I mean Sergei Karasov?"

"A postcard addressed to me at the department came while I was gone. There wasn't any return address, just a short note thanking me for my help and telling me that whoever sent the card was fine. On the front of it was a picture of Mount Rainier. I can't think of anyone else who would've sent it."

"I hope he makes it this time," Howard said.

"What about you? What are your plans?

"My plan is to do everything the physical therapist tells me to do, so I can start using the bathroom instead of a bedpan."

In January 1991 the Chief retired, Captain Headley and Lieutenant Gomez each took a step up the ladder of command, and Sergeant Francis Xavier O'Donnell was promoted to Lieutenant. Operation Desert Shield became Operation

Desert Storm and the combined air power of the Coalition Forces was unleashed against Iraq for six weeks.

In February Keith McGuire resumed his duties as a detective sergeant at the Pacific Grove Police Department. The ground war against Iraq, "Operation Desert Saber," began and ended a mere one hundred hours later in what was an overwhelming victory for the United States and the Coalition Forces.

In March Toshiro Noguchi returned from Saudi Arabia and Neal Upham was reassigned to patrol as the grave shift supervisor.

On 1 April, the day after Easter, Martha Pembroke was sent back to the Naval Postgraduate School, and Howard McGuire returned to his office at the Defense Language Institute.

Made in the USA
Las Vegas, NV
13 June 2023

73387381R00164